COLIN PAYNE

The Hunt For Amelia Clay

Colin Payne

To Jenny, (my favourite Wench)
I hope you enjoy the contents of my imagination, please don't judge me by it!

THE HUNT FOR AMELIA CLAY

For You, thanks for reading my story!
xxx

COLIN PAYNE

Copyright © 2014 Colin Payne
All rights reserved.

First Published 2014
Lord Doggett Publishing.

All characters in this publication are fictitious and any resemblance to persons living or dead is purely coincidental.

ISBN-13: 978-1500497187
ISBN-10: 1500497185

For more information please visit:

www.facebook.com/groups/theshatteredeagle
www.collers100g.wordpress.com

THE HUNT FOR AMELIA CLAY

-PROLOGUE-

How Harry Kilburton Came To Need Fifty Eight Stitches Sewing Into His Face.

No wonder his back ached, the mattress was wafer thin, any comfort or support had long since gone, the bloody thing was like a sheet of cardboard, but that wasn't what was occupying his mind that morning. Sitting on his bed in his cell, the dirty mustard coloured blankets tangled around his legs, Harry Kilburton slurped noisily from the blue plastic bowl containing his *Coco-pops*. 'This Morning' was on the TV, yeah that choir from 'Britain's Got Talent' were on it after the break, twenty two delicious little angels singing in their pretty pale blue dresses, oh what little darlings. He had been waiting for that with a gleeful excitement all morning, the little gap toothed tease who sang the solo, yeah he'd let her have it. He thought back to being at home, Stacey cavorting around the place dancing along to her favourite pop songs, like some little Kylie Minogue, yeah poor little

Stacey, it had been a while, she had no doubt turned rotten with age by now, they all do, it's biology, ruins 'em all eventually. He did miss her though, or at least the memory of her as an eleven year old beauty, that sweet little smile and teasing eyes, God he missed her.

But his reminiscing was interrupted by a metallic tap at his door startling him out of his daydreams, as instantly it swung open.

"You having exercise Harry?" it was Mr Galloway, one of the usual Screws that worked in the Segregation Unit, the fat bastard must have known those little pretties were coming up on the telly, still he had around fifteen minutes, he could get a bit of air then get back for some Harry time, a little bit of special solo entertainment so to speak.

Yeah he liked the idea of that.

"Can I come out for just quarter of an hour Mr Galloway, there's something I wanna watch on the telly?" he replied, yeah just that, quarter of an hour, no more we don't want to miss the little show do we.

"Whatever, it's your 30 minutes Harry, come on then, if your time's so precious we best not waste any more of it had we eh."

The portly Prison Officer opened the door wide, and Harry slipped his Velcro fastened plimsolls on and pulled on the tatty grey sweatshirt, before following the Officer along the landing.

He was skittish, twitching like some wired Meerkat as he looked around, his eyes darting about looking for hitherto unseen threats, although he was always like that and with bloody good reason too, there were the orderlies out cleaning, he didn't trust them horrible bastards, day in day out he had put up with their snide comments through his door when the screws weren't about, pushing him, goading him, who were they to judge him, murderers taking the moral high ground against him, they'd killed people, ended lives, destroyed entire futures, all he did was offer his love and affection, and yet they treated him like the monster, yeah they were bastards, the lot of 'em.

He shuffled along the landing, approaching those two so-called 'trusted' prisoners busying themselves mopping the landing, apparently ignoring him, laughing, probably at his expense, but certainly offering none of the aggression that was usually so prevalent when the screws weren't about.

"Arghh!"

There was no warning, no sign of what was to come, just the clattering of the mop bucket and the flash of something before his eyes, oh shit he was right to be worried, very bloody right. There was a sudden hot stinging sensation as the two razor blades, melted just millimetres apart into a toothbrush handle for callous maximum affect, sliced his face open from his forehead down to the bottom of his left cheek.

For the briefest of moments he could only stand there, stunned, then he fell to his knees screaming as the staff pulled his assailant away from him, the loud piercing alarm wailing as more screws rushed to the scene.

What had happened, oh Jesus what had those bastards done to him?

THE HUNT FOR AMELIA CLAY

All around was the loud banging, as the 'animals' hammered and kicked against their heavy metal doors, the jeers and taunts echoing around the small unit, he could feel the blood literally draining from his wrecked and open face, covering his grubby sweatshirt as it pumped free of his decimated face.

Oh God, again the thought, what had they done to him?

As his fingers probed the large gaping wound he could feel through his severed flesh his bare cheek bone, oh shit, it was *his* bone he was touching.

He knew he should have stayed in his cell, he was safe in there, safe from those savages, and now look what had happened.

Fifty eight stitches they put in his face, just to draw it together again, there was no question of it not leaving a permanent scar, after all it was so cruelly and deliberately meant to, he was just a filthy nonce, it was reckoned he'd even murdered his own step-daughter, as far as those animals were concerned Harry Kilburton got exactly what was coming to him.

-ONE-

Happy Birthday Andrea Clay *Xxx*

It hit the floor with a loud smash, the *Cath Kitson* floral mug shattering and sending its contents spilling over the tiles, shards of white china and hot coffee splashing over the bottoms of the immaculately cleaned brilliant white kitchen units. Andrea was standing there her hand positioned as if the freshly made brew were still in it, oblivious to the hot liquid that just moments earlier had splashed up and scalded her calves.

She was frozen to the spot, staring at the birthday card held in her shaking hand.

To Mum, Happy Birthday.
I love You Lots, and miss you loads and loads.
Lots of love and kisses Amelia
Xxx

What was this?
Some cruel hoax?

THE HUNT FOR AMELIA CLAY

Was this another one of those trolls not content to force the closure of the Blog and *Facebook* site, now escalating things to a whole new level of vitriolic sickness and nastiness?

Why were people like that?

What possible pleasure could they get out of it? Her little girl was gone, did they not understand that? Did they not realise the sheer torment that inflicts upon someone? All that not knowing, always the not knowing, living one's life imagining the unimaginable, every scenario envisaged being the worst possible one.

Where was she?

Who was she with?

And then the worst one, the one that filled every damn waking hour, and then sometimes her dreams as well, what was happening to her?

Yes what was happening to her poor little girl?

That thought was the worst, people wouldn't believe it but even worse than the notion that she may be gone forever, may be... she hated even considering it... dead. No the thought of her own child suffering was the nightmare she had to live with every hour of her life. There was no respite from it, not even some interlude of hope or joy, just the horrible nagging sickening feeling of helplessness, that she was unable to do what every parent should do, be there for her little girl, be there to make it all right.

Yet here it was in her hand, delivered with the bills and junk mail, a birthday card from her daughter, or at least supposedly from her.

But the strange thing was the writing actually looked like Ami's, even down to the smiley face over the letter *i* when signing her name, she was now fifteen, after four years of hearing nothing from her, was it possible she was still doing that silly little thing.

Could it really be from her?

Four years of hoping, wishing, praying, oh my God, was this really from her little girl?

She knew she mustn't become too excited, too optimistic, the spiteful false alarms had come almost on a weekly basis, the bogus sightings, anonymous confessions, the spurious ransom demands, people were cruel that was for sure, and they did exceptionally cruel things, she had never imagined that humankind could be so relentlessly nasty, but please God, please, please, please let this be real, let this be from her.

She picked up the phone, and dialled the number, the number she had dialled so many times before. She knew she should be phoning Paul - her husband - first, or even the police, but they could wait...

"Hello Christoff, it's Andrea, can you come over..."

As a large tear flowed down her face she wiped her cheek with the back of her hand, the bright pink rubber wristband brushing across her face. The wristband *For Amelia*, the imprint of the large daisy next to the italic print, oh please God let it be so, let it be from my lovely Ami...

-TWO-

Because That's Us In A Nutshell - A Right Pair Of Twats

Detective Inspector Henry Manningwell walked from the front of Dunstable Police Station towards their car, DC Denny Black following a couple of paces behind, pushing a salmon pink card folder into his brown leather briefcase as he tried to keep up with his boss, unfortunately all too hurriedly as his fumbling caused it to spill some of its contents onto the wet pavement at his feet.

Oh bollocks, he thought, that's all I need.

"Hold on Manny!" he called to his DI as he stamped around frantically trying to trap a wayward bundle of stapled typed paper under his shoe before it could blow off in the wet and squally autumnal breeze, because one thing was for sure, the last thing any of them wanted were stray pages from the Amelia Clay case cropping up in the press, that was the stuff of headlines, recriminations and almost certainly resignations.

"Come on Denny, sort yourself out, we need to get there, I'm just busting to find out what's happened this time."

It was of course a sarcastic comment, DI Henry Manningwell, or Manny as he was referred to by all who knew him, had become extremely adept at those. Oh yeah he was the real master of sarcasm, Denny thought to himself as he gathered the wet papers up and stuffed them back into the briefcase, well sarcasm and jaded disinterest, not forgetting the unrelenting cynicism and an ever growing lack of motivation. He had seen it all take hold like a slow developing cancer, as each month passed, the likelihood of some fantastic happy ending to it all diminished, and Manny's raison d'être died just a little bit more with it.

But then Manny had been on the case from day one, when with horrible irony, the eleven year old daughter of the Beds County Council Chief Child Safety Officer was abducted from her own home, her parents sleeping in the room next door. At the time it was a job any copper would have climbed over anyone for, the big one, all over the press, plenty of evidence at the scene, it had a result written all over it.

Yeah, it was the job they all wanted, and lucky old Manny got it.

But over time it had just all become a circus, each salacious little detail offering plenty of column inches, but no lead as to where poor Amelia was. Of course it was still a high profile case, everyone knew what Amelia Clay looked like, or at least what she looked like four years earlier, and her mother Andrea was doing everything she could to ensure that her little girl was never forgotten, that no one accepted the fate that unfortunately the country had already kind of accepted.

All around the South Beds area the faded and tattered pink ribbons still adorned the trees, the now yellowing posters were stuck up in shop windows, and the four year old centre spreads from *The Daily Mirror* continued to be on display from homes in almost any given street within the area. Only now the hope had been replaced with some kind of moral obligation to support the Clays, on the unspoken rule that some form of combined community belief would make it all right.

The almost monthly slots on 'Crimewatch' had long dried up, not just as interest faded, but because there was nothing new to offer the public, there were only so many times Manny could wear his best shirt and face the cameras asking people to stretch their minds back years rather than days, then weeks, then months, it was a case that had become the albatross around the DI's neck, and it had dragged him down, changed him, sure he was still a good man, a genuinely good man, but one who had been irreversibly altered by the circumstances that dictated that he was failing in his job.

What a truly depressing place this is, Denny thought, as he drove, or more factually didn't go far at all, along the congested A5 through Dunstable High Street, he looked along the rows of empty shops, fast food outlets, Charity stores, and Payday loan offices, the rain was drizzling down the windscreen of their *Ford Focus*, it was grim out there, horribly drab and grey, and not just the weather, he really didn't like this town at all, it was just an extension of Luton, and that was definitely not somewhere he really wanted to reside. But unfortunately it was where Karl lived, was tied to by work, and he had been well aware of that fact before moving in with him, Dunstable eh, the true price of love.

Once more he pondered the prospect of transferring, even if he had to live in this place he didn't have to work there as well, there was no reason he couldn't commute out of it, the Met or Thames Valley were both looking for detectives, but then how could he just up and leave? Not now at least. Like Manny he had become tied to the Clay case, and although it offered him no joy, no prospect of a happy resolution, he couldn't just flee from it, no he was cursed with his own personal albatross as well.

"So what is it this time?" Manny asked, breaking the silence, interrupting Denny's contemplation of just what a desolate dump Dunstable was and how he was going to escape it. His DI was looking at the A4 sheet of paper in the plastic document wallet in his hand, his furrowed brow rising above the tatty beard that now adorned his face.

"What's the urgent news then, on this wet and shitty morning?" Manny continued, "Has the clairvoyant been in touch, hey Andrea guess who I've seen in a party dress down a well again? Or has Andrea had another one of her dreams, little Ami telling her where she is being held, or has something mysteriously moved in her bedroom again, ooh look her favourite teddy has moved from the bed to a chair, quick call the Police?"

"Oh come on Manny, she's been through hell, let's give her a break for God's sake, she's the kid's mother, of course she'll cling to anything she can. Let's just keep an open mind, see what's happened, eh, it can't hurt."

Manny's dismissal of Andrea had irritated him, he must realise what the poor woman was going through, how she would cling to whatever there was to cling to. Denny didn't have kids, and never fancied it either, which was probably just as well as Karl was severely lacking in the womb department, but Manny was a father, yeah an estranged one maybe, but surely some of that paternal instinct still resided in him somewhere.

"It's not the clinging to anything that gets on my tits, it's the media circus I struggle with, we talk to her one day, she tells everything to Christoff bloody Peterson, and the next morning it's on the front page of *The Sun*, she has a dream and it's all over *Take a Break*, I know she's trying to keep her girl in the public eye, whilst every one cares it makes it all that much more bearable, if they all share the hope, then the hope lives, but that ain't helping us is it? All we do is turn up on cue, get a camera stuck in our faces, and look like a pair of twats on the news. The pair of twats who aren't doing anything. The pair of twats who four years on still haven't a sodding clue. Because Denny you need to be sure on this, that's us in a nutshell - a right pair of twats."

"Maybe, yeah perhaps we are twats, but at least let's be the twats that still give a damn, because if we lose that, well, what's the point?"

Manny said no more, nor did Denny who now just focussed on the traffic snarled up ahead, every so often he needed to remind himself this was Henry Manningwell sitting next to him, probably the best copper he knew, or had ever known, it was his sheer enthusiasm that convinced him to join the team when he had first transferred from the West Midlands, just six weeks after Amelia had been taken. The man had passion, drive, and it had been contagious, they had worked all hours, covered all avenues, no eventuality or possibility had gone un-investigated, all driven on relentlessly by his then eager DI. He wasn't even in charge of the case back then, DCI Robert Barker was lead, but as it dried up, and it became all too apparent there wouldn't be any easy nicking, any happy endings would probably be found elsewhere, then Barker threw it down the chain of command, high profile cases were only good for careers when they ended with a result, and Bob Barker had realised that this one was never going to fit that criteria. No Bob Barker was a shrewd one.

The hypnotic bomp-de-bomp bomp-de-bomp of the window wipers slapping against the bottom of the rain drenched screen was the only sound inside the car, twenty minutes they had been inching along. Denny could see where Manny was coming from with his reluctance to be drawn into Andrea Clay's world, if he was honest with himself he never

THE HUNT FOR AMELIA CLAY

looked forward to visiting the Clays either, each time he saw them their situation appeared to have worsened, like the ribbons festooned on the local timber the public gusto for funding the hunt for their daughter had faded, at least financially. The charity events, bucket collections and media driven whip rounds had long since passed, replaced by the next big public out pouring of sympathy for the most recent young victim of humanity's ability to be so relentlessly cruel to the most vulnerable among its ranks. As Andrea substituted a £60,000 per annum wage as a Local Government Executive for the role of unpaid awareness coordinator for the *For Amelia* campaign, the financial burden placed on Paul Clay became impossible to keep up. Initially the fund raising became more desperate, before the inevitable happened, the Clays began to finance their quest to find their beloved daughter using their own money.

As they approached Harwick Common, the village between Dunstable and Milton Keynes where the Clay's lived in their large now re-mortgaged home, Denny realised he had almost forgotten, he reached into his jacket pocket and pulled out the pink wristband and slid it onto his wrist, it was a lesson he had learnt early on, he needed to be properly dressed when in the company of Andrea Clay.

-THREE-

Andrea Clay And Her Rock, Christoff Peterson.

Andrea Clay was nothing if not a creature of habit, so she did what she always did whilst waiting for the Police to arrive, she cleaned. It was that or take the top off the Pinot Grigio, and at ten past ten that was too early, even for her. So it was that she was on all fours scrubbing away at the floor wiping up the coffee that had long ago been soaked away into the cloth.

She'd had plenty of time to think, get her head around it all, digest the card, the card that DC Black had decreed she shouldn't touch. She had discussed it with Christoff, who was seated at the kitchen table tapping away at his laptop, and as always he helped put things into perspective, placate her, offer some real support, he really was her rock, a role that Paul should have taken of course, but he wasn't strong enough for that. Paul had crumpled long ago, leaving her to carry the burden of actually working to get their little girl back. So instead of her weak and broken husband, Christoff had taken the mantel of supporting spouse, he was her truest friend, and the one person who really understood her, yet he could never be any more than that, at least not while Amelia was gone, everything needed to be right for her return, just as it was, and that unfortunately meant Paul would be there sharing her life when that happy reunion occurred, and not the man she truly loved.

Again she thought of the card, it just didn't make sense, all that time hearing nothing, and then a birthday card. As much as she wanted it to be real, the more she considered it the less feasible it appeared, if her Ami was free, at liberty to send it, then why hadn't she been in touch sooner, and if she were a captive somewhere how was she able to send a birthday greeting?

It was too much for her to really take in, so she scrubbed at the immaculately clean doors of the kitchen units even harder, allowing the vigorous labour to take her mind away from Amelia's plight, although in truth her mind was forever thinking about her, thinking about what was happening to her little girl at that very moment, never.

"Andrea, stop, please, you need to take a rest, you're getting yourself too worked up." Christoff had closed the lid on his laptop and leant back in his chair, that kindly comforting smile on his face. "You need to take a moment, they will be here soon, come sit down, let's talk."

She knew he was right, he usually was, he had that ability to be able to take a step back, see things from a different perspective, that was his strength, well that and the way he was able to communicate with the press. But then that was his job, Media Liaison Executive at the County Hall, that's how she knew him, how they had initially met, before he became the rock dedicating all his spare time to the cause.

Peeling the *Marigold* gloves from her hands, she walked over to where he was sitting, "It's just I'm so confused, my head's a mess, and I feel like I'm just watching on, like some television programme, watching as my life falls to pieces, what if the card is from her? What if it's not? What does it mean?"

She could see him sitting there, behind those greyish blue eyes he was no doubt thinking what to tell her, how to reassure her, what to say for the best, when all she really wanted him to do was take her in his arms and be there, be there forever. She knew he felt the same, or at least she thought she knew, or was she just deluding herself, for they had never broached the subject, there was no point, no reason to, because once they did then it was over, and she really didn't want it to be over.

Maybe there would be a time when it would be different, when her life could be lived as she wished, but that time wasn't now, and as the doorbell rang, she knew that would be them, the Police. Perhaps they would actually listen to her this time, actually pay a bit of attention to what she said, for just once take her seriously instead of fobbing her off with nothing but reassuring nods and smiles.

-FOUR-

The Aroma Of Cif, Flash And Freshly Brewed Coffee.

Manny entered the kitchen following Denny, yeah Denny could lead on this, in fact he didn't know why he had come along at all, yet there was always that obligation for him to attend when dealing with the Clays, it was expected, even though Andrea would only really talk to his DC, ignoring him, of course always with a politeness that let him know it was nothing personal.

He noted how the freshly brewed coffee was struggling to mask the aroma of *Lemon Cif* and *Flash* floor cleaner, with Andrea it was always the cleaning, he looked around the large modern kitchen, everything in its place, like some unfeasibly tidy show home in one of those magazines he only ever read in a dentist's or doctor's waiting room. It made him think of his own kitchen, the cluttered sides, a mishmash of crockery and cutlery, some of the splashes and stains on his units were older than his kids, but then Andrea didn't have her kid did she, her daughter was gone, hence them being in that immaculately spotless kitchen, no she didn't have her child, but she did still have her cleaning.

They were gathered around the kitchen table, him, Manny looked over to Peterson he pondered how the man always managed to be there, even though Paul the actual father wasn't. He was now feeling awkward, it was only since he had sat down that he noticed the dirty footprints across the pristine white floor tiles leading from her kitchen door to where he was sitting, oh bugger it, he thought, that's another black mark against me.

It was Denny who spoke first, once the pleasantries of the coffee and biscuits were out of the way.

"So Andrea, you say you received a birthday card this morning, from Amelia."

The young DC was looking at her, that sympathetic look Manny had seen so many times before, letting Andrea know just how much he felt her pain, empathised with her plight, he noticed the pink wristband on his wrist, yeah he was good, and he had remembered to wipe his feet properly.

"I didn't realise it was from her at first, of course I wasn't expecting it, there were about half a dozen cards in the post, then when I saw it, well…" the sentence just hung there, unfinished, as Andrea struggled to compose herself.

"Can we have a look at it please?" Denny asked, as he spoke he took a pair of latex gloves from his pocket and slid them onto to his hands.

"Yes of course, it's over there," she nodded towards a shelf by the breakfast bar, "after we spoke earlier I didn't touch it again, I left it just as you said."

Manny got up, also pulling a pair of gloves on, and the two Police Officers walked over to where the card sat upon the envelope it came in.

Denny gingerly picked up the card, holding it by one corner with the blue plastic tweezers that came with the large polythene evidence bag, flicking the card open.

To Mum, Happy Birthday. I love You Lots, and miss you loads and loads. Lots of love and kisses Amelia xxx

"And there was no note, nothing else at all?" Denny asked.

"No just that." Andrea answered.

Manny looked at the envelope, postmarked Hemel Hempstead, the previous day, although that counted for nothing as all mail from within a huge radius was processed through the huge Sorting Office in Hertfordshire, he turned the envelope over, there was nothing on it other than the stamp and the Clays address.

"I'm afraid we'll need to take these," Manny said, he could see the disappointment in Andrea's face, "hopefully there may be some DNA or forensic evidence, and we can examine that writing, against some of Amelia's school work."

Andrea looked to Denny, for some kind of reassurance Manny guessed, because Denny was the kind one, the caring one, the one she could trust, "Will I get it back Inspector?"

Manny didn't want to tell her there was no chance, whether it was real or not, it was all she had, all she possessed from four lost years, but the fact was no, she wouldn't be getting it back, she had more chance of getting her daughter back than she did that birthday card. But of course he couldn't tell her that could he, couldn't crush her any further.

"I'm afraid it's doubtful Mrs Clay, at least not immediately, although I will have someone make a copy of it for you, but the main thing is to ascertain whether this is from Amelia, or, and I'm sorry to say this, more likely another hoaxer. What I will do is ensure our people get onto this immediately, and hopefully we can talk later."

Even as he was talking Andrea was still looking towards Denny, then to Peterson, seeking some support, desperate for some argument for allowing her to keep the card, but he could see Denny avert his eyes, no this was evidence and in a case so bereft of evidence it certainly wasn't going to be lost to them for any reason.

"What do you reckon?" Denny asked as he was driving, as they made their way back to the station.

"I reckon that Peterson's seeing to her, where was Paul? If that was my…"

"No Guv', I meant what do you reckon to the card?"

"Oh right Look Denny there's some nasty people out there, some twisted horrible little arsehole is laughing at us as we speak, that's a shame, but the fact he's also laughing at that poor woman is unforgiveable. Let's get it to the lab, see if anyone licked the stamp or envelope flap, check out that writing, see if it tells us anything."

THE HUNT FOR AMELIA CLAY

"What if it is from her, from Amelia Clay?" Denny asked.

Manny gave an involuntary nasal snort, "Oh come on, you know it's not, believe me that's not from her."

-FIVE-

Shit In A Hat And Punch It, What In God's Name Was That All About?

As the large mechanical arm once more cut a swathe through the shit and sludge it was clear to him that the banks were too soft for this kind of work. He'd end up dragging himself into the narrow river if he wasn't careful, he could almost feel the tracks sliding from under him as he attempted to get it done. But if that was what was going to happen then so be it, he was paid by the job, not the hour, so that was the risk he'd have to take. Besides it was only shallow, bugger it, he'd drag himself out quick enough, it was just dirty horrible work that's for sure, and there was no arguing with that.

As he manoeuvred the three small handles the broad bucket at the end of the long yellow arm scraped another year's worth of shit from the sides of the over grown river bank, he looked through the rain soaked screen of his cab, well attempted to, it was pissing down out there, the old decayed wipers that so needed replacing struggled to clear a view for him, in fact he wondered why he had even bothered getting his cataracts sorted last year, if this was to be his view all day. It made it difficult, but it wasn't impossible, after all he could do this sort of thing blindfolded if he really needed to, scraping shit from river banks, it was hardly difficult.

His stomach was grumbling as he dug another load up and deposited it on the far side by the open field, before edging along another five or six feet and repeating the process, yeah this was not difficult, and although he was hungry he'd not stop for lunch, hell he should be done by three, well before dark, even on such a crappy day.

He had worked up to the small foot bridge that led from the cow field to the top pasture, it was as good a place as any to have a smoke, so zipping up his anorak he climbed out of his cab, walking over to the old oak, taking the opportunity to have a much needed piss against its broad wide trunk, before removing a pre-made roll up from his backy tin.

Drawing on the thin cigarette, he looked back along the side of the hedgerow, admiring his work, despite the wet ground that was a bloody straight line he had carved there with perfectly smooth sides, it looked pretty good, even if he said so himself, a real tidy little job. Yep, three o'clock at the latest should see it all done, so all in all a good day's work. As he scraped the thick mud from his boots on one of the trees outstretched roots he glanced along the earth piled up on the far side, he'd go around later and flatten that out, get it all neat and proper looking, then he saw it, about fifteen yards back, hanging out from where he had just piled the earth dredged from that stream.

Bloody hell, shit in a hat and punch it, what in God's name was that all about?

Oh Jesus Christ, was that an arm?

-SIX-

Happy Birthday Sweet Sixteen.

The muck and mud was splashing the side of the dark grey *Focus* as they went through the deep thick sludgy puddles that pitted and pooled down the narrow muddy lane. A couple of patrol cars were parked up on the grass verges, and an ambulance was tucked in tightly against a gateway. They had been phoned on the way back from Andrea Clay's, sent once more to Harwick Common. Manny had let out a defeated sigh upon hearing the news, informed that a body had been had recovered from the side of a river just a mile outside of the village.

Was this it?

Had Amelia Clay been found?

He thought of the girl's mother, no doubt returned to her scrubbing, holding onto the hope that the birthday card was from her missing only child, and here they were about to turn her world upside down.

Happy Birthday Andrea.

***

Denny parked up tight behind one of the patrol cars, and got out and walked to the boot and took out a pair of brightly coloured wellies, and a cagoule, remnants from that summer's Glastonbury, whilst Manny could only shake his head as Denny changed into them. But Denny's footwear wasn't what was bothering him, in missing person cases coincidences were rare, if bodies crop up just down the road from where they were initially taken, then the laws of probability usually hold true.

"Come on," was all he said once Denny was properly attired (well if orange floral wellington boots in any world are proper attire for a copper), before walking towards the wooden bridge where he could see the small cluster of uniformed Police and Paramedics decked out in their hi-visibility jackets. His overcoat collar was turned up, and mud was covering his shoes, caking the bottom of his trousers, he was attempting to pick his way as he squelched through the soft muck, already his shoulders were soaked, but he was oblivious to the weather, he really didn't want this, not at all.

As Denny drew level Manny turned to him, "It's her Den, I know it is, what a poxy horrible day."

They continued walking past the yellow mini-digger, which Charlie Packer had been operating prior to finding their corpse, and over the moss covered slimy foot bridge, their feet slipping and sliding as they traversed it. One of the PCs who had got there first walked over to them.

THE HUNT FOR AMELIA CLAY

"Looks like a teenage girl Guv', no one's touched her, by the look of it the old boy's dug her out and moved the body, it was wet, he didn't notice until he got out of his cab and looked back."

Manny took a long hard look at the scene before him, the rain blowing at what had to be a forty five degree angle directly into his face. He could see it was already taped off, the uniformed Officer, who he knew as Steve Hammond from Dunstable, had done well, hadn't allowed anyone to go trampling over his crime scene, although to be fair his crime scene had pretty much been unwittingly decimated already by some old bloke in a *JCB*.

Ducking under the blue and white tape fluttering in the wind, he walked towards the lifeless human form hanging out of the mud, the upper half of her body, for it was definitely a her, was exposed, the rest buried under the sodden mound of earth. He looked on, his soaking face showing the sadness he was feeling, just staring, all he could think was what a shit job he had, and never more shittier than at times like this. Her hair was matted, over her face, the skin grey, puncture marks and open wounds were all over her head, her lips were a purple blue, she blended in perfectly with the grey drab sky. He continued to stare, half seeing what was before him, half trying to make sense of it in his mind. Her eyes were open, staring back at a world that had let this happen to her, a world where teenage girls are murdered and left by rivers for carrion and vermin to dine upon them.

The girl was clothed, in what appeared to be a dress, oh bollocks he thought, that bloody clairvoyant, please no, don't let it be right, Amelia Clay in a party dress down a well, was a river near enough when it came to supernatural premonitions?

Crouching down to take a better look, the bottom of his overcoat nestling in the wet mud and pools of dirty water which formed on the ground, he saw the brightly coloured badge pinned to the dress, stars and balloons on a bright blue background, *Happy Birthday Sweet 16* in bold red print. Yep, today was a day for birthdays alright. Then he straightened up, his brow furrowing, it wasn't right.

It was her left hand, the hand with five fingers, five perfect, but dead fingers.

Turning, he walked back towards Denny, his face once more giving nothing away, other than how utterly miserable he was feeling.

"Well?" Denny asked, as he lifted the tape for him to duck under.

"It's not her," being all Manny replied, walking back to the bridge. He took out a packet of *Benson & Hedges*, and lit one, drawing on it long and hard.

Denny looked puzzled. "No?"

"No." he blew the smoke out, staring towards the sky, "that's not Amelia Clay, the pinkie finger. As a disability a missing finger is hardly ever the most severe ailment anyone could suffer from, but it is one she'll always have, that finger is never growing back. That girl's someone else."

"Are you sure Manny?"

THE HUNT FOR AMELIA CLAY

He gave a grim smile, "Yeah I'm sure. I have no idea who that poor kid is, but I do know one hundred percent that it's not Amelia Clay."

-SEVEN-

It's Definitely Stacey Hamilton.

"It's Stacey Hamilton. Yes the Stacey Hamilton."

The dozen or so Officers in the room had fallen silent, as they absorbed the magnitude of what DC Floyd Carflour had just announced, whilst the young black Officer pinned the picture of a grinning ten year old Stacey onto the whiteboard, the happy school photo which was in total contrast to the grisly image taken just hours earlier of the corpse, now stuck beside it.

"It was just confirmed, a preliminary DNA match," Floyd continued "South Yorkshire are sending a couple of people down as we talk. This is big, and it's going to shake things up a bit that's for sure."

Denny was sitting back watching Floyd, he was only a DC, if being a Detective Constable was ever an only, but it had to be said that boy could hold a room, he had something about him, a confidence and charisma, people gravitated to him, he had often wondered what that secret ingredient was, what separated the Floyd's from the 'normal' folk, but he guessed it was a quality that couldn't be singled out. As he watched his colleague in his fitted shirt and tailored trousers, the centre of everyone's attention, he once more pondered how if Floyd ever had a change of 'direction' he would be a fully certified gay legend, then 'pulling himself back into the room' he focussed once more on what was being said, annoyed with himself for drifting off.

Floyd, blissfully unaware of Denny's appraisal of any would be legendary status, carried on filling everyone in on what they pretty much already knew. "I presume we've all heard of little Stacey," he continued, pointing to her picture on the board, although he was right everyone already knew who Stacey Hamilton was.

"And also I would imagine everyone knows that her step father, Harry Kilburton had been nailed on as the one who had taken her six years back, and we all presumed murdered her. Of course a court has never confirmed that minor technicality, not officially, but he had been exposed as being a serial sex offender, and after being sentenced for the rape of a neighbour's child, well there may not have been any conviction, but he was rock solid for his step-daughter's disappearance. As we speak he is probably still spending his days segregated in some undisclosed prison for his own safety.

"Yeah the popular view was that Harry Kilburton was as guilty as hell when it came to Stacey Hamilton, that's what everyone reckoned, that's now clearly not the case, at least it would appear for her murder anyway."

Manny was saying nothing, clearly happy to let Floyd continue, Denny was there when he had spoken to him before the brief, and whilst they had been up to his ankles in shit and mud at Harwick Common, Floyd had been very busy.

"It's thought Stacey had been dead for three days maybe four, before her discovery, which coincided with her sixteenth birthday, which without wanting to state the obvious, ties in with badge she was wearing. Now we're not sure how Stacey died, but my guess is it wasn't falling into a bank of wet shitty mud by accident."

As Manny stood up, moving alongside Floyd, Denny considered how his DI had aged, as he often did, he considered himself a great observer of people, of course the beard did him no favours, but then nor did at least a couple of extra stone he had put on, but it was more than that, he looked like he had become someone totally devoid of cheer, even on the days he hadn't been looking at the lifeless form of a deceased teenager, he had lost that little cheery edge in his voice, making him sound permanently dull and miserable.

"Right, there's obviously the big question we need to look at. How on earth did this girl end up on a riverbank less than half a mile from the home of Amelia Clay, two days after her sixteenth birthday? These are two high profile cases, bloody high profile, yet we never had them linked, they were miles apart, not just in distance. Stacey six years ago was a ten year old girl with a truly crappy upbringing. Alcoholic mother who sold herself to fund drugs, booze and fags, and on top of that she was saddled with an abusive good for nothing arsehole for a step-father. Her life was shit, and I mean shit. She vanished whilst home alone as Mum was turning tricks for a tenner or whatever in the back of someone's motor in a Leeds car park and the evil Step-Dad claimed to be out on some park bench getting rat arsed on *White Lightning*.

"Amelia Clay was the polar opposite, from a loving home, as middle class as you can get, the parents were well off, and appeared happy, well as happy as you get living around here. She was loved and cared for. But still snatched from her home, literally whilst Mum and Dad slept in the same house."

He walked around pulling a second whiteboard containing the array of images from the Amelia Clay case next to the one with just the two contrasting photos of Stacey Hamilton.

"And yet Harwick Common. Population bugger all, is our common denominator. Amelia vanishes from there, Stacey is discovered there. Why?"

He paused looking around the room, at the faces watching on, "That my friends is what we need to find out here."

-EIGHT-

Henry Manningwell Stops Off At The Peking Garden For The Old Faithful.

Manny sat behind the wheel of his battered old car, it was nearly ten, sometimes he wondered why he bothered going home at all, what was there for him now? There was the unloving incontinent cat, the TV that only worked when nothing was actually on worth watching, the Computer that kept shutting itself down, and his permanently unmade bed. Oh and of course, a load of memories which just got shittier and shittier, as they became more recent.

His family were now someone else's family, living his dream in the Lake District, only in his dream he was there with them. Yeah some dream that was, they were even looking at changing his kids' names, to avoid confusion and problems as they got older.

Huh, he thought, that would avoid any confusion wouldn't it, except when it came to remembering who their actual Dad was, who their 'biological' father was. But then that was all he was to them now, a genetic connection, more a medical coincidence than an actual Dad.

It was all screwed up, his family affairs - although the only affairs in his family definitely hadn't involved him, at least not as an active participant. Even though Keith, whose surname was now looming so large over his two children's heads earned far more than he did, and had no mortgage, it was his money that was supporting his stay away family, by some logic the calculations indicated that he needed to pay a large chunk of his salary to people who were actively keeping him and his children apart.

Yeah that's so bloody fair that is.

He was only one step away from dressing up as Batman and storming parliament, he was just another father devoid of justice, another man thrown through the mill of divorce with nothing left at the other end but debts and memories.

He parked up outside *The Peking Garden*, it wasn't the best place for oriental cuisine in Leighton Buzzard, it wasn't even the best in the parade of shops it was situated in, but it was where he always went for his old faithful, had done since he was teenager walking home from the pub, when he used to get pissed on two pints of lager and a *Southern Comfort* as a night cap. Special Fried Rice, Chilli Beef and a Pancake Roll, the same as he always ate when eating alone, be that in 1985, 1995, 2005, or now, the greased up old faithful, ideal with a couple of cans, plus any food that may get left would always make a damn good cold and congealed breakfast.

As he waited on the same wooden bench that had been there for over thirty years, he wondered how long those faded *Coke* and *Fanta* cans had been sitting on that shelf for, alongside the dusty Soy Sauce bottle? They had always been there hadn't they? Right next to that year's bamboo calendar, he was sure they had come with the original décor and menu, some traditions just have to go on forever, and sadly some don't.

Looking away from the cans he had been staring at, there it was on the silent TV, the sound off, a helicopter view of his crime scene at Harwick Common, the rolling caption along the bottom…

Police have still to confirm the identity of the body found outside a Bedfordshire village today, although unofficial sources are stating it may be that of the missing schoolgirl Stacey Hamilton…

It then cut to a picture of Stacey, the same one as they had on their white board back at the station, of her angelic smiling face in her school uniform six years back, before once more returning to the aerial view. As the image zoomed out Manny noticed to the top right of the screen the half dozen or so media vehicles, satellites on their roofs, not parked near the river where the supposed story was, but at the end of the cul-de-sac, the cul-de-sac where Paul and Andrea Clay lived, once more in the media spotlight, once more having the horror brought to their doorstep. The screen flicked back to the studio, then footage of George Osborne

THE HUNT FOR AMELIA CLAY

and David Cameron in Zurich on some global conference supposedly putting the world to rights. Yeah what chance did we have with those two wankers putting anything to rights he thought, no bloody chance.

As old George, the *Peking Garden's* owner, was handing over the white carrier bag that contained his Monosodium-glutomatic meal for one, Manny's mobile rang.

"Hello Manningwell," he answered, the phone awkwardly wedged between his shoulder and his cheek, as he struggled to multitask paying George for his food and talking into his precariously balanced mobile at the same time.

"Evening Henry it's Clare Melvic, I'm just giving you a quick bell about those tests I ran on the birthday card. Are you sitting down, because this shook me I can tell you."

"Go on," Manny answered.

"Well like I said it surprised me, but both DNA and prints indicate that the card and envelope have, believe it or not, actually been in contact with Amelia Clay at some point."

She paused a moment, to let the news sink in, "Obviously I'll never give a definite 100% confirmation on anything, you know that, but it's pretty certain that she handled it, and that her saliva was on the stamp and the flap. Cecil's working on the girl found by that river, but as you already know DNA tell us that's just as certainly Stacey Hamilton, apparently the mother's on her way down from Leeds to carry out the formal ID in the morning. I wanted you to know before I went off for the night. Well that's me about done."

Manny rested the white carrier bag back on the imitation pine counter, not sure what exactly to make of the news. He already knew the girl was Stacey, but Amelia Clay had sent the birthday card. Really?

How the hell was that possible?

"Thanks Clare, and thanks for letting me know, it's really appreciated."

"No problem Manny, you have a good night, well what's left of it, and I'm sure we'll see you at some point tomorrow, sleep tight."

A birthday card after all this time from Amelia, and then someone else's missing school girl crops up literally yards away, within hours of each other?

This was all going to get messy, they were linked, they had to be, that was just too big a coincidence.

He remembered from some Geography lesson many moons back that there were close to ninety thousand square miles in the British Isles, all that space, all that land, so why dump the body of Stacey Hamilton within yards of the home of Amelia?

That was some messed up message the perpetrator was sending out, and for whose benefit, was it for them, the Police?

Putting his food on the passenger seat, he sat back in the driver's seat of his car. He could smell the grub, he was famished, he hadn't eaten all day, but knew he wouldn't be able to go home and enjoy it, at least not while it was still

THE HUNT FOR AMELIA CLAY

hot. He pulled the ancient *Kia Sedona* estate round into a u-turn, and although at that particular moment it was the last thing in the world he wanted to do, instead of going the few hundred yards to his house, his food, and ultimately his much needed bed, he headed back towards Harwick Common.

-NINE-

Andrea Clay Once More Takes A Ride On The Emotional Rollercoaster.

As expected the Outside Broadcast vans were still there, lined up between the identical block paved driveways within Barton Close, even as he parked up he could see a woman illuminated by a bright light on one of the cameras, delivering a live feed to a News Cast somewhere out there.

Pulling his coat from the back of the car he saw that mud was still around the bottom of it, he hurriedly tried to brush it off before slipping it on. "Eurgh," he mumbled to himself it was damp and cold, especially around the shoulders and neck, but C'est la vie, none of this was going to be particularly comfortable.

Walking over to the Clays home, he brushed past another camera crew as he walked up the drive.

"Inspector Manningwell, Manny! Can you confirm that the Amelia Clay case is now linked to the Stacey Hamilton investigation?"

THE HUNT FOR AMELIA CLAY

It was Bill Penton, from *Sky News*, he had been assigned the story from near enough day one, and was probably one of the better reporters who were part of the huge circus that had been drawn to Harwick Common over the past few years.

"Too early to possibly comment." Manny brusquely replied, not making eye contact with either Bill or the camera which had swung around towards him.

"Can you at least confirm the identity of the body found, was it Stacey?" Bill pushed on, following Manny up the short drive.

"Sorry, we can't divulge that yet, as I said it's too early to comment."

"Can you comment on the birthday card sent to Andrea Clay this morning?"

How the hell did they know about that?

Well he actually knew the answer to that one. Peterson.

"No I can't comment on that. Thank You."

Manny was disappointed in Peterson, he had hoped that for once he would have held off calling the newspapers or TV companies, just waited to at least find out if it was really from the Clay's lost daughter, for all their sakes. But then he knew that even if it had been fake it would have once more put Amelia all over the papers, and when you're running an awareness campaign you have to heighten that awareness whenever possible.

Manny, stopped, turning to Bill, he nodded towards the camera, "Tell him to do one a minute."

"Give us a moment Robbie," the TV reporter said, whilst nodding in the direction of what presumed was their OB Van.

As Robbie walked away, his camera now pointing towards the ground as it swung at his side, Manny drew in close to the news reporter.

"Come on Bill you know I can't tell you anything until the families have been informed, and that ain't likely to be until tomorrow, at least as far as the body goes. But look, this probably ain't going to come as a big surprise to you, but it's definitely Stacey Hamilton, you know that though don't you, but don't you dare quote me on that just yet. I need to talk to Andrea and Paul now, read into that what you like, and I'm sure if you hang around out here a little longer you'll have a story, after all since when has Andrea kept anything quiet. Now just for the moment please piss off."

Bill gave a little smile, nodded and walked back over to Robbie, calling back as he went, "Thanks Manny, I owe you one."

How he wished Denny was there with him, the young DC who seemed to dovetail into the Clay's way of dealing with things so much better than he did, after all he didn't even have one of those pink wristband things, although he didn't have a wristband of any colour, he never got them, what was the point? He only ever wore anything like that when he used to go swimming as a kid, what was the point of them?.

Within a couple of seconds of ringing the doorbell Paul Clay was ushering him inside, he must have been waiting by

THE HUNT FOR AMELIA CLAY

the door, ready to pounce. Manny quickly scanned the room, there was no sign of Christoff Peterson, it was definitely Paul's turn to be tagged into the ring he thought, before checking himself, was he really that jaded, that coldly cynical? But then he knew the answer to that, yes he was.

"Thanks for coming around Inspector," Paul said leading him through to the living room. Andrea was sitting on the floral sofa, the TV in the background showing the images of the scene just yards away, he could see the expectation on her face, desperate for some good news, after years of relentless doom and gloom.

"I won't keep you any longer than I need to Mr and Mrs Clay. The DNA from the card you received. It is we believe from Amelia…"

Andrea gushed out her joy. "Oh thank God! Thank God, thank you Inspector, thank you so much for letting us know."

"I can also confirm," Manny continued, "that the body we found earlier is definitely not her."

He could see the emotional rollercoaster Andrea Clay was going through, her daughter was alive! How could any mother not be thrilled with that news, but then balanced with the cost of her joy was the fact that someone else would be mourning tonight, someone else's world will have been devastated.

"Is it Stacey?" Andrea asked.

"I'm afraid I can't confirm that, not until the family have been able to identify the body."

Of course he could have confirmed it to her, after all he had already told a journalist for heaven's sake, but then he trusted Bill, someone whose job it is to inform the world of news - preferably exclusives, to hold his peace more than he did Andrea, who would no doubt be calling Peterson the second he had gone.

"The poor people," Andrea's face was wracked with concern for the 'other' family, when she should have been celebrating the fact that Amelia was still alive and had been in touch, but clearly four years of dreading the day that her daughter may be found in such circumstances had made her realise all too well the effects this news was going to be having on another mother, another woman who only ever wanted to have her little girl back.

"I'll make a move now, it's late, we'll no doubt be in touch tomorrow." Manny said, he felt he was intruding, there was nothing more he could offer this couple tonight, he needed to get home, he was tired.

"Thank you Mr Manningwell, we appreciate you letting us know, you don't know how much this means to us," Paul said as he showed him out.

"It was no problem."

Walking back down the Clays drive he wondered how good the news he had just delivered was. Someone out there still had their daughter, and that someone may have killed Stacey Hamilton, very likely on her sixteenth birthday, and then gone to the trouble of placing the corpse practically on the doorstep of the Clays home. That was a pretty mixed up message to be sending out.

THE HUNT FOR AMELIA CLAY

Reaching the gate he came across Bill Penton, smoking a cigarette, ensconced in his obligatory *North Face* thermal coat that all TV reporters seem to crop up in, he was leaning against the wall, nodding to Manny as he approached.

"There's a story there Bill, give them a minute, but when she opens that door, and if I know Andrea you can be bloody sure she will, you want to be the first one up there, maybe suggest she talks inside, get yourself an exclusive. Stay warm mate and have a good night."

It was well past half eleven by the time he finally got home, but he was unlikely to be able to get off to sleep, not just yet. Fumbling with the key he struggled to unlock the front door, as the white plastic bag containing his supper hung from his wrist and he balanced two four packs of *Carlsburg* with his fingers looped through the plastic rings. Finally he got the door open and walked in, Urgh!

Cat piss.

What was it with that bastard cat, why wouldn't she just go outside, or better still just die? He'd even put a litter tray down for her to use, but no she'd rather piss on his front door mat. He took a large step over his threshold, and after clearing a space placed his beers and carrier bag of food onto a kitchen worktop, heading back to his door with a spray bottle of *Jey's* Cleaning Fluid, drenching the offending area, although he had no intention of getting on all fours and scrubbing at it, at least not tonight.

Walking back to his living room he decanted the two tin foil trays onto a plate, which may or may not have been washed up, still it looked clean enough. He sat in his armchair with his lukewarm congealed food on his lap, and one of his beers poured into a tall glass, the consummate bachelor, the lonely old copper home alone. Using the remote he flicked the TV on, there was Bill Penton, he had got into in the house before Manny had even got home, in front of him sat the Clays, on the sofa, tempering their joy of hearing that their daughter was very likely alive and had sent Mum a birthday card, whilst offering their sincerest condolences to the parents of whoever had been found earlier that day.

He slowly shook his head as he ate his food, what was this all about, what did it mean?

-TEN-

Rising Stock, And Vague Blurred Memories.

It was still dark, the morning daylight doing little to illuminate the room, the sun buried beneath the menacing black clouds, it was going to be another miserable day, but not for him. Sitting in the leather office chair in front of his PC monitor in his small office Phillip clicked the link on the *BBC News* website which informed the nation that a teenage girl, identity unknown, had been discovered dead in a field at Harwick Common, although he knew exactly who she was, and how she had got there. She had been a prized asset, for six years, he had grown close to her, refined her, polished her, cared for her. It hadn't been easy, at times he had felt like Henry Higgins to her young Eliza Doolittle, after all she was hardly an eloquent individual, in fact when he had first met her he had been unaware any child could be so badly brought up, so rough and uneducated, but he had persevered, just like training a dog, it had taken time and patience, but it had been worth it. Unfortunately - but inevitably - she had become of little value, literally outgrown her usefulness, although her loss was rather tragic, it had considerably increased the value of the other half of his 'portfolio'.

He stirred the coffee in his mug, whilst still transfixed by his PC monitor, "Oh poor Stacey, my poor little angel, you were such good company, what a shame these things always have to come to an end," he said to himself, before switching to another window on the screen, as he began to type...

My dearest friends, I do hope this message finds you all in good health, and high spirits. It's been a little while since we last met, so please accept this as a cordial invitation to what I'm sure will be a very special evening of wine, fine food and exquisite entertainment at the Tuesday Club, the Greatest Show On Earth...

No poor little Stacey, it really is such a shame we sometimes need to say good bye, but unfortunately nothing lasts forever, but ho hum, life goes on.

Whilst Phillip typed his invitation, not forty yards away, three stories above in the attic room that once was occupied by the household staff, Amelia Clay lay on the cast iron bed, dressed in one of the white cotton and lace night gowns she wore permanently between her daily baths. Staring blankly at the pale blue striped wallpaper beyond the screen of the small TV that sat upon the dresser, but she wasn't in the mood for video games or DVDs, in fact she wasn't in the mood for anything much. Today was one of those 'black' days, those days that came so often, one of those days where even the tears can't relieve the morose pressure of the unrelenting miserableness she was feeling. That's why she was staring at the wall, trying to fill her head with emptiness, make her mind devoid of any thoughts at all, because on the black days thoughts are never good.

But an empty head isn't an easy thing to achieve, there's always some thought popping up, always something.

'Uncle Phillip', or the 'The Pig' as she preferred to call him, although never to his face, had brought her breakfast up around an hour earlier, oh God how she hated him, oh how she really hated that man. But for all his evilness, and she was so sure that was what that Pig was, horrible and evil, he could cook. Ha, some redeeming feature, in four years the only good thing she could say about him was that he could cook. She resented the fact that she gave him credit for anything, found the remotest thing about him worthy of a positive response, but she had learned early to distance herself from the link between that man/monster/pig and the food he provided, otherwise she would have starved long ago. Last night was a fine example, fish in a white sauce with nice crispy potatoes and green beans, and a slice of cake. But it was that cake that had reminded her so vividly just how much she hated him, her mother's birthday cake he had said, why did he do things like that, what possible pleasure could someone get from being so horrible, so remorselessly cruel?

Abandoning her attempts at keeping an empty head, she surrendered to her thoughts, imagining how her mother's birthday had gone, pictured being there, desperately trying to drag the memories from past birthdays, but only ending up with blurs, vague pictures missing the sharp detail she so desperately wanted to recall. It was strange there wasn't a day that went by when she didn't think of Mummy and Daddy, yet had she forgotten how they looked? She was sure she hadn't, but was it possible that those people she loved so much could have had their true faces replaced by images of characters from videos or films, because with each day passing she knew those faces were becoming lost forever. She wondered why he had done that thing with the birthday card, he had never bothered before, it was strange, but then if everything was to make sense she wouldn't be lying there, chained to a bed, dreading her own birthday.

Always dreading that day, always wishing she had no birthday, in fact always wishing she had never been born at all.

-ELEVEN-

A Grieving Parent - Someone Better Call Denny Black.

Sitting in Dr Clare Melvic's office, a cup of coffee, the first of the morning in one hand, and a chocolate *Hobnob* in the other, Manny was intently listening to Clare as she gave him her opinion.

"Right this is only a preliminary overview, don't go quoting me on this. We've still to do the autopsy but I'm pretty sure Stacey Hamilton died of asphyxiation, she was placed in the ditch post mortem, killed somewhere else, probably moved within a day of dying. I'd say she's been dead for four days, give or take a few hours, which would have coincided with her sixteenth birthday. Not much of a day for her heh."

She took a large sip of coffee, and offered Manny another biscuit. He was fascinated by Clare, in this day and age of TV shows portraying pathologists and Scene of Crime Officers as young beautiful go-getters, out there solving the crimes themselves, whilst living the glamorous but dangerous life, Clare was the antithesis of all that. She was a short fat woman in her early fifties, her teeth were atrocious, no doubt due to the fact that her mouth seldom was ever without chocolate, cake or biscuits in it, her chin had more whiskers than his - and he had a full beard - and the idea of her leaving her lab complex, except to go home or get some more food, was ludicrous. But she was the best at her job he knew, if she said she would do something she would do it, and she was seldom wrong, although that was probably due to the fact that she never committed to an opinion 100%, always left that element of doubt in there, because in her eyes there was nothing that was a nailed on certainty.

"The nasty lacerations to her face were also post mortem," she continued in between eating her biscuits, "I'd say caused by the wildlife whilst she was out there, rats, foxes, who knows what. Examinations show that she had likely engaged in sexual activities very recently, there was evidence that she was on the contraceptive pill, and there were signs of vaginal trauma, she had certainly been involved in full intercourse within the past week, and probably for a long while before that from what I can tell, and there was also indication she had been anally penetrated."

"If you look at these photos," she handed him a small digital camera showing the dead girls arm, "look at the right wrist Manny, the skin has an almost shiny look to it, like a band, it's similar with the left ankle. It's pretty certain she was secured by something, perhaps a manacle or maybe a handcuff, and was kept like that for a fair old time, it certainly looks like she was held captive.

"One thing I noticed though, her teeth are in remarkably good condition, as are her nails, so she was looked after, fed a reasonable diet, she's not skinny, nor fat, considering she was a prisoner for five years, she was, rather ironically, a very healthy teenage girl."

Manny was looking at the digital images of the wrists, he pictured her tethered to a radiator or old metal bed, some dirty paedophile lurking in the background, the same bastard who had decided that at sixteen he didn't need Stacey Hamilton anymore, yeah that piece of shit had looked after her really well. But he knew Clare Melvic was a woman of medicine and science, not emotions, she had told him that before on more than one occasion, she couldn't do the job if she started to *care*.

Of course she cared about the victims, how they had lived, and how they had died, but not enough to keep her up at night, not enough to become emotionally involved, no she didn't *care* for them that much, she needed that detachment, as did Manny, only Manny had somehow forgotten how to keep it in place, how to divorce himself from missing girls and murder victims. He envied Clare on that front, her nights free of nightmares, flashbacks, and hauntings, and no more so than now.

"Any sign of a struggle before she died?" he asked.

"Nope, no defence wounds, no juicy DNA under nails, nothing."

"Could she have been drugged, before he killed her?"

"It's possible but early results from toxicology report no medication in her system, there's no sign of recreational drug use either, her bloods appeared clean and healthy."

"So he fed her, made her brush her teeth, then abused her whenever he liked, for six long years, chained up waiting for him. Then as soon as she's no longer a child he kills her." Manny was talking to himself more than to Clare, he knew Clare would correct him, and she did.

"Supposition Manny, *I* never said that."

"No, I did. When's Mum due?"

"Floyd's been in touch, now that is one good looking boy you've got there Manny, if I were twenty years younger…"

"If you were twenty years younger Clare I'd be chasing after you never mind Floyd, but that doesn't answer the question of when Mum's getting here."

"If you'd let me finish I was saying Floyd's picking her up from the hotel, should be here within the hour."

"Good I'll kick around, now let's have another brew shall we."

Manny never liked doing the stuff with grieving relatives at the best of times, so he did what he would probably always do in such instances, he called Denny in to offer the supportive shoulder, play the caring face of the Bedfordshire Constabulary Major Crimes Unit.

As Shirley Kilburton gasped and wept as Clare pulled the sheet back to reveal her deceased daughter, Denny offered the kindly words and the arm around the shoulder.

THE HUNT FOR AMELIA CLAY

"Oh why, oh why, not my Stacey, please not my Stacey," the mother wailed.

Manny watched on as Denny went to work.

"I'm sorry Ms Kilburton, please take your time, this is never easy for anyone, I'm so sorry for your lose." The young DC was talking in that reassuring voice, although Manny knew he was 100% sincere, this wasn't some act for him Denny really did care, but he was also aware that whatever he said would offer no help, no real assistance, Manny doubted if the anguished mother was even hearing what he was saying, but it was just good to say it in a reassuring voice all the same.

Just standing back silently, Manny could see the old track marks up her arm, the home made tattoo on her wrist, HK in a heart, Harry Kilburton, the lowlife who had been in the frame for this kid's murder. She stank of booze and fags, leaning over the corpse on the metal table, her lank hair nestling on the forever still face of Stacey Hamilton as her tears fell upon the daughter she had last seen as a ten year old.

He had to stop himself from judging, cut it out, he told himself, her grief is every bit as valid as any other mother's her sadness just a potent as the grief Andrea Clay would have experienced had that been Amelia beneath that sheet.

He felt ashamed of himself that the thought had even come into his head, recalling what Clare had said, how she had been *looked after*, how well would Shirley Kilburton have looked after that girl?

Yeah he felt ashamed for thinking it, but he had thought it all the same. Yet that lank haired smackhead crying her heart out wouldn't have tied her up for five years and violated her until she was actually the legal age of consent before killing her.

Who was he to judge.

He had no right, his right - no his duty - was to find the man who did this.

-TWELVE-

There's Over Seventeen Hundred Registered Sex Offenders In West Yorkshire.

The room had fallen quiet as the two detectives from Leeds addressed Manny's team in the large open office, the first a DS by the name of Johnson was a tall man in his thirties, although every neatly trimmed hair on his head was silver. He spoke with a broad Yorkshire accent. In his hand he held a large white vinyl ring binder, which he lay on Manny's desk.

"Stacey Hamilton, abducted when she was ten years old from her home on the East Riding Estate, in Leeds. It was widely thought that her step-father, Harry Kilburton, a known paedophile was responsible. Although we couldn't prove it at the time, still can't, we reckon his horrible dirty finger prints are all over it, he may not have killed the poor girl, but he certainly had a hand in her disappearance."

As he spoke Johnson was flicking the plastic pockets within his binder which showed photographs', like some illustrated modern day Brothers Grimm story book, first Stacey, then a picture of her home, her bedroom - where it was thought she was taken from - then a picture of Harry Kilburton, as he went on he turned the pages, adding life to the bleak cold facts.

"Despite one of the biggest investigations Yorkshire has ever seen, at least outside of the Ripper case, we came up with pretty much nowt. It was thought by most of us that Kilburton had murdered her and disposed of the body, although never officially, the case had kind of petered out, it was increasingly looking like it would remain unsolved."

Johnson shrugged, more a recognition of how Police work can sometimes be, rather than a reflection upon the failings of any investigation. As he spoke his colleague, a DC introduced as Cain Willoughby, watched on remaining silent, he was a similar age to Johnson although opposite in appearance, being little more than five foot five with jet black tightly curled hair.

"Obviously now things have taken a dramatic turn," Johnson continued, "apart from their ages there had been little to link Amelia Clay with Stacey, although as you no doubt know our people had come down when Amelia was first taken, there was no tangible connection to be found."

Manny flicked through the pages of the binder Johnson had now left lying on the desk, the pretty schoolgirl, grinning for all she was worth for the camera, no indication of the booze, drugs and unsuppressed danger that had awaited her when she returned home each day, just a normal pretty little kid who had no doubt cleaned her teeth extra well that morning as well as thoroughly brushing her hair, in preparation for the annual school picture.

He looked at the image of the seventies house, surrounded by a fence that appeared to have been made up from no more than splintery pallets and rusting wire, the girl's bedroom with clothes and toys everywhere, what had happened in that room that day?

What horror had been bestowed upon Stacey Hamilton?

Then the picture of Harry Kilburton, the hollowed out cheekbones, eyes sunk deep into his head, the stubble over his face flecked with grey, his mouth closed, but Manny just knew that his teeth would resemble a row of neglected brownish tombstones.

Harry Kilburton, what's your role Harry, he thought, where do you fit into all of this?

As if reading his mind DC Willoughby spoke, "You don't get more archetypal than that eh? He certainly looks the part, doesn't he."

"When did you last talk to him?" Manny asked the young DC.

"A few months back now, we're about his only visitors, at least twice a year we go, and at least twice a year he tells us nothing. That ugly face got even uglier last year, someone took a razor to it, he ain't exactly the most popular resident in his prison."

"And he gets no visitors at all?" Manny enquired.

Johnson answered, "Not that we know of, we've checked the visits register, just us, his lawyer a couple of times, certainly no family or friends, Shirley disowned him, although we're sure she knew what she was marrying into, but him bringing his hobbies into the house probably saw an end to that undying little loved up marriage."

"And Shirley, we're happy with her are we?" Manny asked.

"Her alibi stood up, she was with some punter, turning tricks at the time, she's a mess is Shirley, made some pretty bloody stupid choices in her life, but she had nothing to do with this, not directly anyway." Johnson answered.

Micky Page, Manny's DS, was looking over his DI's shoulder at the folder, "Who else did you have in the frame for it? Besides the wicked step-dad? Were there many other suspects?"

Johnson gave an ironic laugh, "There's over seventeen hundred registered sex offenders in West Yorkshire alone, four thousand in the whole of the county, we weren't short of suspects, but it kept coming back to Kilburton, he was our prime suspect."

"Well you got that wrong didn't you." Micky derisively replied, gaining himself a withering look from Johnson. Manny noticed, Micky should really keep his mouth shut sometimes, or at least give it a bit of thought, after all they hadn't exactly set the world alight when it came to tracing Amelia's abductor, which now looked very likely to be the same person as Johnson and Willoughby had failed to find.

THE HUNT FOR AMELIA CLAY

At least the Yorkshire men had managed to identify a prime suspect, which was more than they had achieved.

The point was clearly not lost on Johnson either, who merely retorted, "Perhaps you can now ask all those you pulled in about Stacey can't you?"

"We'll have to give Mr Kilburton a bit more company I think," Manny said, ignoring both the sergeants, "pay him a visit, see what he has to say."

"Yeah good luck with that." Being Johnson's reply, before adding, "see how long you last before you want to put a scar on the other side of his face, the bloke's a real test that's for sure."

Leaving Manny's office the two Yorkshire Officers promised to transfer everything in the binder into an electronic file, as well as all the other evidence they still had, this was now Beds (or more accurately Beds and Herts as the Major Crime Unit was a joint cross county department), case and as such they would now be responsible for collating everything.

As they discussed the logistics of moving so much evidence and reports that it would require a van, Johnson smiled, "That's a lot of paperwork Inspector, and I mean a lot, there's over 700 interviews alone in that lot, like I said we've a lot of wrong 'uns up our way, sorting through that is going to take a lot of time and patience, that may be a good job for Detective Sergeant Page I reckon."

Manny smiled back, "Oh I'm sure it will be in good order, plenty of signposts to what's relevant and what's not, we'll be in touch to sort it all out."

He went back to his office where Micky, Floyd and Denny were, "Tomorrow we're going to see Kilburton, apparently he's sitting in the CSU at Woodley Grange just outside of Milton Keynes, so it's no huge journey, Den you come with me, Floyd you can see his wife, Shirley, she's going back up north tomorrow, so it'll have to be first thing in her hotel, she's expecting us. So if I was you I'd ensure no one drinks too much tonight, which if Bob Barker is paying for anything shouldn't be too big a problem."

-THIRTEEN-

Detective Chief Inspector Robert Barker Has Left The Building.

The low beamed ceiling accentuated the unintelligible chatter and laughter, as everyone got into that weekend feeling, Manny was standing at the bar among the huddle of early drinkers all eager to get their first rounds in, just wishing he was somewhere else. *The Queen's Head* was busy, all the youngsters from the offices and shops meeting up, he never liked this place since they had 'done it up', ripping the heart and soul out of it, and replacing it with a 'retro' refit, a mock heart and soul for a new generation. Its beer was overpriced, in direct contrast to its bargain give a way micro waved gastronomy, where everything was 'Buy one Get one free', never mind the quality, just look at the picture of that plate covered by the behemoth of a meal, and when it came to *The Queen's* food, quantity definitely had the sway over quality.

Televisions were hung from any given vantage point relaying silently the tennis from Portugal, which no one at all was watching, but it had to be on all the same, it was the new tradition, every pub had to screen obligatory wall to wall sports, heaven forbid people were actually left to amuse themselves.

As he loaded the four beers onto the metal tray, keen not to end up with them all down his front, he once more pondered how he really didn't want to be there, and not just because he didn't care much for the surroundings, he'd never got on that well with Bob Barker, and never really wanted to, although by the same token he had nothing really against the bloke either.

After all Bob was Bob, and good luck to him.

Unlike the other two DIs under Honest Bob's command Manny didn't see himself as a game player, he'd realised that in an institution where they habitually promoted everyone one step above their abilities, he had no desire to climb any higher, it was most definitely just a job, a vocation perhaps, but definitely not a career. Although he still had seven years until he hit 55, and the road, he knew exactly what his pension was worth and he sure as hell didn't need that last minute jump up the pay scale to get by.

As he manoeuvred to the table he glanced across to where Tony Goldstein and Eddison Pond were sidling up to their now departed DCI, arranging games of golf they no longer needed to actually play now that Bob Barker had officially left the building, although both were far more interested in brown-nosing Chief Superintendent Critchlow who completed their little circle, all setting themselves apart with their superiority, a little clique they had clearly barred Manny from.

He shook his head with resignation, before walking over to where Floyd, Denny, and Micky were sitting.

"Not chatting with your mates?" Micky asked as he took the drinks from the tray Manny was holding, placing them in front of the others.

"No, I'm stuck with you three by the look of it aren't I." Manny replied sitting down and supping the top from his pint.

"Who's replacing him then, who's the new boss. You must know, oh for God's sake tell me it's not that clown from Luton?" Floyd asked.

Manny shook his head, thankfully it wasn't who Floyd was referring to, otherwise he would have been off pretty rapidly too, following Bob out of the door.

"If by that clown from Luton you mean my good mate Sean Hampton, then no it's not that clown from Luton. You may as well know, it's no secret, at least I don't think it is, they're drafting someone in, from the Met. Apparently they shut down part of the Anti-Terrorism Unit, and this guy needed a job, just at the right time."

"Yeah good luck then Manny," Micky chimed in, "I heard it was him, apparently he's so far up the Home Secretary's arsehole, they have to give him size 15 boots, just to stop him being totally sucked up there, she found him the post herself I was told, foisted him on us. He's just an axe man, fifteen percent savings over three years they want, that's his job, cut and run, we won't be seeing much of him, but the whole force will be driving around in shit heaps like yours Guv', if anyone wants directions to the nick they can just follow the trail of rust."

"Yeah well let's wait and see shall we, and there's nothing wrong with my car Micky."

Manny tried hard not to show any amusement, his car was a running joke among his team, for some reason classic Korean automotive engineering was something of a source of mirth and ridicule, but what wasn't funny was what he had heard about Bob's replacement, it was pretty much the same as his sergeant had relayed, well it was no secret, there were big savings within the squad being demanded, and who ever took the poison chalice which was Bob's old role was the one being tasked with finding them, as once Bob had signed on the dotted line to go he clearly didn't need that kind of battle as a prelude to tending to his roses and playing golf.

Manny used to enjoy nights out like these, it was part of the camaraderie of working within such a tight environment, and he got on well with all three of them, but he knew he had to drive home, it was in the back of his mind all evening, whilst firmly lodged in the front was the image of Shirley Kilburton sobbing over her daughters corpse. The heroin addicted prostitute who had married the dirty kiddie fiddler, hers was definitely not the face the papers would be leading with in tomorrow's editions, because that didn't sell copy, the last thing they wanted to feature would be the image of what little Stacey would probably have turned into had her abductor not intervened, no the world wanted to remember the toothy ten year old, the stuff of media campaigns and public sorrow.

Manny knew he was being harsh, but also that he was right, although he didn't share his thoughts with any of the others, he felt none the better for having them.

-FOURTEEN-

Adrian Howard Pays The Price For Pissing Off The Wrong People.

As Manny sat at the table, only really half in the conversation about Bob's replacement contemplating when was the soonest opportunity to flee and go home, the man who had got Bob Barker's job was unpacking the last of his possessions from the cardboard boxes in his new home.

Kneeling before a large cardboard box full of nothing VHS tapes, even though they never owned a VHS player, Adrian 'Frankie' Howard looked around his new surroundings, for some reason he had expected that around twelve hundred a month was going to rent them a mansion, one of those huge Country Houses you see in the broadsheet's property sections. Instead it had got them a rather small semi-detached cottage in the sticks. Admittedly it was a pretty good location, the small garden backing onto the canal, a mile or so outside a village called Ivinghoe, and even though it had done nothing but rain since he had arrived, he knew that on a nice day this was something special, but then for twelve hundred a month it should be. It had been the view that had swayed him, well actually it had swayed Catherine his Canadian partner, they had looked at a few places out that way, but this had been the one she had fallen for, so as in all the best relationships it was the one they moved into. How he had come to this he wasn't sure, living with someone again, sharing his life, how the hell did that happen? His long term plan was always to meet someone else, of course it was, he was a human and humans aren't solitary animals, but somehow he never envisioned it would be like this. It had been a bit of a whirlwind at first, but now things were settling down, it had been well over a year, it was all natural, he was loathe to use the phrase, spout such new age crap, but Catherine was right, there was something 'organic' about what they had, and setting up home together was the right thing to do.

He'd got a long weekend off, then he was due to start, working in the Major Crime Unit at Dunstable. He'd spent all his career in London, and until recently would have been happy to spend what was left of it there, but things had changed, this was about as good a move as he was going to get. Barbara Shaw, the Home Secretary had been as good as her word, he'd got the kind of move he wanted, although she didn't have that much choice. She had also made it clear that they were now even, he could expect no more favours, it was his move, but his move to fuck up. Her parting words being that if he followed form, she'd be taking great pleasure in sitting back and watching him burn, a great deal of pleasure indeed.

He'd seen the newspapers, he was a big believer in timing, and in this case it really was everything. His new Unit were heading up not just the Amelia Clay case, but the investigation into the murder of Stacey Hamilton. Two massive cases, he'd get stuck in from day one, lead from the front, it'd be good to be working free of all the political bollocks, none of the interference from Whitehall and Thames House, actually not just investigating, but jailing those responsible, catching the bad guys without the worry that in doing so you were somehow betraying the 'state' and killing any career prospects you may have left in the process.

He moved over to the patio doors, plucking the bottle of 12 year old *Glenfiddich* from another cardboard box, pouring a large shot into the white mug that had previously held a coffee, yeah, he thought, this is all new. Sipping his scotch, standing beside his piles of books and vinyl stacked up awaiting shelves to miraculously appear, he watched a canal barge just a few metres at the end of the small lawn, only just visible through the twilight that had descended far too early, even for that time of year, tut-tutting by, the smoke rising through the small chimney sticking out of its green gloss roof, light shining through the tiny lace covered portholes. Catherine walked over and stood beside him.

"Pretty fricking nice eh?" she said, drinking from a mug of coffee, her free hand picking up one of Frankie's books, as she looked at the cover before placing it back on the pile. "Thanks for agreeing to it Frankie, me a home bird hey, who'd have thought that, but hell man I really did fall in love with this place, I can't believe we're here."

THE HUNT FOR AMELIA CLAY

He smiled, "I'll have to take up fishing you know, otherwise that glorified river's just a big waste of time."

"You do whatever you like, bringing me here has just earned you all the Catherine points you'll ever need in life, I love this place, I just love it." But then a slightly concerned look came over her face, her tone changing completely, "So this new job, you've not said much about it, is it really what you want honey, because we can get by, you do know that, you don't have to do it if you don't want?"

Frankie stared out of the window, watching the barge disappearing behind a large bush as it made its way towards the locks a hundred or so yards down the canal, then he turned to her, "I haven't got a clue to be honest. I always saw myself seeing the time out at the ATU, never thought too much about moving, or being kicked out on my arse. So no I'm not sure if it's really what I want, but we'll see I guess. After all how bad can it be?"

-FIFTEEN-

Amelia Clay, The Chained Rabid Dog, And Her Eternal Nightmare.

She hated him, every day she had to remind herself of that fact, never let him get an edge, never allow him to be thought of in any other way. He would try and be nice, pretend to be some kind of kindly parent, but he wasn't, he was just the 'The Pig', and that's how she regarded him because he didn't deserve anything else.

The object of her hatred was now standing before her, for it was that time again, her thirty minutes of being unchained from that bed, her time to bathe, use the toilet and do whatever she damn well pleased behind that white gloss painted door that afforded her, Amelia Clay, the only privacy she truly had each day. Regular as clockwork he would come, eight in the morning, and eight at night, every day of her life, the life that this man who called himself uncle had robbed from her so cruelly.

But then it wasn't everyday was it, there were the special days, those awful horrendous special days, when 'The Pig' didn't unchain her for the purpose of bathing, washing, or using the loo, when he never freed her for her much anticipated moments of solitude, instead she was unchained for *that*, and *that* was what she dreaded so much, more than anything, *that* was the worst thing about her wretched life. Birthdays, Christmas, Easter, any occasion that would normally be special for a child were just nightmares, only they weren't nightmares were they. Nightmares aren't real, they can be terrifying, scary, absolutely horrid, but they are not real. They may seem like it at the time, but you can always tell yourself that they are not happening, everything will be OK, just fine in the morning. But in her world everything was not OK, nothing was just fine in any morning, the mornings that would see her hurting, hurting and bleeding in a way no girl should hurt and bleed. The fact was that nothing was OK on those mornings, everything was just bad, and as bad as bad can be. Because the nightmares, that weren't nightmares, would see 'The Pig' present her to a host of other 'Uncles', a load of other horrible Pigs, evil Pigs, repulsive fat ugly Pigs, Pigs that hurt her, hurt her so badly. Just thinking of it made her scrunch her eyes shut tightly.

Make it go away, she told herself, make it go away, clear your head Ami, make it go away.

But it wasn't going away, how could it?

Tethered to that bed over twenty three hours a day, like some rabid dog, by the fifteen foot chain that was her jailer, her captor, but not her tormentor, no it would never go away. She knew every link of that stainless steel restriction between her and any route out of there, every single identical link, there was no weak spot, nowhere that might give with some encouragement, it was cold solid steel, and it kept her there, kept her where Phillip-what-ever-his-name-was wanted her.

He was no uncle, no, he was just a very very horrible Pig.

As he placed the key in the handcuff she looked away from him, unable to make eye contact.

"What an awful day it's been out there Amelia, just rain, rain, rain, you'd never believe it was only a few weeks away from Christmas, now don't forget to clean your teeth properly and brush your hair…"

The foul Pig was talking, although she never acknowledged him, she knew what Christmas had in store for her, as it did for the past four years, so cruelly followed by New Year's Eve, just six days later, another party, another one of his sick revolting parties, she continued looking away from him, focussing on the TV in the corner of her room, the TV which was now switched off, but the same one which played the DVDs and videos, never actual telly programmes like the news and stuff, but it was still the TV that was her only window to a normal world, a world where not everyone was cruel and sadistic, a world where people didn't do those things to other people, a world she had lived in once, a long, long time ago, oh so very long ago.

-SIXTEEN-

The Girl In The Bath, Contemplating The Long Fruitless Wait For Prince Charming.

"Only five more minutes Amelia, and don't forget to do your teeth."

She sank her head under the water, her eyes tightly closed, closing him out, silencing his tapping at the door. What did it matter to him if she cleaned her teeth, what business of his was it? But then everything was his business, and she knew exactly why he wanted her to have nice teeth, to look pretty, to be just right for his perverted depraved friends. She raised her head out of the water, her ears blocked, that dull silent drone allowing her to shut out the sound of him immediately outside the door, she thought back to when the dentist had visited the house, she didn't know exactly when, it was sometime between her thirteenth birthday and Easter, she recalled how he had looked at the bad tooth, then did the filling, the only filling she had ever had in her life.

COLIN PAYNE

Remembering how he had looked so kind, had been so nice to her, recalling how she whispered to him between spitting into the sink, pleading, begging for his help, for him to call the Police, in the hope that he was somehow her saviour, her rescuer. After all he was a dentist, they were nice people weren't they? Their job was to help people, making them alright, there to stop the pain, but she was to cruelly find out that he was just another 'uncle', later recognising his face at a party, that revolting sweating piggy face, as like so many others that night he forced himself upon her, got inside her, he wasn't kind, he wasn't someone to trust, he was just another one of them.

She knew there was stuff she could do, stuff that would make them leave her alone, she had seriously considered cutting her face at one point, slicing herself so badly, in such an ugly fashion that no one, no matter how sick and depraved they may be, would ever want to look at her, would ever want to touch her again. She could just break the glass in the window, and cut, and not stop until there was nothing pretty left, she could do it before he would be able to get in and stop her, do it quick, but she always resisted, always the hope that one day this would be over, one day she could be normal again, but when that would be she had no idea.

But she knew she couldn't go on like this, and once more looked out of the unbroken window, across the roof tops that formed part of the huge sprawling building she was imprisoned within, and over into the woods far beyond. Every day she looked out, and never had she seen a soul out there, never. No one to call to, no one to help, no one to save her, but then even if she did attract someone's attention, call someone, how was she to know that it wasn't just another dentist, another Phillip, another Pig.

It was down to her, she now recognised that fact, there would be no Prince Charming arriving, freeing her with love's first kiss, or climbing the walls, pulling himself up by her long braided hair, to liberate her from her very unhappy ever after. No there would be plenty of revolting loveless kisses and hair pulling coming her way, she was all too aware of that, but never from any Prince Charming.

She looked down, immediately below the window was the drop, the drop that would no doubt lead to nothing but her death, and although there was little to live for at that moment, she still wanted to live, wanted to go home to Mummy and Daddy, she closed her eyes, again picturing their faces, them smiling, as she enthusiastically called for their attention as she rode her first bike, the little purple one, around the close where they used to live, them waving back as she peddled for all she was worth.

Opening her eyes she once more considered her potential escape route, she knew it so well - because she had looked at it so often - there was a small ledge approximately a metre below, about 3 inches it protruded, it ran along the side of the building, towards the slate roofs a story down. That ledge, it had become fixed in her mind, ingrained in her imagination, hundreds of times she had thought about it, lowering herself down, inching along it, then somehow dropping down onto the top of the lower part of the huge house.

That was as far as her plan went, how she would still get down she had no idea, how she would get away was not in reality something she had foreseen, not properly, but that ledge, it was her way out. She needed to be brave, to be courageous, to take that decision, and actually prepare for the day she was going to do something.

"Amelia, that's it, it's time to come out, please don't make me come in, I try to treat you like a big girl, you must respect my rules darling."

"I won't be a minute, please don't be angry, I only want to clean my teeth properly."

But that time was not today.

-SEVENTEEN-

Henry Manningwell And Denny Black Meet Horrible Harry.

Manny looked around the spotless and sterile gate lodge of Woodley Grange, it wasn't his idea of what a prison should look like at all, there was no sign of any rodent infestation or the Victorian severity that he had encountered on previous visits to other jails, in fact as a lifetime tax payer he felt a little aggrieved, this place looked positively welcoming. Whilst he and Denny stood before her, the Prison Officer behind the bullet proof screen was guiding them through the checks they were required to have before entering the modern 'Cat A' prison. They had both been photographed and their finger prints scanned by the infrared biometric panel before them, they had been stripped of phones, pagers, memory sticks, or any other electronic gizmo they may have had, and were led to what Manny reckoned resembled an airport check in.

As he watched his shoes and belt travelling along the conveyor belt that ran through the massive x-ray machine,

Manny rather self-consciously curled his big toe in, now all too aware of the hole it had been poking through in his sock, he was sure it hadn't been there when he got dressed that morning, but that wasn't something that he rigorously checked as a rule, as his shoes would normally remain firmly on his feet all day. He was also forced to acknowledge just how much weight he had piled on of late, having seen how his waist band had folded over on itself, free of the belt, struggling to hold back the heaving stomach which he had created by over indulging in too many take away meals, an excess of beer and no exercise whatsoever. He breathed in as far as he could as the poor Prison Officer, who had been tasked with searching him, ran her fingers inside the under-stress waist band, before forcing a smile as she reunited him with his belt and shoes.

Jesus he thought, I need to lose weight!

After walking through a labyrinth of corridors they were shown into the bleak and austere interview room where they would be meeting Mr Kilburton. It was almost bare but for the table, three tatty chairs and a tape machine. On the walls were posters warning of the consequences of smuggling items into the prison, how 'Security Is Everyone's Responsibility' and rather bizarrely an advertisement for a forthcoming production of 'A Midsummer's Night's Dream', which was being held in the prison gymnasium prior to Christmas.

"Do you fancy a bit a Shakespeare Guv?" Denny joked nodding towards the poster.

"Never did get it Den," Manny snorted, "load of old tosh if you ask me."

"I don't know I did some at University, in fact I had a role in that play."

Manny groaned, "Oh come on, surely you're not that predictable."

"What?" Denny protested.

"Don't tell me, your Bottom went down really well."

Denny shook his head, "If you're going to spoil all my punch-lines I'll just shut up."

"Good." Being all Manny replied.

He liked working with Denny Black, the lad usually knew when to speak, when to have an opinion, and when best to just keep quiet, but clearly had gauged it wrong on this occasion, Manny wasn't in the mood for any of his end of the pier humour, he wasn't particularly looking forward to meeting the man they could now see approaching the door, flanked by two surly looking members of staff.

Harry Kilburton shuffled in to the room.

"Just ring the red bell when you're ready, not the green one mind, that one gets you plenty of unwanted attention. We'll leave Mr Kilburton in your safe hands," one of the escorting officers said before they both left, locking the half glazed door behind them.

Manny looked around to where the two bells were positioned on the wall, located just over Denny's shoulder, he presumed the green one must be the alarm.

He then turned to Kilburton, Yorkshire's number one suspect, he was skittish, he looked scared, glancing through the Perspex panels that revealed the other interview rooms, clearly distracted.

"Good morning Mr Kilburton," Manny opened, "I'm DI Manningwell and this is DC Black. We're here from Herts and Beds Major Crime Unit, we're investigating the murder of Stacey Hamilton."

Kilburton stopped his fidgeting, the mention of Stacey's name getting his now undivided attention.

"We'll be taping this interview, and I would like to make it clear that we are just interviewing you, you are just helping us, you are not under arrest or anything. Your attendance is not compulsory, and you may request a representative if you wish."

Kilburton said nothing, but Manny could see how his demeanour had changed, he was licking his lips, as if he was actually relishing their chat, Manny suspected he wanted all the gory details, wanted to know what the press hadn't said, there was no sadness, or upset that they were talking about Stacey in the past tense, her demise appeared to have set about no negative emotional response what so ever. He watched on, Kilburton's left knee now jerking up and down, yeah this piece of work was actually excited, a minute ago he had been shitting himself, now he's getting off on it, he thought, Manny glanced towards Denny, who was also watching Kilburton, his DC's face was the picture of restraint no emotion on view at all, yeah he was good.

Manny had taken an instant dislike to Horrible Harry, as the press had dubbed him, but then it would be very hard not to. He saw the scar running across the length of his entire face, it was impossible not to see it, he imagined the scene at the time, how much blood must there have been? The face flapping open revealing muscle and bone, he noticed where the stubbly beard now resided, the strip where the hair failed to grow, like an old railway line through wild undergrowth.

Did he deserve it?

Of course he did, but it wasn't justice, not for what happened to his late step-daughter, no it was Manny's job to deliver that form of justice.

He switched on the large twin tape machine, which emitted a high pitched beeping sound before both the spools rotated in perfect unison.

"For the benefit of the tape I am Detective Chief Inspector Henry Manningwell."

"I am Detective Constable Dennis Black."

He then addressed Kilburton, "Can you please say your full name and date of birth for the tape."

"Harry Kilburton, sixth July 1977." It was the first words he had spoken since he had sat before them, his voice was gruff, forty a day gruff, and Manny thought that if he was only in his late thirties, then he must have had a bloody hard paper round as a kid. He instantly sized him up, he looked at least sixty, his grey pallor, the skin coated skull of a face, his rotten teeth, he didn't look well, and he certainly didn't look under forty.

"Please can you confirm your relationship to Stacey Hamilton." Manny asked.

Kilburton initially said nothing, his head cocked to one side examining the two Police Officers, particularly Denny, he gave a smile, or at least Manny supposed that was what it was supposed to be, his mouth offering instead a crooked variation, where the twin blades had sliced across his lips. When he did speak it was a slow and deliberate rasp, "She was the wife's kid."

"And how did you get on with her, what was your relationship like?"

Again the horrible crooked smile.

"Oh it were like Romeo and Juliette, we were right star struck lovers were me and Stacey."

Manny looked on impassively, before Kilburton let out a laugh which turned into a cough.

"No I'm kidding, she were Shirley's daughter, I were never your ideal Dad, but I never touched her if that's what you're asking, too close to home."

"Really? Wasn't the neighbour's child close to home?" Manny asked.

Kilburton just grinned, "Yeah but sometimes you can't help who you fall for can you?"

"She's dead now, Stacey, how does that make you feel?"

"Not a lot, do you have any fags, I'm dying for a real smoke, you know proper cigarettes."

"No I've given up," Manny lied.

"Hmm, how do I feel about little Stacey? It's a shame I guess."

"You guess?"

"Well like I said she weren't my kid, and she is kind of to blame for all this in't she. Not that I'm bitter or anything, you know with me being the forgiving kind n'all, but really such a little tease, I can't odds it, she was asking for it, really pushing it all the time."

Manny fixed him a hard stare, he remembered Johnson's heads up, about him being a 'test', he now knew exactly what he had meant, the bloke was a 'test' alright.

Kilburton was leaning back in his chair, no longer the frightened rabbit, he was now having a bit of fun, he clearly knew what he was saying, and appeared to be revelling in his provocative act.

"You ever been to one of theme parks Inspector?" the grinning prisoner asked.

Manny said nothing.

"Well imagine you're a kid, let's say at that *Alton Towers* place, and all the best rides are the ones you can't go on, no matter how much you may want to, how appealing they may seem, they're out of bounds. Well that was Stacey for me, don't get me wrong I'd love to have ridden on that ride, I could have gone on it all day, every day, really had fun, scream if you wanna go faster. But no I weren't allowed was I. So imagine the kid at the amusement park, if they then take away that ride, the ride he can't go on anyway, what does it matter to him, if anything he's glad to see it go, no longer missing anything is he."

Yeah Manny was just about ready to put that scar on the other side of this little shit's face.

"That's one way of looking at it Mr Kilburton, one perspective. Another way would be someone took that girl, a little girl you were partly responsible for, they held her for six years, the girl who should have been under your care, subjected her to God knows what, then murdered her. That's the perspective I'd go for, that's the view most people would take I'd say." Manny was speaking calmly, but there was a definite edge to his voice, Denny was sitting back still watching, just seeing where Manny was taking this.

"Yeah well I in't most people, I'm special I am." Kilburton again coughed after speaking.

"So what part did you play in Stacey's disappearance?" Manny had changed tact, the ambiguous tone in his voice gone, that wasn't so much a question as a fact he was stating, "Come on Harry, where do *you* fit into all of this?"

Kilburton again laughed, and once more broke into the coughing fit, wheezing and gasping for air to refill his spluttering lungs.

"Is that cancer Harry?" Manny asked.

"Sorry to disappoint you, it's just a chest infection." Kilburton answered, wiping the phlegm from his lips with a scrunched up tissue. He was right, that had disappointed him, it was almost something he had hoped for, the idea of Harry being in pain until his terminal decline was a thought that appealed to Manny.

"So go on, enlighten us, what part did you play in it all Harry?"

Harry Kilburton thought for a moment, as if tempted to actually answer before tempering his thoughts prior to speaking.

"There're many things you don't understand Inspector, you think I'm the only nonce in the village eh? That Harry is unique in his tastes and desires? Oh come on, the world's full of us, people you don't understand, people who have to live lies, just because we were born in the wrong place and time. Look at history, how many Kings were shagging little girls, marrying them, that's our royalty, our great British heritage, we're all nonces at heart."

He broke out coughing again, but was clearly eager to go on, to continue enlightening Manny as to how things 'really were'.

"What you see is the tip of the iceberg, do you think we all live on shitty council estates in Leeds, that we're all on the dole, well do you?"

He watched Manny for a reaction, then laughed, that horrible rasping, wheezing laugh, "The rich, the famous, MPs, doctors, lawyers, millionaire business men, shit even Policemen, a whole world of us, it's happening everywhere, every day, little secret worlds you know nothing of, societies and groups getting on with it, yet you still think I took Stacey, oh you're so bloody wrong, you in't got a clue, it's going on all around you, and yet you still come to me like I have all the sodding answers. Yeah I probably do know more than you do, but who ended up with Stacey five years after she went? That's like asking who's driving the car I sold five years ago, people sell things on don't they."

Manny, slowly shook his head, this bloke was a shit, but he knew something, he was right about that at least, he knew more than they did.

"So Harry, who took her, did you? Did you sell her on like some second hand motor, one careful owner, no mileage on the clock, was that it, you were just the salesman?" Manny could see Kilburton was keen to talk, the corner of his mouth, at least the one that still functioned correctly was twitching, whilst a string of spittle just hung from the other side.

"Well was that it, you sold your step-daughter, how much? How much was Stacey worth to you?" The ambiguous calm was now gone, Manny was leaning towards Kilburton, in his face, pushing him. But Horrible Harry had played his game, had his fun.

"See that bell Inspector, the red one, the one that sees my personal assistants come back to fetch me, well you ought to be pushing that, because that's me done."

"Oh no we still have questions for you. Go on tell me, who took Stacey, you know, I know you do, who took her Harry?" Manny nearly had him, this man was keen to spill his guts, he may not have realised it, but once he had started he was prime for a bit of confessing, he wouldn't be able to stop himself, Manny just needed to press the right buttons.

Harry again wheezed and coughed, spitting on the floor before them, "No you in't got no more questions, that's it. Now like I said, for the benefit of the tape I no longer wish this interview to continue, now push the sodding bell, I'm done here, I'm doing my time, I told you I've nothing to do with it, now piss off."

Manny pressed the 'stop' button on the tape machine, and took the two tapes out, handing them to Denny to seal and label, before reluctantly pressing his finger against the small red button.

THE HUNT FOR AMELIA CLAY

"You know Harry, I reckon you can tell us so much more, and I intend to prove you're involved in all of this, maybe not killing that poor little girl, but yeah you know where she went. We'll be back, believe me, you can be sure of that."

-EIGHTEEN-

"You Weren't My First Choice You Know, In Fact None of The Board Favoured you."

"What do you think?" Manny asked as they drove back.

"I think he's a nasty bit of work, you know he probably had a hard on whilst you were talking to him, he was playing with us, and enjoying it," Denny answered not taking his eyes off the road as he spoke.

"Yeah, but how involved is he?"

"With Stacey probably very, he practically told us as much, but how does that tie in with Amelia? I mean, there's no link with him and the Clays, I can't imagine Andrea ever inviting him down from Leeds for a dinner party."

Manny shook his head, "Hmm is there even a link there at all, is Stacey's killer creating it himself by choosing to leave her there, is he leading us on? Perhaps we'd have been better churning through those files before going to see that piece of work."

THE HUNT FOR AMELIA CLAY

Denny smiled, "Or roughly translated, when we get back get stuck into all that paperwork they gave us."

"Am I really that predictable?"

As Manny and Denny made their way back to Dunstable, DCI Adrian 'Frankie' Howard was sitting outside Chief Superintendent Edwin Critchlow's office on the second floor of Bedfordshire Police Headquarters in Kempston, just outside of Bedford. He was browsing the photographs and paintings dotted around the walls, as the secretary stopped her typing and smiled at him, "He won't be long Sir, he is expecting you."

Of course he was expecting him, although how warm the welcome would be Frankie didn't know, when put on the spot by the Home Secretary, months earlier, he'd plucked the first place he could think of out of the air, he had a friend who lived out this way, and he had lost his licence driving through a village in the county, otherwise he may just as well have blurted out Strathclyde or Devon and Cornwall, now he was sitting outside his new boss's office he was wondering on the wisdom of his decision. He had of course 'boarded' for the job, but that had been a formality, he knew he could have turned up pissed and naked and would still have got the post. It wasn't the ideal backdrop to a new life, foisted on them by probably one of the most odious women in Britain, but better than being scattered around the Met which is what had happened to the rest of his team.

"Mr Critchlow will see you now, please go through," the secretary informed him, again the warm smile.

Entering the office Frankie could see it was certainly well appointed, a large mahogany desk, with an almost throne like matching wooden chair, floor to ceiling bookshelves along one wall, and filling the others another host of pictures, photographs and plaques, ornate badges from foreign forces, commemorating visits and exchanges, Hong Kong, New York, Toronto. There he was the man sitting in front of him in at least half a dozen photographs shaking hands with people who Frankie didn't recognise, as well as the obligatory picture from the day he passed out of his training, he had one just like it, the group shot, only his was buried in packing cases somewhere back at his new home.

This was their first meeting since Frankie had attended the interview, he had noted at the time how the Chief Superintendent was younger than he had expected, around the same age as he was, he stood from behind his desk holding his hand out.

"Adrian, welcome to Beds, just wanted a chat before you started at Dunstable, please sit."

"Thank you Sir." Frankie replied.

But the welcome had evaporated almost as quickly as it was offered.

"You weren't my first choice you know, in fact none of the board favoured you, yet here you are, strange that isn't it. Congratulations."

Frankie wasn't sure how to respond, so just nodded and said, "Thanks, I think."

"Let's save the thanks for the time being. Let me tell you about the Major Crime Unit, we're a joint force initiative in partnership with Hertfordshire. We have four teams spread over the two counties, each headed up by a DCI, all answering directly to me. You're heading up Team 3 which is based in Dunstable. You'll initially have three DIs each leading a sub-team. Murders, rapes, serious crime, it's all under your umbrella. It's a huge work load, but the results speak for themselves. That's the good news. Unfortunately in these troubled economic times we're not immune to the savings in public expenditure that everyone is expected to be making. We need to trim between 15 and 20% off of our budget across all departments, including yours. I need to make savings, and as such you need to make savings.

"I hear you're a good manager Adrian, that's good, because that's what I need, not a Policeman, not an investigator, I need you to manage this, manage these transitions for me, and of course for the force."

Frankie needed to put him right, his new boss appeared to be talking to the wrong person, or at least he hoped he was. "Sir, I should point out I'm not from a financial back ground, I'm a detective, it's what I do, and I do it bloody well but..."

Critchlow interrupted him, "No you were a detective, remember that Howard, *you were*. Because in this role I need you to think beyond that, out of the box, but just in case you need help here I'll offer you a clear and precise overview. You have three sub-teams at Dunstable, each with an Inspector, two Sergeants, and four Constables. I want that changing to two sub-teams, and in each I want an Inspector, two Sergeants and five Constables. Now I know you don't come from a financial background, you've just told me that, so let me help you out here, that offers me a saving in salaries of a lot of money."

Frankie felt sick, what the hell was he coming in to?

He wasn't some bean counter or hatchet man ready to slash and run, he was a copper, a good copper at that. Was this his punishment for getting one over on the Home Secretary, was this her last laugh. He tried to twist the conversation back to policing, something he understood, something he relished.

"I know of the Stacey Hamilton case, and the hunt for Amelia Clay, both of which come under Team Three I believe, can I ask what are the unit's other priorities?" he asked, desperate to return to firm ground.

Critchlow merely smiled, "Manage my budget Adrian, that's your priority, that's all you need to concern yourself with, at least for now, like I said that's your role."

"Just manage the budget? Just make the cuts. Can I ask one thing, how free am I to shuffle the pack? I want to bring in three of my own people, is that on the table?" Frankie asked.

"As long as you stick to the template I have laid out I don't honestly care, there's spaces to redeploy within the force, you can use who you like, just show me the savings. Now if there's nothing else I'll get Joanne to show you where your office is…"

"You mean I'm working out of here, not Dunstable, I'm sorry Sir, but how does that make sense?"

THE HUNT FOR AMELIA CLAY

"It makes sense Detective Chief Inspector, because I say it makes sense. For the time being I want you here, free from distractions, free from business you don't need to be involved in, like I said your priority is the budget, everything else we can look at later, now if that's everything…"

The first of the pile of files plonked on to his desk, theylanded with a loud thud, sending a little cloud of dust into the air. Denny just stared at it open mouthed, it had to be over a foot high, all bound with cloth straps tightly fastened with small metal clips, an A4 sheet of paper on top with just five words written on it *Harry Kilburton one of six*.

He groaned as he untied them, urgh God where to begin?

They appeared to be in almost random order, and looked like it had been literally years since anyone had last looked through them, oh Jesus, what a bloody mess, he thought.

Taking a bit of logic he started where he presumed would be the best place to look, the thickest one.

Harry Kilburton Interviews was written in black felt tip pen down the spine and across the front. Opening the cover there he was, unscarred but still ugly as hell, his photo taken with him holding a card with his name written upon it. Then the index page offering a date and time for each of the written transcripts of the interviews the Police had conducted with him, there were dozens of them, ranging from 'no comments' to pages of denials. No wonder Yorkshire were so pleased to see the back of this case.

-NINETEEN-

The Horrible Pig And His Exciting News.

He had that look on his face, that devious slimy look that meant something bad was going to happen. He had that look when he had one of his surprises for her, and his surprises were never pleasant. Yet whatever it was he was keeping it to himself, at least until she had taken her bath.

It was the evening, it was dark and raining, really raining out there, Amelia was sure she could still hear him just the other side of the door, his repulsive breathing, was he watching her again?

Hundreds of times she had run it through her head, and each time had talked herself out of it, it was too dangerous, if she slipped she would fall, and if she fell that would be it. She wasn't Spiderman, there was so little to cling onto, but, there was always that but, what if she didn't try, didn't try and help herself? No one had come to her rescue, rushed to her aid, and no one likely would now. Stacey had gone, where - she didn't know - but she wasn't at the last party, and she had always been there at the parties, it was just her now, her and that Pig that called himself an uncle, and that was too lonely a situation for anyone to put up with.

Amelia placed the towel over the door knob, obliterating the keyhole, and waited to see if he would come bursting in, but no, nothing. She silently pushed open the sash window, and hung her head out, her hair blew in the wet wind, clinging to her face, and like a hundred times before she looked down at that tiny ledge, she was in just her nightdress, far down below she could just make out the crates stacked up, and the large cylindrical orange gas tank.

Would they break any fall?

Or only make the injuries worse?

She turned her head and looked along the wall, about three metres along there was another window, then a bit further on another, then the short drop onto the slate roof that butted onto that part of the building, the roof that offered her a sure footing, a route out of there.

She hesitated, was she being mad?

She hung a leg out of the window, and then swung the other out, her belly lying flat against the wooden frame, it was like she was acting out some dream, there was a surreal quality to it all, like it wasn't actually happening, as if she were watching on from outside of her own body.

She slowly and deliberately took the weight with her arms, easing her mid-rift up, lowering her legs gently down the side of the wall, her toes extending desperate to make contact with the narrow ridge she knew was there. Suddenly she panicked, all too aware of just how high up she was, how very far from the ground, just as she lost her footing, her outstretched toe sliding from the narrow ledge it had only just located. She struggled to support herself as her knee scraped against the abrasive brickwork, slipping down, she was all too aware of the skin than had been peeled off due to the horrible stinging sensation she felt. Her heart was in her mouth, her arms tightening their grip in the window frame as she scrambled back up, now realising the foolishness of what she had just done, desperate to get back to the safety of the bathroom, her chest pounding, she felt sick, that was awful.

There was a tap at the door, "Are you OK, I can't hear the bath running darling?"

She silently pulled the sash window closed, and hurriedly moved to the bath and turned the taps on. She had made her mind up, as stupid and mad as it had been she was going to try it again, even though she was terrified, she should have done it earlier, for this was no life, but there was no way she was capable of that, she would have been blown clean off that narrow ledge, but soon, it had to be soon.

"Hurry up Amelia, I have something to tell you, something exciting, I can barely wait, it's so exciting! I think I'll just burst if I try to keep it in any longer!"

It was him again, of course it was him, who else would it be. She wished he would just burst, explode in a mass of flesh and gore, disappear from her life, her wretched nightmare of a life, but he wouldn't would he, he would be there the other side of the door, always there.

***

THE HUNT FOR AMELIA CLAY

Drying herself off, she took the fresh nightdress from the pine chest of drawers in the bathroom, identical to the others, and slid it on, ensuring that her grazed knee was well hidden. She didn't want to make him angry, she knew she couldn't delay any further, and as she opened the door, as she knew he would be, he was there sitting on the chair at her dressing table. She walked to him as if programmed, her left hand held out, no words, no eye contact, no communication at all, and like he had done now over a thousand times before he placed the steel handcuff attached to the chain - which was in turn connected to the large steel ring on the wall - upon her wrist, his hand remaining on the back of hers, she forced herself not to flinch away, not to recoil with disgust, as he stroked it gently, his fingers lingering far too long over her soft skin, before he slowly pulled them away.

Please let that be it, please God don't let him stay the night, she thought, as she fought to hold back her tears.

She walked over to the bed, not looking back at him, desperate for him not see the effect he was having, and climbed under the white cotton duvet, turning her back to him, scrunching her eyes shut tightly, hoping with all her might that he would just leave.

"Well don't you want to know the exciting news?" he asked.

No she didn't!

Because there was only one kind of news this Pig ever delivered and it was far from exciting. Tears trickled down her face, she couldn't hold them back any longer, as he continued, his well enunciated words stabbing into her very heart, each one tearing her apart.

"Well I must say you can be an ungrateful little bitch can't you!" his tone had changed, she could hear the spite in his voice, it was how he went, how he acted before he would punish her, she flinched, was he going to hurt her now.

"I'm sorry," she whimpered, "please tell me your news."

"That's better."

His voice had returned to its normal level, once more calm, like he was reading a small child a bedtime story or something. "There's going to be another party, it's this Tuesday, that's just five days away, and believe me it's a special party, let's call it a late birthday party for your mother. Lots of people are coming, it will be fancy dress, isn't that exciting."

It was no such thing, it was awful, it was the last thing in the world she wanted to hear, yet the one thing she was expecting him to say, knew he was going to come out with. She couldn't say that to him, couldn't tell him how bad that was, she had learnt that lesson early on, it wasn't wise to argue with him, it was a mistake she had only made a few times before, she could see the signs now, knew how to behave when he began to turn. The marks still resided on her back, the raised welts now shiny scar tissue, left upon her as her permanent reminder not to talk back to 'Uncle Phillip', as if the usual punishment hadn't been enough to deter her from repeating her mistake. She sobbed as he fussed around, collecting her plate, cutlery and glass, from her evening meal.

THE HUNT FOR AMELIA CLAY

"Oh I expected you to be pleased, you are pleased aren't you Amelia, please tell me you are, because I need you to be pleased, we all need you to be pleased, no one wants to go to a party full of miseries do they? What fun would that be for anyone?"

She nodded her head, unable to talk, scared that her sobs would illicit another punishment.

"Good, because I don't ask much in return for caring for you, don't ask much at all, but when I do ask I need you to do exactly as I say, you do understand that don't you?"

Again she just nodded, she was biting the top of the duvet, stifling her anguish, gagging her pain, because she understood all too well.

Tuesday, just five days away, apart from her birthdays and the usual holidays, the special parties were always on a Tuesday, but not this time, her mind was made up, she wouldn't be going, she had been to her last party, and she was sure of one thing, she would never go to another.

-TWENTY-

Harry Kilburton Decides That If No One Else Is Going To Help Him, Then It Is Time To Help Himself.

Shit that hurt, what the hell were they thinking, he had told them there was no way he could move to a normal location, he was a nonce, and a notorious one at that, but they knew that didn't they, knew he'd be eaten alive on C Wing, a tiny sprat to be devoured by the far bigger fish, eager to offset their horrible dirty secrets by highlighting his, it was only a matter of time in such a location before they came for him. Yet still they had moved him.

He again punched the wall, he looked at the back of his hand, his knuckles skinned, the sore red tissue all too obvious, the blood smeared across not just his hand but the graffiti and cream paint on his cell wall, but he needed to punch it harder, do some real damage. Again another crunching smack, Jesus Christ that hurt! One of his knuckles was now disjointed and mashed up beneath what was left of his tattered skin, oh fuck that was painful.

That should just about do it, he said he would show them, show them they couldn't keep him there, and he wasn't wrong.

Wondering if in fact he had taken it too far he rang his cell bell, that hand looked bad, and felt a bloody sight worse, but let them deal with that, that was their worry, theirs to put right. He could hear the high pitched whining of his bell, deliberately fashioned to be that irritating, impossible for the overworked screws not to hear, and just as impossible to ignore. And sure enough here they came.

"What?" the face the other side of the dirty observation panel asked, "What's up?"

Harry was sitting on his bed, he said nothing, just held his smashed and shattered hand up for the officer to see, smirking as he did so, yeah he said he'd show them.

The officer scrunched his eyes to focus on what was before him. "That's not too clever is it Harry, I'll put you down sick for the evening."

The steel flap closed obliterating Harry's view of outside his cell, no that wasn't what was happening, that was not how this was going to play out! He jumped up from the bed and rang the bell again, once more the same face appeared.

"I want to kill myself I'm suicidal! You need to open a watch!" Harry shouted.

He could see the officer shaking his head, before the sound of the key in the lock and the door opening, a sharp metallic clonk as the door was locked open. The resigned looking warder walked in, yeah he couldn't ignore that, he had to do something now.

"Sit on your bed Harry," he said as he pulled up the plastic chair in the cell so that he was sitting level with him, "Go on, I'm all ears, tell me what's up?"

"Well it's like this," Harry had his attention, he'd be out of there within the hour, "I'm scared for my life on here Guv', really scared, everyone knows what I'm in for don't they, everyone knows I'm Horrible Harry, and they'll all want a piece of me won't they, all wanna be the one who slashes me, scars me again, I'd rather be dead, I really would."

The officer looked far from sympathetic, a world weary look of irritation instead was on clear display.

"Really?" he answered, "You really think you bruising your hand is going to get you back on the numbers, back in your little isolated world? Look mate, the Governor himself had you moved, you've been risk assessed as able to cope on here, the Seg was full, no room at the inn, this is you for the rest of your sentence Harry, accept it, try and integrate, it's not so bad on here, there's plenty on the wing who are in for all sorts, just get your head around it. If you hide away and refuse to come out, get yourself on suicide watches, well you'll draw attention to yourself, paint a big target on your back. You really do need to give it a proper go."

"Give it a go, are you mad? Look at my face Guv!"

Was this fool even listening to a word he said, was he really that damn stupid? "Look! There's a clue right there as to what people think of me, what happens to me, please I'm begging, get me off of here, I can't come out of my cell, I swear down, I can't even get my own dinner, for God's sake man, help me, please I'm begging you."

"Like I said fella, not my decision I'm afraid," the officer said standing up and walking towards the small metal door, "what I will do though is put you on a watch, get a nurse over to take a look at that hand of yours, make sure you're OK, and I will try to talk to Mr Hargreaves, see if we can't get you back to the Seg. In the meantime be sensible Harry, it's your hand not mine, I'd be looking after it a bit better if it were mine, you've made your point, that's hurting no one but yourself."

"Wait!" Harry called out, "I need to speak to Inspector Manningwell, as soon as possible it's urgent. Get someone to contact him straight away, I mean it, it's important."

That was it, if they weren't going to do nowt for him, if they weren't going to help him, he needed to help himself, he'd tell the copper all he knew in exchange for a move if he had to, after all he couldn't be in any more danger, yeah he'd tell him everything.

-TWENTY ONE-

It's Just A Very Simple Request.

Once more the detectives from Dunstable were in the interview room, the twin tapes running. Before them sat Harry Kilburton, he appeared even more twitchy than when they first met him, his hand was bandaged up into a thick lump, and he was fidgeting, his leg vibrating as his foot could be heard tapping as if he were wired up to some low voltage electrical socket. He was clearly afraid, and Manny figured that was a good thing, it was Harry who had requested this meeting, and urgently, so it was Harry who would be doing the talking.

The DI sat back observing him, he'd done the formalities for the tape, and was now just leaning back watching, allowing the odious specimen in front of him to contemplate what he wanted to say, letting him stew in the awkward silence. Denny was likewise remaining silent, happy once more to let Manny run on this one however he wanted.

Harry's tapping foot competed with the ticking from the clock on the wall as the only noises in the room, as the two Police Officers watched the prisoner in front of them, then

THE HUNT FOR AMELIA CLAY

Harry suddenly burst into one of his coughing fits, rising to his feet as he bent over, a thin line of stringy spittle dangling from his mouth, before wiping it away on his grubby sweatshirt sleeve.

"I need to move back to the Seg," he suddenly blurted, "I need to go straight away Inspector, I can't stay on no normal wing, it in't happening."

He sat back down in his chair, before continuing, his voice still rasping from his rattling chest.

Manny raised his eyes, what a waste of time, he didn't care where Harry resided, he wasn't particularly fussed if he was safe or not, in fact he no doubt would only get what he deserved, but what he was concerned about was being called in urgently for this, didn't he have enough on his plate, he looked at his watch and went to rise from his chair, but Harry again pleaded.

"I'll tell you stuff you need to know, damn it, I'd tell you anything. You wanna know who's been playing on little Stacey I'll tell you that, really I will, but I need to be safe, because if I tell you that, then there's no way I'm staying on bloody C Wing, it in't hard, this in't no rocket science, you get what I'm saying. Now you need to talk to Governor Hargreaves, get him to move me back where I'm safe, and once that happens I'll talk, I won't bloody stop talking, do you get me?

Now I don't know who killed Stacey I really don't, but I do know who took her first of all. You get that name, once I'm back in the Seg, and I know for a fbloody fact that's a very big one for you."

Manny watched on, once more sitting down, bloody hell he wasn't expecting this, not at all, Harry had his interest.

"So let me get this straight Harry, you know who took Stacey, and you are now prepared to co-operate and tell us who that was?"

"If I go back to the Seg, that's what I'm saying."

"So let's not piss around any further, this seems pretty straight forward to me, who took her?" Manny asked.

"You in't listening are you Inspector," again Harry went into a bout of coughing, before once more composing himself in order to continue, "I in't saying bugger all until I'm in the Seg with a promise that I'll be staying there, in writing, from Governor Hargreaves, thems my terms, nothing until then. Now you and your queer little friend here would be wise to go and talk to the Governor pretty bloody quick, for all our sakes, but I'm saying nowt until you come back with something that helps me, do you understand, you wanna know who took little Stace', then you gotta play your part."

Manny didn't like taking instructions from criminals, especially shit like Harry Kilburton but this was too good to turn down, this was his shoe in, he wanted things to get moving, and quickly.

"OK Harry, we'll talk to him, I can't promise anything though as I have no power here, but we'll talk."

"That's what I figured, funny that eh. But you be sure to stress to that bastard how important it is, because if you don't move me, then I in't saying jack shit. Are we clear?"

THE HUNT FOR AMELIA CLAY

"Oh I think we're perfectly clear." Manny said, before ringing the bell on the wall, summoning Harry's escort back to the cell he dreaded so much.

"Well I wasn't expecting that." Manny said to Denny as they were escorted towards Governor Hargreaves office on the other side of the prison. "We'll hang around here, once they move him we'll get him straight back in, see just how much he does know, because if he really does know who had Stacey then I want to be talking to them before this day's through. This could be it, this could be the break we need on this."

"Look Guv', I don't wanna be the miserable one here, God knows that's your role, but don't you think he'd say anything to get his way, get back to where he feels safe?" Denny said, keen not to dampen Manny's optimism, because it was a nice change to see him so upbeat, but all too aware that someone that scared would indeed say anything to get what they want.

"We'll find that out won't we, but only if he gives us that name in the first place, let's get this sorted, let's get him moved back."

-TWENTY TWO-

The Intransigent and Belligerent Starched Shirt And Regimental Tie.

"I'm sorry Inspector, but Mr Kilburton stays where he is."

Manny looked dumbfounded, it had been a simple request, nothing extreme, he wasn't asking for Horrible Harry's immediate release, or a move to one of those Butlin-esque Open Prison's, or anything that would even slightly inconvenience this pompous arse sat before him. He'd asked nicely, humbly, respectfully, but the look on Reginald Hargreaves's face said it all, it was stony, unmoving, clearly showing no sign for negotiation nor manoeuvre, that was his answer.

"But you don't understand Mr Hargreaves, this is not just about Kilburton, there's a murder case this ties into, and probably more importantly a missing persons investigation, he may hold the key to everything, I need you to…"

Hargreaves interrupted, his voice cold, "No *you* don't understand Inspector, Mr Kilburton is a very manipulative individual, and I am not as easily manipulated as you may

THE HUNT FOR AMELIA CLAY

be. I do believe he has conditioned people in the past, experienced people, and this may be the case here. He is located on C Wing because he has been assessed as suitable and safe to be there. He does not dictate otherwise, not in my prison, now unless things have drastically changed I still have full jurisdiction over such matters, and unfortunately for you, you do not."

Manny struggled to come up with his response, his mind full of words he wanted to toss into Hargreaves direction, but also aware that they would do nothing to benefit his position, and probably contribute greatly to him getting in the shit. The Prison Governor was shuffling some papers, and observing his PC monitor, clearly indicating that the discussion was over, he was a tall man, in his early fifties, the starched shirt and regimental tie knotted tightly around his neck giving a clue to not just his background, but his belief in structures and hierarchies.

"Please Mr Hargreaves," Manny said, keen not to delve into pleading, but also aware that this was something that he really needed to happen, "just let me explain how important this is, let me have a little more of your time."

"I'm sorry Inspector, I think we're done, at least on this request, you can of course communicate through our Police Liaison Officer, which correct me if I am wrong is the normal channels we would deal through, but I do believe this particular matter is closed."

Hargreaves gestured to the Prison Officer standing behind them, "Please show the Officers out, good day to you both."

"We need to see Kilburton before we go, I need to speak to him." Manny said as he got up.

"I'm sorry, we're going into a patrol state soon, that won't be possible, like I said earlier please feel free to make another appointment through our Police Liaison Officer."

His mind was whirring reliving not just the entrenched stupidity of that prick Hargreaves, but Harry's offer to give up Stacey's abductor, give them the information that may actually help find Amelia, by now he should have that name, they should be heading to wherever Kilburton's information took them, not back to the 'nick'. But this wasn't over, Manny wasn't just going to let this go, this wasn't something he could just accept without any argument, just carry on with a resigned smile and pragmatic shrug of the shoulders. He had tried to contact Critchlow as soon as he got in the car, but he hadn't even got past his secretary, he'd left a message to contact him back as soon as possible, only to be told how busy the Chief Superintendent was. He knew he was busy, the bloke was always busy, but bloody hell this wasn't a request for more stationary, pens or even a new photocopier, this was something that really was urgent, what could he be doing that was more important than this? A girl's life was at stake here, and that meant more to him than some arrogant pen pusher's schedule.

There seemed no logic to it, they weren't asking much, why on earth wouldn't the prison agree to it? In fact once he had the name of whoever took Stacey then he didn't really care if the Governor went back on his word, he felt no sympathy for Horrible Harry Kilburton, he wouldn't lose any sleep at all if they had one over on him, put him straight back on that wing he was so scared of. But to just arrogantly dismiss his request without any thought, just because some over paid civil servant could, well that was just crazy, it made no sense at all.

"You OK?" Denny asked, he was no doubt aware that no, Manny most definitely was not OK, he was very pissed off, but that was Denny, he liked the lad, but really what a dumb bloody question.

"No I'm not OK," came his curt reply.

"Wanna talk about it?"

Was he really that thick skinned? He'd surely worked with him long enough to know when he didn't want to talk. But before he could answer the question he really didn't want to answer anyway, the DC was again talking. "Look it may not be my place, you being my boss, and a bit of a misery, but I'm worried about you Manny, you're…"

"No you're right Detective Constable, it isn't your place, just leave it eh, we're all entitled to a bad day, please just leave me to wallow in mine."

Denny said no more, just went back to staring ahead, watching the road, Manny wondered, had he been too hard on him? He meant well, but he wasn't in the mood for Denny's homespun caring, and the need to always cheer him up, Jeezus, he was entitled to be miserable sometimes, everyone was.

The rest of the journey had been strained, Denny pulled the car up into the parking space, neither of them had said a word to each other, just drove in silence with their own similar thoughts. Manny got out of the car, he felt uncomfortable, not just with what had happened back at that prison, but physically uncomfortable, his trousers were much too small, he had long abandoned the notion of fitting into the suit jacket, but now he really needed to buy some new strides, either that or actually face the inevitable conclusion that he needed to diet, had to start sorting himself out. He was all too aware he had let himself go, but was apparently powerless to fight back, and not just his physical appearance, but his lust for life had disintegrated, as had his love of the job, he lived alone on a staple of cheap lager, take away meals, and indigestion tablets. He didn't sleep at night, he couldn't relax, and he had bugger all to look forward to. He needed to snap out of it, but how, what was the magic solution to a terminal decline in self-esteem? It just appeared to be a miserable merry go round spinning in some vicious circle, there was no getting off or pausing, shit he needed to give himself a good kick up the arse, only not today, he was in no mood for self-improvement and positive thinking. So in answer to the earlier question, no he wasn't alright, but that was none of Denny's bloody business, he wasn't about to open up to him, pour his black heart out like thick oil on water, that wasn't how they worked, it wasn't the relationship that they existed within. Four years they had been teamed up, but he doubted Denny even knew the name of his kids, no doubt because he had never mentioned them to him. He had his life, and he had his job, the two may have spilled over in his world, but as far as Denny Black was concerned they were two definite separate entities.

As he walked through the entrance, Denny following, a uniformed officer called over to him from behind the desk, "Inspector Manningwell, the new DCI is in your office, he said to let you know as soon as you got in."

Manny nodded, bollocks that was all he needed, yeah that was just about crowning his day off nicely.

-TWENTY THREE-

The Day Harry Kilburton Missed His Pie And Chips For Lunch.

Where the hell were they, those two coppers, it had been well over two hours, they said they'd be back, what were they playing at, did they think he was joking? Harry Kilburton lay upon his bed pondering his next move, what to do to get somewhere safe, his hands were trembling as he rolled another match stick thin cigarette, why hadn't they been back?

His door was suddenly unlocked, at last, he thought, but it wasn't that Manningwell bloke, or the young poof who had said bugger all, it was just a screw.

"Dinner's up."

That was it no more said, no explanations, no reason for his saviour not returning, just the instruction to get his food. Well they could forget that, he wasn't going out there, go out to get his face sliced up like raw meat, bugger that, he got up and slammed his door shut, he'd rather starve. He lay back on his bed, lighting up his 'burn', sod it, he was hungry, his stomach was growling, and it was pie and chips today he could smell it in the air, why were they doing this to him, messing him around, he'd played the game, hadn't caused them any problems, it weren't fair.

He could see the stream of prisoners passing by his door, occasionally one would kick it as they went by to get their dinner, hissing some unintelligible abuse in his direction, and although it was common place, and he really should be used to it by now, he knew he was right to stay locked in, he may be hungry but that was better than facing them. Again his door opened, once more the screw standing there, "You really not eating Harry?" the white shirted Officer asked, "I ain't pissing around keep coming back, and I certainly ain't no waiter."

"Nah, I told you I in't safe, I'm not leaving this cell."

"You're choice mate, it's you that'll be going hungry," being the only response as the door again slammed shut.

Then once more the door kicking and abuse as the others returned to their cells with their meals. He screwed his eyes shut, when that copper did return he had a good mind to tell him to piss off, messing him around like this, but then that was just being stupid, he had no choice, he had to give the name up, his safety was now all he was worried about. Suddenly his thoughts were interrupted as he could hear shouts from out on the landing, metallic food trays smashing, and the squalls of radios, followed by unmistakeable shrill wail of the alarm sounding throughout the wing.

There was something kicking off, that was plain to hear, and it sounded like a fair few of those out there were involved.

"Out, Out! Withdraw!" It was the sound of the screw who had seconds earlier closed his door, shouting above the din. Then he heard a loud scream, he ran to the observation panel in his door, the metal flap was open and he could see the chaos going on around him on the ground floor. Bloody 'ell, he had been spot on staying where he was, not venturing out there for his grub, the staff retreating as fast as they could, the hoard of prisoners chasing them towards the gates at the end of the wing. Blood flowing from a female officer's head, another two dragging one of their colleagues behind them, a hail of missiles rained down as they made their exit. Then with a loud echoing bang as the metal doors that allowed them their safe exit were slammed shut behind them, and suddenly he felt sick, really sick, as he realised there were no staff on the landings left, they had all gone, all fled to safety.

This wasn't good.

He could hear the jeers and shouts of abuse as around two dozen men pushed pool tables, chairs and anything they could against the doors, spurred on by the others still locked in their cells, piling up a barricade to ensure that their captors had no easy route back in.

As the minutes went by they had exhausted stacking high anything that wasn't bolted down, he could see them out there, congratulating themselves, laughing and chanting, as initially they just kind of milled around, before looking for their next course of action. T-shirts were now worn covering faces, like Arab head dresses. The food that was being served was being devoured by the mob as they wandered around munching on pies and chips.

Those officers had to come back in soon, return order it had to be only a matter of time before they'd be charging in, batons flailing teaching that scum a lesson, because if they didn't, then he was in trouble.

-TWENTY FOUR-
Detective Chief Inspector Adrian Howard Introduces Himself.

"Adrian Howard."

Standing before Manny was a tall man dressed in a smart dark blue suit and white open necked shirt, his hair was neatly cropped, he appeared in his mid forties, his hand outstretched, and a warm smile. "Sorry to gate crash your office, but I needed somewhere to set up, apparently I'm expected to run a unit from twenty fucking miles away, what kind of set up is this? No don't answer that I'll work it out for myself. Henry isn't it?"

Manny shook Howard's hand, "It is indeed, although most people call me Manny."

"Good, I wanted to talk straight away, shut the door Manny and sit down please. As you are a detective, and I'm told quite a good one, you'll no doubt have deduced I'm the new DCI. I must admit I'm keen to meet everyone and see where we are on things before I get on with anything else. You're heading the Amelia Clay investigation, right, and almost by default the Stacey Hamilton murder investigation.

They're two biggies, a lot of work, and a lot of pressure, are you up to it?"

What!

What the hell was this bloke saying, he had shaken his hand then was already putting the boot in, what sort of bullshit was this, 'are you up to it'? He needed to talk to him about Kilburton, see if he couldn't pull some strings, after all this new DCI was supposedly in league with the Home Secretary of all people, he had power, he had the connections to put Hargreaves in his place, but he had thrown Manny, Kilburton suddenly pushed back in his mind, he needed to see what he was on about first.

"I'm sorry Sir, what are you saying? What do you mean am I up to it?" He knew he looked shit, tired, fat and jaded, but what sort of presumptuous crap was this?

"What I mean Manny is I've been here an hour, it's no secret that I have to make changes, trim the department down, and already I've had people tell me that you're my best bet for losing a DI, that you're not on your game, on the way out. Now that's not very nice I know, but let's be a bit brutally frank here, people are telling me you're not up to it, I need to ask you, because believe it or not, I think you may be able answer that question better than anyone else around here. So, hence my question, well are you up to it?"

Manny looked wounded, but Howard continued, "Before you fire back, I've also had people tell me you're a bloody good copper, not a politician or some yes man who will do anything for a sniff of promotion, but someone who cares about the job, and the people with that opinion are in your team. So tell me which is right?"

Manny stood up, and made his way towards the door, the door of his own office, before leaving he turned to face Howard, his finger pointing at his new superior, "Look Detective Chief Inspector, I can't be bothered to play games, I really can't be doing that, if you want to listen to what they say about me, then crack on, I've a murder case and a missing girl to find, and believe me at this moment that's all I'm concerned about, you do what you want to do. Now if there's nothing else, let me know when you've finished with my office, it is after all still my office, as I've work to do."

Damn him, he'd chase up Critchlow instead, this bloke was clearly some moronic oaf, and if this was a taste of what was to come, then perhaps he would be better off well out of it, get a fresh start elsewhere, only he couldn't could he, he had to close the case, find Amelia one way or another, that was business that couldn't be left unfinished.

Howard laughed out loud, Manny was struggling to make him out, what was funny?

"Sit down. I said sit down!" Howard barked, then more gently added, "Please. Look actually there is something else. Tell me what's the score, I need to lose staff, I need to make changes, what do you reckon, you must have your own ideas, go on, what's your take."

Manny stood where he was, "All due respect, but really I don't believe you, have you not heard a word I said, can I not make it any clearer, I don't care, I'm sorry but I'm not putting anyone forward for job losses or transfers out, that's your job, my job's catching the man, or men, who took Amelia Clay, very likely murdered Stacey Hamilton and this is doing nothing to help that, now you can do whatever you damn well please, but do not, and I mean *do not*, hinder my investigation."

Howard again smiled shaking his head. Getting up from behind the desk he walked around to where Manny was standing, "You know you're the first person to tell me that, everyone else has plenty of ideas on who's going and staying, and a fair few of them involved you getting fucked off out of here. You should know that apparently you're washed out, lost the appetite, tired and lethargic, coasting to your pension. There you go, they were quick enough to offer up their opinions, not you, you are the first one to actually mention a case, talk about an investigation, Police work. Excellent, let's not piss about anymore, tell me about Amelia Clay, for a start what happened at the prison."

"Sorry, you know I went to the prison?"

"Of course, the wicked step-father, what's he saying Manny? What's Harry Kilburton got to say for himself?" Howard answered.

He was surprised, he didn't expect Howard to be clued up on his movements, on the case, not on day one.

"He wants to talk Sir…"

"Frankie, call me Frankie. It appears no one uses their real names in this place."

"Well Frankie, he wants to cough on who took Stacey, says he knows, says he will tell us."

"So why are you here talking to me, and not banging some fucker's door down? Who is it?" Howard asked.

"He won't say until he is moved back to their Segregation Unit, for his own protection, he's a vile man, a right piece of work, he's already been done over once, had his face scarred, and very likely to happen again. He'll tell us anything to move to where he thinks he'll be safe."

"So what's happening?" Howard looked puzzled, not unreasonably he clearly couldn't fathom why he was talking to Manny in this office instead of his DI being elsewhere pulling someone in.

"They won't move him."

"What? Who won't move him?"

"The Governor there refused to move him, the bloke's an arsehole, he refused flat, reckons we're being taken in by Kilburton, manipulated, he even had us escorted out."

"Well fuck that, come on let's go, let's go talk to this prick. He won't move him, I've never heard such shit, what a load of bollocks." Howard was heading out of the office, "Well come on, we've wasted enough time, if I have to move him myself I will, let's go get that name."

-TWENTY FIVE-

"We're Coming To Get You!"

Half an hour had passed and still no staff rushing in. What the hell were they playing at, what were they doing out there? He had been pacing around his cell, but all the anxiety and fear had brought on yet another coughing fit, Harry was now on all fours, gasping between prolonged coughs and wheezes, as he fought to refill his lungs with air, tears filled his eyes as his chest heaved with the pain. They had told him it was just a nasty infection, but it had been kicking around for weeks now, apparently immune to the ever increasing quantity of antibiotics they had been pouring down his throat three times a day. The Prison had a duty of care to him, why was he still choking his lungs up? He again considered getting on to his brief, they didn't give a damn about him, they were supposed to be looking after him.

Hah!

Looking after him, who the hell was looking after him now, trapped in his cell whilst a mob of blood thirsty murdering bastards rampaged on the wing, empowered to do whatever they pleased. Again the coughing, he looked down at the long string of phlegm that hung from his blue tinted lips, thick greenish snot flecked with tiny spots of blood, what kind of bloody care was this?

But his suffering was interrupted as suddenly there was a banging at his door, like it was being hit by something heavy.

"Yeah ya fucking nonce, we know ya in there, ya dirty ripper!"

Harry turned and looked at the oblong glass opening in his door, a hate filled face snarling abuse obliterated any view other than the look of sheer aggression and vile hatred.

"We're coming for you nonce, we're coming to get you, we're gonna' fuck ya up you dirty horrible scum."

He could see the face shouting the abuse, then it moved to one side to be replaced by an older, but equally threatening head.

"It's you Kilburton, we're coming for you, you filthy kiddy fiddler, say ya prayers you paedo bastard, you're getting it!"

The face pulled back and there was a loud 'crack', he could see the glass separating him from the mob buckle in, it had shattered in the pattern of a spider's web, the centre of which being the point of impact.

Again another 'crack', it was now bowing inwards, he could hear the frenzied kicking at his door, as they took turns to look at the cowering spluttering mess on the floor. Harry huddled into a ball, sobbing between coughs.

Another crack and bits of glass rained down on the curled up form as the table leg broke through.

THE HUNT FOR AMELIA CLAY

The chaos was louder, as a man in his late twenties shouted through the now unobstructed opening.

"String up Kilburton, it'll be quicker for you, just string up nonce."

Harry had stopped coughing, his lungs now seemingly not being his brain's priority, "Please, leave me alone, please," he begged.

But his pathetic plea only heightened the glee of the excited thug looking through at him. A plaited length of light green sheeting was dangled through the opening, swinging from side to side.

"We're coming to get you, and it's going to be long and painful you nasty little shit. Make it easy on yourself, string up, go on, do it!"

Harry lay there, shuffling back against the back wall, still cowering, the face at the door spat across the cell, then another face belonging to someone else who likewise spat on him, then another, and another, as the mob took turns to revel in Harry's suffering.

As he shivered in a curled up ball, covering his face, he felt a sharp blow to his ribs as a fluorescent tube was thrown through the opening, slamming into him, before shattering. He could hear the cheer from out on the landing. Why was no one helping him, where were the prison staff, they were supposed to look after him, where were they, why weren't they protecting him?

"String up ya filthy paedo pervert! String up!"

He couldn't see who was shouting it, but he felt the plaited length of shredded bedding hit his head, "There you go

Kilburton, we've made it easy for you, go on hang yourself you worthless dirty ripper, because if we come in there we're taking you apart piece by piece and feeding you your own dirty rotten little cock and balls. We mean it Kilburton, string up!"

Harry was weeping, now uncontrollably, he was done for, fuck it, he was actually going to die, more bits of furniture hit him, as parts of a smashed up TV stand were hurled towards him.

He had no choice.

Big balls of lighted newspaper landed on the floor, the smoke once more kick starting the coughing, then more paper, scrunched up and alight, the smoke causing the dozen or so prisoners to move away from the door as it began to billow back out onto the landing.

Inside the cell Harry struggled to his feet, his lungs hurt, they hurt so bad, as they now filled with smoke, already unable to drag in enough fresh air to cope, Harry knew this was his time, the smoke lowering to envelop him, he bit his finger tip, hard, blood instantly appeared and he wrote on the wall just two words, TUESDAY CLUB.

He picked up the length of rope fashioned from cotton sheets, a noose already there at the end, and stood on his chair, standing on tip toes, desperately trying to hold his breath as his head entered the acrid clouds of black smoke, threading it through the bars of the high window, now fighting to breathe, the smoke getting thicker and thicker, goaded on by the jeering mob outside, taunting and threatening him, showing him no pity, no sympathy, just blind hatred. He placed the noose around his neck, they were right, he had no alternative, no choice, he was sure of that, they would kill him anyway, they were animals, murdering animals. He wouldn't give them the pleasure.

He kicked the chair away, his airways were instantly obstructed, there was no crack of his neck breaking, no instant relief, he was instead suffocating, being strangled through his own volition, his hands tried desperately to loosen the noose, fighting to free himself as he swung, his legs kicking out wildly in pain and desperation.

Oh shit, in Christ's name, what was he doing?

"Clear the landings, clear the landings!"

At three entry points the riot trained Prison Officers stormed in, body armour under their blue overalls and dark blue helmets glistening as they charged in at pace, forming an un-breachable line of long plastic shields, the prisoners excitably leaping around outside Harry Kilburton's cell door moved away, retreating from the oncoming far from thin blue line.

"Clear the landings, Clear the landings!" the Tornado Team instructed, and only a lunatic would have done anything else. Within seconds the 27 prisoners that had over run C Wing were kneeling on the floor at the far end of the wing, hands on their heads as instructed.

It was chaos on there, the smell of fire and smoke dominated the landings, those still in their cells were banging against the thick metal doors that separated them from the newly arrived prison staff, insults threats, jeers and abuse echoed around as the rioters were led away one by one. Once it was clear that no further threat existed on the open landings the attention switched to the cell with plumes of smoke billowing out of the smashed observation panel, it was immediately doused in water from one of the nearby hose reels, but it was still full of the acrid clouds of black poison, the staff donning the bright yellow smoke hoods entered, feeling their way as they went, blind to obstructions and hazards.

Harry Kilburton had been dead for too long.

It was a grisly find for the three officers, groping in the smoke only to find the cell's occupant suspended at the far end. As he was cut down, and his body pulled from the cell, they went to work on him, but all present knew the simple fact, you can only keep people alive, not bring them back from the dead.

All the pumping of his chest and breathing into his soot covered blue framed mouth was not going to change that status, he was Horrible Harry Kilburton, the notorious kiddy fiddler from Leeds, not Lazarus.

No he was dead alright.

-TWENTY SIX-

"I May Be DCI Howard, Although It May Be Better For You If I May Not Be Him."

As they approached Harrocote Road, the broad tree lined boulevard that led to Woodley Grange Prison, it was blatantly clear that something was wrong, and not just something in minor hiccup category. Manny could see the lines of Police and Prison Service vehicles that were parked on either side of the road, as well as the Outside Broadcast vans desperate to get as close to the scene as possible.

Damn!

That would be it for the immediate future, he knew that if something was kicking off inside then there was no chance of him nor his new ally getting in there, no way to confront the belligerent Governor Hargreaves about his intransigence over Harry Kilburton, there was no chance at all.

Manny drove their *Vauxhall Vectra* to the barriered gate wondering what was going on in there, as he drew level they were stopped by a Police Officer in a fluorescent jacket.

"Sorry gents you won't be able to go in there for the time being, there's an incident in progress, could you please turn around in the space just over there and head back in the opposite direction, once again sorry for any inconvenience."

"DI Manningwell and DCI Howard, Herts and Beds Major Crimes, what's happening?" Manny asked holding out his warrant card.

"We're not totally sure Sir, it's gone off in there, big time, there's been a riot, a nasty one by the sound of it, the Prison Staff are in charge of dealing with everything within the walls, whilst we've got the outside. But no one from our side's going in, so perhaps you'd be better coming back another time. Like I said you can turn around just over there."

Manny nodded, and threw the car into a three point turn and as advised drove back in the direction they had come, although he had no intention of just going back to Dunstable.

"Please tell me you're not just going?" Howard asked, he sounded perplexed, as if doing what a fellow Police Officer had instructed was somehow the most inappropriate course of action imaginable.

"Of course not, I'm going to park up though, then we can find out what's happening."

He thought of Horrible Harry, his pleading to get off the wing and back to segregated conditions, what if he were caught up in this, he'd be shitting himself, he would now be even more keen to spill his guts to preserve his own neck. That bastard stubborn Governor needed to back track on his decision a bit sharpish, this was all valuable time, although what exactly Howard was going to do to make him change his mind so readily he had no idea, he had asked him several times on the way, and all he got in reply was that they would play it by ear, everyone could be persuaded to change their mind providing the incentive was big enough.

"Over there, over there, there's a space over there, between the two vans." Manny was shaken from his thoughts by Howard, who had clearly seen a parking space along the crowded route. He pulled the *Vectra* up onto a grass verge, well after a bit of to-ing and fro-ing as he struggled to manoeuvre into the tight space.

They both got out, and walked back towards the prison entrance. Dozens of Police Officers were milling around, clearly the Police had the poor end of the deal, there was little for them to do except hang around, unless dozens of murderers, rapists, terrorists, or any combination of all three suddenly came bursting through the front gates, or abseiling down lengths of bedding from the tops of the high walls that surrounded the place, they were just there because some contingency plan said they had to be.

Howard approached a small group of officers who congregated around the back of one of the numerous minibuses, laughing and joking, hot drinks in hand.

"Who's in charge?" he asked one of the group.

The Policeman looked at him for a moment, then turned back to his conversation, taking a sip from his polystyrene cup as if Howard didn't exist.

"I said who's in charge?" Howard again repeated, only this time there was little politeness in his enquiry.

The Officer looked irritated at again being interrupted in his conversation, "Hold on a mo', someone obviously can't see I'm talking," he said to the others before addressing Howard, "And who may you be?"

"I may be DCI Howard, although it may be better for you if I may not be him, but fuck it, I am. So, constable, if it ain't too much trouble I'd appreciate a simple answer to what was a pretty simple question. Now I didn't come to play Where's fucking Wally, although I think I've found him anyway. So please tell me who is in charge here, and where can I find him or her, then you can get back to wasting tax payers money and I can get on with my job?"

The officer clearly thought better of arguing the point, simply replying, "Inspector Francis, she's over by the Mobile Control Centre I believe."

Howard was already walking in the direction the officer was pointing, Manny following, it had been a few years since he had seen a higher ranking officer throw so many fucks into someone, it was like going back twenty years, although how well that kind of style of management would go down with some of the others within the unit should they ever find themselves on the receiving end he could only imagine.

THE HUNT FOR AMELIA CLAY

"What's wrong with some people Manny," Howard was saying as he walked, "Manners cost fuck all, I mean it doesn't hurt just to answer someone does it, some people are just plain rude."

Manny followed Howard into the Mobile Control Centre, which was in reality a converted coach with the addition of telecommunications and CCTV monitors. It was immediately clear to see who Inspector Francis was, she was leaning over the shoulder of a uniformed constable, directing him on which camera feed she wanted to see next. Manny could see the images from C Wing on the screen she was watching. There were dozens of Prison Staff in full riot gear wandering around, smoke was obstructing some of the view, and he could see the Firemen dousing down various points within the building. The images were black and white, yet surprisingly sharp, the place was a mess, broken fixtures and furniture littered the floor, smashed up pool tables, chairs, notice boards, and there were papers scattered everywhere, literally centimetres deep in places. But whatever had happened had by the look of it been resolved.

Manny cleared his throat, more to get the Inspector's attention, who was engrossed by what was on the screen, than to actually clear any obstruction.

She turned towards them, "This is a restricted area. Can I help you?"

Her voice was brusque, and there was no doubt that she was definitely not welcoming any uninvited guests.

"DI Manningwell, DCI Howard, Herts and Beds Major Crime Unit, we're here…" Manny began, but was cut short.

"Yes Inspector you are here, but this is neither Bedfordshire nor Hertfordshire, as you can probably see we have a major incident in progress, and I'm a little bit tied up, so if it's me you need to see please phone Milton Keynes Police Station at a more convenient time, if you're here for any other reason, well I'm not aware why that may be, so likewise feel free to contact me at Milton Keynes Police Station. Now if you'd excuse me, may I ask you to leave this area."

Manny wasn't sure what to say, but he was quite impressed with Jane Francis, she was in her late thirties, early forties, but possessed a very obvious air of authority. It was clear that this was her domain, but he still needed to see Harry Kilburton, "Look I appreciate you're busy, we were here to see a prisoner, he's connected to the Amelia Clay and Stacey Hamilton cases, Harry Kilburton, obviously that's not going to be on now, but can you at least tell us what's happened here?"

Francis took her eyes off the screen she was watching and for the first time actually looked at them, her brusque dismissals now replaced by curiosity, "Harry Kilburton you say?"

"Yes." Manny answered.

"Follow me," she said, walking down the length of the Control Centre to a quieter part of the vehicle. "Look you're not going to want to hear this, but I'll tell you all the same, it's not a hundred percent certain, it was chaos in there,

THE HUNT FOR AMELIA CLAY

absolute chaos, but we believe Mister Kilburton took his own life during the riot."

"Oh this isn't happening, please tell me this ain't fucking happening!" Howard exclaimed.

"I'm afraid it already has Sir." Francis said, "Although as far as suicides go he may have had some assistance, we're looking at the video footage, there was a fair old crowd around his door, and although none of them actually accessed his cell, we do believe he was pressured and coerced into acting. I'm sorry gents but you won't be talking to Mister Kilburton, at least not without the aid of a medium."

She gave a grim grin, then her face returned to its previous state, she clearly regretted her joke, glib comments weren't her usual stock in trade.

"Can we go in?" Manny asked, pretty much aware of what the answer would be.

"Not my scene, we have only just got people in there ourselves, but I'm pretty sure that you won't be stepping anywhere near that cell, not today anyway."

Manny looked at Howard, wondering whether the uniformed Inspector was about to fall foul of his tongue, but Howard just gave the briefest of smiles before saying, "Thanks for your time Inspector, I can see you're busy, we won't take up any more of it."

As they walked back to the car Howard turned to Manny, "Coincidence? What do you think, our terrified paedo's about to name names and now he's dead, not more than a few hours after you see that retarded idiot of a Governor and tell him he's got to move?"

"Well Sir, the world's full of coincidences," Manny answered, "But I don't reckon this is one of them, mind you if it ain't then we've a very awkward conversation with Hargreaves coming up."

-TWENTY SEVEN-

Bill Penton Shares Home Baked Cookies And Freshly Brewed Coffee With Andrea Clay.

It had been a busy couple of days, the Amelia Clay story had gone global again, now it was linked with the death of Stacey Hamilton the nation's hunger for the tragic tale of the missing girl had been reawakened, and Christoff Peterson hadn't been slow in getting Andrea out there to talk to the world's media. Bill Penton had received the call just the day before, Christoff offering the 'exclusive', so a half hour 'Special' had been hastily arranged, a one to one with Andrea Clay and himself, the reporter that had been there from the start, a mutually beneficial bit of telly, although Bill Penton knew that both *Sky* and him would be benefitting more out of the show, as the programme was being plugged mercilessly in advance, seven thirty on *Sky One*, the hotspot on the flagship channel, with at least four repeat showings throughout the week, it was a biggie.

He could smell the freshly baked cookies as he and the crew set up, Andrea always the perfect hostess, even at the beginning her coping mechanism had become domestic chores, tidying, cleaning, cooking, she would fill every spare minute making her home an idyllic place ready for her daughter's return.

Christoff sidled over to him as he was getting rigged up with the tiny microphone on his shirt, talking in hushed tones to ensure that neither of the Clay's could hear him, "Poor Andrea, she doesn't know what to think, this has tipped her world upside down. The card was one thing, but them finding Stacey Hamilton like that has rocked her. It's out there every day, just yards from her front door. You be sure to go easy on her Bill, I mean it, no nasty stuff."

Bill slowly nodded, he knew Christoff from a while back, they had both worked together for a short time before going off in their current directions, "Don't worry, I'm not about to go adding anything, you've seen the questions, so has Andrea, I'm not out for some salacious tabloid hatchet job, you know me well enough by now, please give me some credit."

Christoff remained stony faced, "There's very little credit left for anyone in this, just be sure to go careful," then almost as a reluctant add, on threw in a half-hearted, "please."

Bill didn't particularly like him, he never really had, he suspected that there was more to his relationship with Andrea than just an advisor cum friend, he had seen the looks, the glances, their body language around each other.

THE HUNT FOR AMELIA CLAY

Of course maybe he was reading it all wrong, Peterson was after all not just the man who dealt with the media in what was a media driven circus, but he was clearly her emotional crutch as well, but in his mind he was convinced that Christoff Peterson was sleeping with her.

They were almost ready to go, Bill was in the kitchen sitting at the table, the bowl of fruit in the middle no doubt replenished that morning, with Andrea and her husband Paul sitting the opposite side. Paul had, as usual, decided not to participate in the interview, although this was no surprise to anyone, he was never at ease in the spot light, he sweated too much, and looked awkward on camera. Initially it had made the public believe he may have been connected, the nervous uncomfortableness betraying some unsaid secret, although never a genuine suspect, there had always been something about him, something that didn't sit well with either the people or the media clambering to fill column inches and air time. So it was Andrea, his wife, who had always been the media's face of choice, plus with rumours of a marital split in the air it was decided that the two of them wouldn't present the solid united front that was obviously required.

Bill was going over the questions he would be asking, one last time, ensuring that nothing would be taking his interviewee by surprise, causing dead air or unwanted tension. But by now Andrea was the consummate talking head, the media had become her ally, she had learnt to deal with the intrusion, and had managed through Christoff to manipulate, at least as far as they could, the press and TV companies into working for them and their quest to find Amelia. Nowhere was that media bond stronger than with him, no doubt helped considerably when *Sky* had donated an undisclosed sum to the 'For Amelia' campaign and a handsome reward for information that would ensure her return, a couple of years back.

They were seated in the Clay's living room, Bill in the large armchair, Andrea on the settee, besides it the small table with flowers and the picture of her missing daughter, just to the right of the shot, but in the frame all the same.

Bill was in a dark blue lamb's wool jumper and white cotton open necked shirt, he wanted to go for the casual look, Andrea a grey blouse and black knee length skirt, she was wearing makeup, but only for the benefit of the lighting people, this wasn't about her, it was her words that were important, the message was everything, and the message was that Amelia was out there, within yards no doubt of someone who was watching the broadcast.

"OK are we ready to go?" Bill asked the crew, the director nodded back. There was no need for any preamble, or introductions, the edited in voice-over would be doing all that before transmission, along with the brief outlay of the story for anyone who could possibly be unaware of it, so Bill launched straight in.

"So Andrea, please tell us how it felt when you received the card from Amelia?"

THE HUNT FOR AMELIA CLAY

His voice was reassuring, the tone perfect, he was a reporter after all, not an interviewer or seasoned presenter, but he was also the face associated with reporting this case, and the producers were keen to let him run with this one.

"Well Bill it is so difficult to say, I so wanted it to be from her, so very much, to believe that this was a message from Ami, but…" she paused for a moment, the camera zooming in slightly as she did so, "… but as you know in the past, all the hoaxes, all the false sightings, some of which were no more than malicious cruelty, it was more than I dared to hope. Yes if you ask what I felt, then it was hope."

Again Bill's reassuring voice, "Then the Police confirmed it was from Amelia."

"Yes, that very night."

"That must have been an emotional moment."

Andrea again paused before answering, "I can't express in words just how happy it made us, to know she was out there still. I always knew she was, but to have it confirmed, well it was like a dream come true. But then…" There was another pause, a longer one this time.

The camera cut to Bill, looking sympathetic, but not interrupting, then back to Andrea, the eyes now watering as tears began to flow down her face, yet when she spoke her voice didn't change tone or pitch, "… she's still not home is she, still not here where she belongs, safe with us. Someone out there is still keeping us from her, and to that person I ask, no plead, please let her return, please let my Ami come home."

The tears were flowing down her cheeks now, and a quiver had come into her voice, out of camera shot Bill silently gestured to one of the crew to bring Andrea a glass of water. He knew this wasn't going to be easy, although Andrea had indicated she was happy with the questions when they had run through them, he still had to breach the finding of Stacey's body, just a few hundred yards away, questions that had sounded fine less than half an hour earlier now appeared callous to him, uncaring and brutal.

Andrea dabbed her eyes with some tissues and sipped from the glass the assistant had handed her, Bill took a moment to allow her to compose herself, the editors could sort it out later, this wasn't about her misery, her torment, he didn't want it to be thirty minutes of just someone's pain, although that obviously would be reflected in the finished programme, but he wanted to show the hope too, counter balance everything with the news that yes Amelia was still out there, still able to be found, that this was a good thing, that needed to become an even better event.

"Take a minute," he said as he himself also sipped from a glass, "there's no hurry."

"It's OK, let's go on." Andrea replied, "I'm ready, go on ask the question."

Bill smiled a reassuring smile, and nodded to the camera man to let him know they were going again.

"The discovery of Stacey Hamilton's body, so near to here, must have been hard for you, what were your feelings when you heard a girl had been found?"

THE HUNT FOR AMELIA CLAY

He wondered whether the question had been delivered too coldly, aware that Stacey also had family, a family he was due to meet soon, yet it was obviously a question that needed asking.

"Well Bill, it was devastating news. Only that morning I had received the card, then to hear she had been found so near turned my entire world upside down. First of all there was the notion that it was my Ami laying out there, my little girl. I was dumbstruck, shell shocked, no that doesn't do how I felt justice, I was ripped apart, from the inside out, the whole world was turned upside down. Then when we found out it wasn't her there was a brief sense of sheer relief."

Again Andrea paused, Bill thought how impressive she looked, like some stateswoman before him, the mature yet attractive lady, coping under extreme pressure, he had to admit to himself he found her attractive, perhaps that was why he resented Peterson so much. She took another drink from the glass before her, then blew her nose before continuing, apparently once more composed and back in control, "But that sense of relief was all so brief, because that was someone else's daughter, that was someone else's little girl, I didn't have the right to be relieved, feel any happiness, how could I? There was the overwhelming grief for Stacey's poor mother, Shirley, that could have been me, I kept telling myself, that could have been me."

They continued talking, again and again Andrea pushing the point that someone out there knew where her daughter was, someone a neighbour, a postman, milkman, paperboy, may have seen Amelia. After well over an hour and a half Bill reached the last of his questions, it had gone well. He did wonder at the beginning, when the tears had appeared, whether Andrea was up to it, but he should have known her by now, it wasn't about her, she'd put herself through anything if it meant a safe return for Amelia.

As the crew removed the mic from Andrea's blouse she hurried off returning with a huge plate of cookies, the ones they had smelt cooking when they arrived, and Paul, marginalised for the interview, was suddenly put to use fetching the teas and coffees.

Bill chewed on a fine example of Andrea's baking prowess, he felt bad, he was there offering hope, if only through his ability to provide her publicity, but deep down he knew, pretty much knew for sure, that Andrea Clay was never likely to see her lost daughter alive again.

-TWENTY EIGHT-

Frankie Re-Unites The Band, But What About Yoko?

It had to be admitted, he may at this moment be the biggest selfish prick she had ever met, but he had damn good taste. Frankie's place was pretty nice, no it was more than that, it was very nice indeed.

What was this about though?

For all the time that Sylvia Hardacre had worked with Frankie at the Anti-Terrorism Unit he had never invited her, nor any of the others around to his home, even though at the time it was just around the corner from where they worked. No, he was the almighty power which they had all orbited around at work, yet it had always been that work was work and home was home, and he had maintained that stance resolutely all the time she had known him, no matter how tight knit they had become in their jobs, he had kept his private life just that. And yet here she was, with fellow Constable Alice Parrachio and their old Sergeant Felix Fernando, invited to Chez Howard for dinner and a drink.

Hah, she thought, dinner and a drink, how cosy was that, what was it he wanted? Because she was damn sure it wasn't just to catch up or reminisce over old times. It was the first time they had all got together since the ATU had been disbanded, or strategically reorganised as the hierarchy had decreed, and it was awkward.

Throughout the ten years they had worked together she had trusted Frankie with her life, and that was no exaggeration, yet they had all ultimately felt betrayed by him, and none more so than she. After all he had just gone off, on some kind of glorified extended gardening leave, and whilst away his kingdom had evaporated, with them being cast asunder with no say or input into their professional futures, redeployed to various stations around the capital, The Red House, the base they had inhabited for so long turned over to Special Branch as part of the amalgamation of the Met's resources.

This was the first she had seen of him since, he had clearly been able to sort things out for himself just how he wanted, setting his home up close to his new little number at Dunstable, whilst they were shifted into any shitty role the Met had deemed appropriate. Although she wasn't too bad, in fact she had landed on her feet, falling into quite a nice posting at Hampstead, with a possible shoe in to CEOPs, something she quite fancied.

Felix on the other hand had been off work, sick, well actually he was sick of living any decent life, even twelve months after the 'tragedy' he was still wallowing in his own private hell of grief and guilt, a very broken man, who was also very reluctant to mend. She had lived with him for a while, but moved out after she had hooked up with Craig, her now boyfriend, although she still kept in touch, but he had changed so much, and there had been little sign of any changing back.

Alice had been crapped on from a great height, having only just joined the ATU she hadn't the experience or influential friends to keep her in a decent job, she had been handed back a uniform, and was pounding the streets of Cricklewood, wondering why the hell she had ever transferred out of Thames Valley, seduced by their host's promises of a better life fighting terrorists and saving the nation only a few months previously.

Hmmm, what did he want?

But this was Frankie, so one thing was for sure they would find out quick enough.

As Catherine, the Canadian ex-film journalist cum ex-spy, Frankie was now residing with, waxed lyrical about the vistas and views over the Chilterns and the joys of rural life, Sylvia could see the awkwardness that she was feeling was also present in her old boss. He looked preoccupied, his partner's words drifting through him, it wouldn't be long now before they found out what he wanted, as that tell-tale twitch in his right eye was going ten to the dozen. She could smell their dinner cooking, it smelt good, but she wondered if he would be able to wait until they were sitting at the table before revealing the true purpose of the evening.

Whilst Frankie twitched, Felix was standing by the French windows dressed in what looked like a thirty year old corduroy jacket and equally old jeans, the irony being he had actually dressed up for the occasion, he looked distant, although he always looked distant now. Alice was standing beside him, listening to Catherine's enthusiasm for her new home, but she appeared to be casting furtive glances towards Sylvia, looking to her for a lead, this was all too edgy, there was a definite elephant in Frankie's well decorated, open plan, room with a view, and that elephant was that they had been stitched up, and as far as she was concerned it was by their old DCI.

As the others were clearly leaving it up to her, Sylvia thought she had no choice, she couldn't go on like this all evening, politely bottling it all, saying nothing, so she took a deep breath, what else was there to do, but just ask? As Catherine took a break from her enthusiastic descriptions of their new home and went to the kitchen to get more drinks for her guests, Sylvia took her opportunity.

"Oh for God's sake, this is silly, we know each other well enough to speak openly, let's be straight shall we?"

The others had gone silent, three pairs of eyes fixed in her direction.

"You dump us like we're shit," she continued, "not a bloody word from you, whilst you set up home and feather your nest at some small town Police Station. Not a blooming dickey-bird, couldn't even make a phone call to explain, then you just invite us here like this. So excuse me if I'm being rude, but to coin your phrase, and I'm quoting you here Frankie, either piss or get off the pot, we're all thinking it, so why are we here then?"

Even as she was talking she was wondering how it had managed to come out like that, but it was what she was thinking, all bottled up, so it was probably best to just say it as it is.

Frankie smiled, that slightly lopsided smile, "Fair question. As you so eloquently request I'll get to the point then, I haven't just invited you all here to show off my new home, although you must admit it is a bit nice, in fact I want you all to appreciate that it's highly unlikely a further invite will be winging its way in the post any time soon, so make the most of it. There is a reason why I asked you all here, I'll just say it, I want to reform the band."

He was looking at all three of them as if to gauge their reactions, see what response they had to his statement.

"What?" Sylvia said, putting her glass down open mouthed.

"I want all three of you to join my department, come work out here." Frankie continued, "I've cleared it, the jobs are yours if you want them, I can take on who I like, and I want you three, I've a good base for a team, I want you three to finish it off."

Sylvia appeared irritated, "Oh just like that, come move out here everything will be hunky dory, is that it, why we're here, so you can flannel us?"

"Yes Sylv' that is it! That is it in a nutshell. That is it exactly. Now you may feel aggrieved at some personal slight I may have inflicted upon all three of you, but believe me I didn't shut the ATU down, Alice I didn't post you in Cricklewood, I wouldn't do that to my worst enemy, the place is a shit hole and I didn't give you back the black and whites, although judging by the get ups you used to turn up to work in that probably wasn't a bad move by the force, and Sylvia no matter how good you may think it's going to be, you do not want to be watching web cams of dirty old perverts whacking themselves off whilst trying to get in kids pants. What I can offer you is decent Police work, work that'll make a real difference to people, and the chance to work together again. Now what do you think?"

"Do you really for a moment believe we're going to just smile, thank you and come and work in bloody Dunstable, join your little band, do you really think that is going to happen?" Sylvia fired back.

"Actually yes I do, well maybe you'll be the Yoko Ono in this little reforming scenario, but Felix and Alice have already said yes. I knew you would be the one who needed the persuasion, hence you coming to my house, eating our lovely food, and enjoying my sparkling wit and repartee, which as I already have made clear is all something I hope you're not getting used to. So if you really want to know what tonight's about, it's about you Sylvia, just you, it's about getting you on board."

"Well," Sylvia huffed with a pronounced disapproving look, "that food had better be a bit special then hadn't it."

-TWENTY NINE-

Gerald Draper, The Man With A Golden Ticket, Cuts Amelia's Hair.

He held the strands of hair in his hands and ran his fingers through them, surveying the long locks as they fell free from his grasp. She had absolutely beautiful hair, truly lovely, but then she would wouldn't she, she was a totally wondrous little creature, a sublime being, so fresh so innocent, and yet so utterly desirable. Of course it was unfortunate that she was aging, already well past her prime, but then this was Amelia Clay, the ultimate forbidden fruit, the holy grail of unobtainable love. And here she was, her hair in his hands, her slender and pale neck revealed as he, Gerald Draper, lifted that long luxurious mass of hair from the back of her head. Sometimes life just offers up gifts that even the likes of him are not worthy of.

Phillip, as he was instructed to address him, although he knew this man by an altogether different moniker, had called him up the previous night, 'a special request for a man with a special gift' he had said, he needed her hair done in preparation for the party, and he trusted no one else to do the job. Of course it meant a morning away from the salon, and the problems that would cause, among his clients that morning were an actress, super model and the wife of the leader of the opposition, none would be happy to hear that the great Gerald Draper would not be behind the scissors when they sat in their chairs, but he left instructions with Marco, his assistant, to inform them that he had been called away on urgent family matters, to apologise profusely, and generally placate the pampered bitches, up to and including cutting their rotten hair for free. For this was an opportunity he could not turn down, not only would he be working on the most famous young head in Britain, but part of the payment for his labours was a golden ticket to the party, and at a reduced rate!

Yes, a golden ticket, he had of course imagined what it would be like to actually sample the delights that Amelia had to offer, he had been present at other parties, had seen other golden ticket holders indulging themselves, living out what were his fantasies, but this time others would be envious of him, would be wondering what he was feeling, what joy he was experiencing, and it was all just a couple of days away!

Amelia was seated on a chair in the middle of her bedroom, she was saying nothing, just obediently sitting where she was, he felt a little awkward, he was so used to striking up conversation with his clients, it was a skill he was almost as proficient in as cutting hair, yet Phillip had been adamant, he was to say nothing to her other than what related to what he was doing, only touch her when totally necessary, and whatever he did relay nothing of what was happening in the world in general. It was made clear to him that this was an honour no one else was deemed worthy of, and he was not to abuse it.

Phillip was sitting on Amelia's bed, watching on, observing him like some hungry hawk, he looked impatient, like he just wanted this over with, wanted him out of his home, it was off putting, he had no problem with being observed whilst he worked, judged and assessed, because he knew he was the best, but there was an air of menace about this man watching him so intently, it unnerved him a little, he felt a slight tremor in his hands, although not enough to hinder him in his work.

"So what do you want me to do?" he asked Phillip, knowing that Amelia had no say in any of this, no opinion or no views would be allowed, her captor had made that plain, and she clearly appreciated this as she just stared silently to the front.

"I want her hair to look as it does in the pictures." Phillip said handing him a flyer, one of the hundreds of thousands that were circulated or stuck up over the past four years. "You cut it exactly as it was, I don't want her to look any different, she's not some whore or one of the vacuous tarts whose hair you normally cut, so don't make her look like one."

Gerald just nodded, pursing his lips as he did so, well that was a bit uncalled for, he thought, manners cost nothing, he definitely didn't like this man, but then he knew what he was capable of, none of which would endear him to anyone. Still he was paying a fee far greater and desired than any other he had ever received, so what did it matter what he thought of the person paying it?

As he planned how he would tackle what was really an all too simple task, he felt a wave of sympathy for the girl, that man was not someone he'd want to be spending his time with, but then the end did justify the means, and what was happening was for the greater good, and that included him, well it definitely now included him.

He took the spray bottle and dampened Amelia's hair, and taking a last look at the picture he began to cut, initially taking a good four inches off the length, as he did so he could hear the stifled sound of her sobbing, just noticing her shoulders twitching as her beautiful young head remained perfectly still. He took another look at the picture, lying beside the chair on the small dressing table, his brain had gone into overtime, yes, it was worth it, ignore her, she's playing mind games with you, she's trying to get into your head, you have a golden ticket Gerald, you have the promise of delights very few men will ever experience, he had spoken to Phillip, there were only eight such tickets available at this party, all the others were just silver or bronze - his usual choice due to financial considerations - but not this time, one haircut and all of this would be yours!

He cleared his head, consciences were for the weak, for those not prepared to take what they could have, and as he stroked the loose hair from around her ear he felt the stirring in his pants, he felt his true feelings making themselves

THE HUNT FOR AMELIA CLAY

known, oh God he would soon be enjoying this creature to the full. He couldn't help it, as he manoeuvred to cut the other side he deliberately brushed his erection against her back, Amelia Clay's back, oh Jesus, just two days. He stayed there working close to her, he could feel his cock pushing against her young body…

"Gerald, can I have a word." It was Phillip, interrupting his moment, he had risen from the bed, "Just outside for a moment."

Phillip followed him out, closing the door as he left.

"Yes Phillip…"

But before he could say anymore Phillip slapped him across the face, hard, with an open palm. Gerald recoiled bringing his hand up to his head to protect it from further attack.

"What the hell did you do that for?" he whimpered, as he cowered drawing away from his attacker, rubbing his nose to check for blood, what had he done to deserve that? What was he playing at? Was there more to come? Oh please no don't let him hurt me again.

"You never touch her outside of a party. Never! I explained that to you, that was made perfectly clear, do you think I'm blind, well do you? Do you think I'm bloody stupid or something?"

Gerald could see the rage in his eyes, he looked terrifying, it was as if those eyes were burning, alight with some intense fire. The whimpering hairdresser shook his head, "No Phillip, no."

"Good, we'll let that one ride, call it temptation, the agreement still stands, but if you ever do that again outside of a party, then heaven help me I'll cut that hard dick of yours clean off with your very own scissors. Now get back in there and finish the job."

-THIRTY-

'The Tuesday Club' Horrible Harry's All Too Brief Farewell To A Very Cruel World.

Whilst the forensic team meticulously combed around on the now prisoner free wing, Manny and Denny were shown into the cell that had less than 24 hours earlier been the home of one Harold Kilburton. Denny looked around, they could only observe from the doorway, but what they saw told a very vivid picture. The broken shards of glass scattered around the door way, bits of furniture lying around the cell, which he surmised had been thrown through the now unglazed observation panel in the door, and the lingering smell of smoke. There were the large ash like balls of what was once some tabloid, and lots of blackened smaller bits of paper, covering the floor like dark snowflakes, there was smoke damage to the cupboards, up the walls, even on the ceiling, and most tellingly there was the tightly plaited ligature still dangling from the window bars, cut just by the noose, no doubt to release the body suspended from it, where it had mercilessly tightened and strangled Horrible Harry.

Denny, like everyone else was dressed in a white paper suit and was breathing through the paper mask, he imagined their would-be witness in there, trapped, totally and pathetically helpless. There had been no one to help him, save him from his inevitable horrific demise, at the mercy of a rabid mob baying for his blood with skewed righteousness, people whose crimes were no doubt just as heinous taking some kind of vengeance on behalf of the good and innocent of our society.

He pictured Harry begging, pleading for his very being, he knew how scared he had been, and also how justified that fear had been.

Just what had he endured in his final moments?

What desperation must he have felt to have taken the route he did?

The route that saw him released from his incarceration in a steel box in the back of a black van, robbing society of its justice, but also taking from them the one decent lead they had to find Amelia Clay. Amelia Clay, the girl they now knew for sure was still alive, but also the same girl whose very existence may now rest on the whim of the killer of Harry's own step-daughter.

He had to remind himself, that was what this was about, not the death of Harry, because that in itself would be causing no one any sleepless nights, but with him went some of their hope, no that was the real tragedy here.

THE HUNT FOR AMELIA CLAY

"No way to go is it."

Denny was shaken from his trance like imaginings by Andy Bruchia one of the Thames Valley detectives who was with them at the door.

"It must have been hell in here, just looking at the CCTV, they were like animals." the young policeman continued.

"Where are they now? The ones who were rioting?" Denny asked him.

"All over the show, they were all shipped out last night, dispersed around different prisons to keep them apart, we've got some miles ahead of us to see them all."

Whilst the two DCs were talking, Manny was looking at some A4 photos he had been given earlier, shots of the cell from various angles.

He looked up from them, "What's this one about?" he asked, showing Bruchia the close up of the word 'Tuesday Club'.

Bruchia looked at it, before answering, "It was written in what they believe to be blood, probably from a wound he had on a finger. Apparently it was fresh, so whatever it's about he wrote it just before he killed himself. There was no note, nothing else really, well not relating to any last words, so that's all he had to say for himself by way of his farewell to a cruel world. As famous last words go he didn't leave us a lot did he."

"Maybe he has, we'll see, can I get a copy of all these?" Manny asked holding up the photos.

"Yeah, keep them, we guessed you'd want them when you arranged to come so had an extra set printed, there's more of them, we'll sort it all out before you go. Is there anything else you'd like to see?"

"I'm not sure. Has the prison Governor been spoken to yet?" Manny asked.

"Not as far as I know. He's in, but I'm not aware anyone from our side has interviewed him yet, obviously he's on our list, but not exactly at the top, he wasn't at the scene or anything. He's been helpful enough."

"Yeah I bet he bloody has." Manny answered.

Denny again stared into the cell, he knew they needed to go in, have a good root around, but this wasn't their crime scene. He noticed a still soggy cardboard box under the steel bed, papers protruding from the top, it had somehow escaped being ignited, was there something in there? Perhaps the information they needed, but then from what he could see there was just old newspapers sticking out, he'd request copies of any correspondence before they went, but it was clear that Harry Kilburton was someone who didn't have much in the way of personal possessions, there wasn't a lot there that any un-grieving relatives would be arguing over in some solicitors office when it came to the reading of the Last Will and Testament of Harold Kilburton.

Manny moved away and Denny followed, he knew who his DI wanted to talk to, and he also knew that the conversation was unlikely to occur that day.

"I want to speak to that arrogant prick, I want to hear what he's got to say for himself, I want to see that smug bastard's face, now he's got a paedophile hanging from one of his cell windows. I want to be looking him in the eye and asking him why he didn't move that horrible fucker when he could. And that is an answer I really want to be hearing straight away."

-THIRTY ONE-

Amelia Clay Imagines A Way Out, Whilst The Two Foul Pigs Squeal at Each Other.

The two foul pigs squealing at each other, she wondered what 'Uncle Phillip' had done to the fat pervert, she could hear his pathetic whimpers and protestations through the door. She glanced over at the shiny scissors sitting abandoned on her dressing table, and just for a moment, the briefest of moments, she pictured herself plunging them into her 'uncle's' heart, deep into his chest, twisting and turning, the blood oozing out onto her hands, spurting everywhere as she withdrew the metallic blades before plunging them back in again, and again.

But then the reality, she was still chained to the wall, what chance did she have, she'd be dancing around like a scrap yard dog, her would be victim just staying out of reach, and then there was the hairdresser, could she really kill two men, even if she was emotionally capable, did she have the strength and speed to stab them both before they moved out of range, or beat her down to the ground.

Of course she didn't, but for an instant she felt free, even if just in her mind, she was momentarily happy. Had she got it wrong, did she really need to escape by some almost death guaranteeing route, when she could grab her freedom another way?

The door opened and the two men walked back in, the fat hairdresser was silent, she glanced over towards him before hurriedly returning to staring straight in front of her, but at least that horrendous hardness in his trousers had disappeared, as he went back to cutting her hair, utilising those scissors for which she had such a different use. She suddenly felt strong, invigorated, because now she saw a future, a future that would be happening in less than 48 hours. Now she had a different idea of how she was going to get free, and it was one which was suddenly appealing. Again she closed her eyes, yes she would be able to do it, she envisaged the blood again, could almost feel it on her hands, she didn't care anymore, for four years she had been the victim, four years of playing this man's games, well not anymore.

As the hairdresser cut, now ensuring that his private parts were well away from her body, she pictured it again and again, 'Uncle Phillip's' painful demise. Even as she looked in the mirror and saw the horrible straight fringe that man had sculpted just over her eyes, it didn't upset her, not now, not now she had an alternative to all of this. She glanced down, making sure that her head remained perfectly still as instructed, and saw the leather wrap that contained the hairdressing equipment, combs, brushes, clips, and more scissors, all just inches from her bare feet, laid out wide open, she inched her toes towards it, invisible under the large black cape that the hairdresser had draped upon her prior to starting. She wondered at just how mad this was, how she had given it no thought at all other than an image of that swine's lingering death, no consideration of any consequences or repercussions, yet that didn't worry her, because nothing could be worse than she had already endured.

As 'Uncle Phillip' saw Gerald Draper out of the room and guided him towards the door apologising as he went for the earlier misunderstanding, Amelia sat in her chair, once more left alone. She looked at the mirror, her face emotionless, the same hair 'style' recreated as when she had been a normal girl, a girl who had yet to understand the evil that people were capable of, a girl who didn't know what virginity was, let alone that it could be taken so prematurely, a girl with day dreams and hopes, wonderfully unachievable aspirations and goals, a girl who never realised that one day she would be sitting chained up in a room with a pair of scissors laying hidden beneath her feet.

She lifted her foot and leant down picking up the five inch blades, moving over to her bed and pushing them under her mattress. Only now did any notion of what may go wrong enter her head.

What if the fat hairdresser noticed them missing before he left the building, would he and 'Uncle Phillip' come rushing in, would she be ripe for another beating, but was that something he would do so close to a party, even in one of his rages?

Oh God what had she done?

But it was no use worrying about that now, she had already done it, and the thought of meekly just handing them back, perhaps explaining that the fat hairdresser had dropped them or something, was not an option, at least not if she ever wanted to get back to that life she now remembered less and less.

-THIRTY TWO-

Seven Hundred And Twenty Nine Million Tuesday Clubs.

"Seven hundred and twenty nine million results Manny, that's seven-hundred-and-twenty-nine-million. There's a fair few Tuesday Clubs out there."

In the large open plan office that the Major Crime Unit populated, Floyd Carflour handed Manny the printed sheet, *Google* marked at the top, and the first half a dozen search results stacked up below, yeah he was right three quarters of a billion results for 'Tuesday Club'. It had been just over two hours since they had returned from Woodley Grange and the grisly scene of Kilburton's self-inflicted end, and unsurprisingly Governor Reginald Hargreaves had been unavailable to speak to them. Manny had been keen to nail down what exactly this Tuesday Club was, but all he had ascertained from Floyd's initial sweep of the internet was that it was an extremely popular name for a group.

Floyd leaned back in his chair and continued, "Not too many of them are signposted to paedophiles or child kidnappers unfortunately. Football clubs, OAP tea dances, discounted cinema tickets, radio shows, games, well you name it, it would appear people do it on a Tuesday, no wonder there's nothing on the telly on a Tuesday night, what's the point everyone's out at clubs." Floyd laughed, though clearly more out of exasperation than any amusement at the proliferation of clubs occurring on Tuesdays.

This hadn't been what Manny had wanted to hear, not at all, that many search results just meant they were further away from anything than they were before Horrible Harry had used his own bodily fluids to give them such a vague and totally shitty clue. Manny pondered, yeah that was some clue, the average bloke has eight pints of blood in his body, that's a gallon, even taking into account how scrawny that bastard Kilburton was, he could have at least spared a bit more to have made things clearer, that's even if it did relate to their case, maybe he was just fucking about with them, was this his last laugh, just some cruel goose chase he was sending them on?

But Floyd didn't need telling the obvious, Manny needed him to dig deeper, to keep probing.

"And yet Harry Kilburton spent his last moments on this earth writing it in his own blood," he said, partly to Floyd, partly to himself, "so I'm guessing it's something we need to know, because at this moment in time it's all we've bloody got. Search it with a few key words, there's hundreds of them they use, check that directory and add them to 'Tuesday Club' I want a list of the thirty most likely on my desk by five, get Denny to help, and try and rope in any one else who's kicking around, come on let's go on this one."

As Manny returned to his office, the door to their work area flew open and his new superior officer, Frankie Howard, breezed into the room, behind him were three other people Manny didn't recognize. The new DCI walked straight towards Manny's office which was situated in the far corner of the large open plan area, calling, "A minute if you can," as he swept by.

"Close the door please." Howard said to Manny as he made himself at home behind his DI's desk, the three people who were following him waiting awkwardly outside the door.

"Henry out there are DS Felix Fernando, and DCs Alice Parrachio and Sylvia Hardacre. They are joining your team as from right now."

Manny went to speak, but Howard gave him no opportunity, continuing, "As you know part of my remit is to reorganise the Unit, and this is part of my reorganisation. Before we go delving into the realms of 'why wasn't I told' or any other such pertinent questions, this is not open to further discussion or debate, it has happened already, rubber stamped and all official. They will be here on a permanent basis as from now."

Howard then called the three into Manny's office, still not allowing his DI to speak, "Sylv, Felix, Alice, this is DI Henry Manningwell, he will be your boss, he heads up this section, he will I'm sure brief you on all you need to know. Now Manny please can you bring the rest of your team into the office, and make sure one of them brings some brews with them, I want to talk to them all, but I need a drink even more, what's the deal with the heating in this place, we're going to need to get that looked at it's like it sucks the moisture clean out of you."

A few minutes later Denny Black traipsed in carrying a tray of assorted mismatched mugs and chipped cups, joining Micky Page and Floyd Carflour, along with the others. Manny could see by their faces that meeting their new DCI was not something that was filling them with unbridled joy, and none more so than Micky, would his sergeant be able to keep his mouth shut when Howard revealed his new 'team', Manny doubted it, keeping his mouth shut was hardly Micky's speciality, although pissing people off certainly was.

"Right," Howard began once they were all squeezed into the comparatively small office, "I'm Detective Chief Inspector Howard, I'm sure you are aware of my new role, and I hear through the grapevine that there's already an opinion as to what I'm here for. Now some of what you may have heard is probably true, but take it from me that some will be total bollocks. Hopefully we can sort out which is which now, because one thing I don't take to is rumours, especially ones which are totally spurious. With me are DS Fernando, DC Parrachio and DC Hardacre. They are now part of this team, and along with you folks will form up this unit."

Manny could see Micky whispering something to Floyd, something he was sure wasn't of an exactly approving nature. But Howard either never saw it, or simply chose to ignore it, as he continued.

"Now as my rank would suggest I normally do the inappropriate questioning, talking out of line, and throwing any fucks into any conversation that may need fucks throwing in, and under normal circumstances you would all nod approvingly and agree with me. It's what I do, and I'm pretty good at it, so please when it happens to you don't complain, I sat a lot of exams and went through a lot of boards to earn that right, and I don't intend to surrender it quickly. But, and this is quite a rare but, this is not a normal situation, so before I start talking about where we are with investigations and what we're up to I'm going to give you all the chance to introduce yourselves to each other and me, and as frankly as you like question me on anything you wish, well anything that relates to work that is. Now whatever you say isn't going to prejudice how we later get on, well not much, although it may be wise to be a bit careful, you know keep it all a bit civil and courteous, but let's pretend there's no rank for the next five minutes, and as long as you don't take offence by the answers, I won't be offended by any questions. Are we clear?"

There was a general murmuring and nodding of heads, but the only thing that was really clear was that not everyone was reassured that this was necessarily a good thing, especially Manny who watched on, his eyes flicking from Howard to Micky.

"Who's first then?" Howard asked looking around the room.

THE HUNT FOR AMELIA CLAY

As Manny had imagined he would, it was Micky who spoke up first, "Micky Page, Detective Sergeant, been on Major Crimes for about four years. Yeah I've got a question, and believe me no offence is meant by it, but you did say to ask away, so ask away I will. The word is you're here just to slash costs, a kind of hit and run merchant. I've been told you're here to save Head Quarters a shit load of cash, no matter what the effect may be on us, then you'll piss off somewhere else. Now I'm no mathematical genius, only got a GCSE grade B in Maths, but, and like I said no offence to anyone here, how does you bringing three new faces into our little world, three people who know nothing of what we're about, or where we are with our cases, help with anything, especially when you need to be shipping people out? Please tell me how does that make any sense what so ever?"

Howard smiled, although it hardly appeared to be a particularly warm facial gesture, before picking up a mug from the tray and taking a sip.

"Eurgh, good God, that is a truly awful cup of coffee."

He put the mug down and turned his attention back to Micky, "It makes sense DS Page because they are three people I know will do a fucking good job. Simple as that. Yes they may be my people, but they're also damn good Police Officers, and I'm not just saying that because they're here. I do though get where you're coming from, and kind of appreciate your honesty, after all I did ask for it didn't I. In a way, you're right though, I have been brought in to make reductions in expenditure, that's spot on, it's not my field of expertise I must confess, and I'll be totally honest, I'm not overjoyed to be given that role. Although now I know you have certificates in Maths I may be coming to you to help with my sums, there you go that work at school wasn't a complete waste was it. But despite what you may have been told that's not all I'm here for, and anyone who thinks I am is very, very much barking up the wrong fucking tree. You all need to be very clear on that one, now I mean that, you'd better not be thinking I'm just some bean counter, because that is not how I want us to work together, we are clear on this one aren't we?"

Howard took another sip from his coffee, and looked around the room for confirmation that all were in fact clear, before continuing, "Now my office may be miles away, but I'm afraid I won't be. This is my department, and as such this is where I will be basing myself. Now I've got loyalty to no one, staff cuts are going to happen, but the fact that you're here talking to me now, and not meeting with me this afternoon, means you can presume that it's not going to be you shifting over to some other department. Although I may have been a bit premature with one of you, whoever made this brew better up their game and pretty sharpish, because this is a truly shit cup of coffee, but we'll hopefully learn from our mistakes. So congratulations you're stuck with me. As I said I have meetings planned with what are going to be some very unhappy people this afternoon, and I'm not relishing that, but that's my problem, and I will deal with it. All that crap is separate from what is going to really matter, and what really matters at this moment is finding Amelia Clay and whoever has her, before she becomes the late

THE HUNT FOR AMELIA CLAY

Amelia Clay. Now if I've got things wrong and you think anything else is remotely more important than that one all-encompassing task, and I include Police budgets in that, then please speak up, because if that's the case then I may have got my choices seriously wrong and I may be needing to speak to you after all this afternoon. So if you really want to know why these three fine officers are in here with me sacrificing a life in the Metropolis to come and work in Dunstable of all places, it's because we've more chance of finding that girl, and the murdering bastard that has her, with them than without them. Everyone appreciate that little fact?"

There was silence.

"I'll take that as a very big 'Yes Guv we fully appreciate that'. Now that's good, that's very good. So please continue introducing yourselves, but let's make this quick, because I really want to get on with some Police work now. With regards to the Clay case we're back to day one, everything, and I mean every little thing, gets looked at afresh, I want a new pair of eyes all over this. I want you to pair up, DS Page I want you to team up with Parrachio, Carflour, you're with Sylvia, and Black you'll be working alongside DS Fernando here, I want you to get to know each other, but more importantly I want everyone looking at this as though it happened yesterday. This is one case as far as I'm concerned, a murder and abduction, by catching Stacey's killer, we hopefully get Amelia back. No one's ruled out. Today we start again."

-THIRTY THREE-

DCI Howard Wants A Fresh Start.

Starting afresh?

This case had been running for four years, there had been literally thousands of hours invested in it, and yet Howard wanted to start afresh. Manny was sitting the wrong side of his own desk, and in the chair he would normally be sitting in sat the source of his irritation, DCI Adrian Howard, or Frankie as he was told to call him. Everyone else was now out in the open office, trawling the net and records for some sign that one particular Tuesday Club was more than just a harmless mid-week activity.

"We've questioned him time and time again Frankie, Paul Clay is clear, it's all in the case notes, the transcripts, the reasoning, the conclusions. He's not our man." Manny was talking with a slight tone of exasperation, this was wasting time, and there was enough for them to be doing without chasing suspects who they didn't suspect of anything.

"But now I wanna talk to him, and to his wife whilst we're at it. Eighty percent of murderers are known to their victims, in the case of children that's close to ninety percent, over half from within the same home. You can't argue with statistics Manny, you can doubt them, fucking question them as much as you like, but the law of averages and probability say that Amelia Clay has a nine in ten chance of knowing the person that has her. Hence there's a nine in ten chance that it may be Mr or Mrs Clay, or if not them then someone they know well." Frankie answered, whilst flicking through a file of papers on the desk before him.

"But Amelia hasn't been murdered has she. And we're treating this as the same case as the Stacy Hamilton murder, in which case the killer, stroke abductor, certainly doesn't come from the same home, will not be known to both of our victims, nor the Clay's in all likelihood, they've been through enough Frankie, us turning up at their home to question them doesn't help at all."

"No you're right," Frankie said putting the small pile of papers he was flicking through back on the desk, whilst pushing his glasses up onto his forehead, now focussing exclusively upon Manny, "Us going to speak to them at their home is a waste of time. I want them both bringing in, into our interview rooms, and I want to talk to them both separately, like I said this is going back to day one. We start again, no one is ruled out, because in four years I can't believe we haven't missed anything, that everything is just spot on. I want them here. And I want to interview them both personally, now get someone to fetch them in, because only one thing really matters in this, and that's finding that girl alive.

-THIRTY FOUR-

Paul Clay Remembers The Night His Daughter Disappeared.

It felt awkward, sitting there in the cold austere interview room, with Paul Clay across the table. He was never a man who looked at ease, and Manny knew what he had been through over the last four years. He was someone living with the guilt of not protecting his young daughter, the self-torment of knowing that in the one place she should have been safe and secure, she hadn't been. He was the man who knew that whilst he had slept that night four years previously his daughter's life was changed and ruined forever, and he would have to live with that fact, that was Paul Clay's cross he would always bear. Whilst his wife had presented the strong face of the Clay family to the world, Paul wasn't even capable of showing his in public. The man was an emotional wreck, barely held together by medication and regular counselling, he was living the nightmare every day, for him there was no release, no respite, just the pain of knowing, and equally of not knowing, what had happened to his beloved daughter.

Manny had argued that this wasn't the right thing for them to do, that neither Paul nor Andrea warranted questioning, especially in this fashion, but Howard had listened to none of it, so here they were.

He looked across at Paul, head bowed, biting his bottom lip. There was a palpable silence in the room.

"Hello Mr Clay, please allow me to introduce myself, my name is DCI Adrian Howard, I'm now heading up the investigation into your daughter's disappearance. You really must excuse me bringing you to the station like this, but I was keen to speak to both you and your wife as soon as I could, I do believe that there is no substitute for good honest verbal communication. Let's face it I could stare at typed files all day, but nothing will be as clear as actually talking to someone. And I'll be honest here, clarity, that's what I'm after."

Manny watched on, saying nothing as Frankie offered his hand across the small table that separated them from Paul, he could see Paul looking at it with a kind of cautious suspicion, before briefly shaking hands with the man who had just introduced himself to him. Paul said nothing, but gave a weak smile.

Frankie continued talking, "Can I get you a cup of tea or anything, perhaps a cold drink?"

"No I'm fine thank you Mr Howard." They were the first words Paul Clay had uttered, since he was brought to the station, he hadn't even really protested when they had told him they were bringing him in, unlike Andrea who had had plenty to say on the subject, but Manny knew that wasn't unusual, it had been thus since he had first met the Clays, Andrea the communicator, Paul the mute in the background, always in the background.

"Okeydokey. But please don't mind if I sort myself and Henry here one out, I'm parched, are you sure I can't tempt you?"

"No really, I'm fine."

Manny could see Paul was anything but fine, but Frankie continued, "I should also advise you that our conversation will be taped, and should you require it your legal representative can attend this interview, although I really just want to go back and get a picture of that night. But as I said you can have representation if you wish."

"No that will not be necessary. I'm not sure how well Mr Manningwell has explained my situation to you, but I don't generally like to discuss these things, my counsellor tries to encourage interaction about it, but it's not easy." Paul Clay sounded quiet, his voice tailed off to a whisper, with the word 'easy' being barely audible.

Manny had indeed discussed Paul's reluctance to talk about the case, but that had only intensified Frankie's desire to pull him in for questioning again, he could see Frankie watching their victim's father intently, examining his face, his mannerisms, almost sitting back and just staring at him. It did little to alleviate any awkwardness within the room. Manny was inwardly urging Paul to 'man up' to present himself as the person who they had already cleared of

THE HUNT FOR AMELIA CLAY

suspicion. He was watching him withering under Frankie's scrutiny, come on Paul pull yourself together man, he thought as he could see the tears welling in Paul's eyes.

After what appeared far too long a pause Frankie again began to talk. "What I want you to do Mr Clay is talk me through the evening, the evening when Amelia was taken from her home. Please take your time, we're in no hurry."

"But I've already done this, so many times before." Paul half-heartedly protested.

"Not to me sir. As I said, in your own time. I find it helps when thinking back to first close your eyes, draw a big mental picture, you know get the whole scene set up in your mind's eye, then just tell us what you see. Nothing should be considered too trivial, nothing not worth saying."

Manny saw Paul look to him for some kind of assistance, hmm not a lot he could do to help him out, even though he could probably recite line for line what Paul was going to tell Frankie, so he just nodded for him to carry on.

Paul closed his eyes.

"I came home from work around seven o'clock. Andrea and Amelia were both home, Andrea in the kitchen cooking dinner, Ami was doing her homework, on the dining room table."

He closed his eyes tighter, before continuing, "She always did her homework, she loved school, really loved it, she worked so hard. Well then I went to the kitchen, spoke to Andrea about her day, before going to change. I don't think I spoke to Ami, other than to say hi, she would always tell me off if I interrupted her school work," a brief smile came onto his face, but it quickly evaporated as he continued, "yes, I went upstairs to change."

Paul opened his eyes, rubbing them briefly, "Is it possible to change my mind on that drink, I'd quite like a glass of water if that is OK."

"No problem," Frankie replied, "I'll have someone fetch you one right away."

Frankie got up and walked to the door, calling out the order for two coffees and a water, before returning to his chair. "I appreciate how distressing this is for you Mr Clay, but please continue, you got changed then what?"

"Then we had dinner, Ami had cleared the table, well after a bit of badgering from Andrea, she was in a bit of a sulk, she said she hadn't finished, but the food was ready. We ate, we always liked to eat at the table, as a family, discuss things, I think it's important," again he paused. "Or at least we did, it's one of the things that has lapsed now. Anyway we had our dinner then afterwards Ami went back to her homework. I remember it, it was a Geography project on rivers, she took so much pride in it, colouring it all in. We watched television, whilst she did her work in the other room, it got to nine, and Andrea chased her to bed, that was it really."

"But unfortunately it wasn't it was it Mr Clay, unfortunately that was far from it. So what happened then?"

There was a change in Frankie's tone, not so much aggressive, but just that little bit demanding, any sympathy was replaced by a kind of inquisitive cynicism.

THE HUNT FOR AMELIA CLAY

Once again Paul looked to Manny for some kind of intervention, but Manny once more just nodded for him to continue, but his gaze was broken as Denny Black came in with their drinks, handing each of them a polystyrene cup.

"Please continue," Frankie said before taking a sip, Manny guessed that his young DC must have learnt the lesson of how the new boss liked his drink, as Frankie made no complaint, not taking his eyes off of their interviewee for a second.

"Well then Andrea and I watched some TV, before going up ourselves, we went up about half ten, yes I remember the time as the News had just finished."

"And when did you realise that Amelia had gone?"

"It must have been about half past two in the morning, I was going to the bathroom when I noticed she wasn't in her room."

"You're sure about that time Mr Clay?" Frankie asked.

"Yes I'm sure."

"And what did you do?"

"First of all I called out, quietly at first, I didn't want to wake Andrea, then when she didn't reply I called with more urgency, Andrea then got up, we looked all around the house but she wasn't there. For some reason we checked outdoors as well, that's when I called the police."

"Now I want you to really concentrate Mr Clay, what made you check in on your daughter? What made you look in her room at two thirty in the morning?"

Paul Clay looked puzzled, like Frankie had just asked him some unfathomable conundrum which was impossible to answer. He cleared his throat before continuing, "The door was open I guess, I could see she wasn't there, her bed was empty."

As Paul finished speaking Frankie was already on his feet, "Thank you Mr Clay if you could wait here for a minute or so I'd like to speak to Mrs Clay now.

As Frankie and Manny walked down the corridor Frankie stopped, "Was he sleeping with his daughter?"

"What!" Manny replied.

"Clay, was he abusing Amelia? He gets up at two thirty and goes to her room, now I've had kids, and I can't remember ever making a detour when I'm having a night time piss to look in on them, not at that age, it's not something you do is it."

"We've considered it, of course, but only as a case of elimination, we've not considered Paul as either an abuser, or a suspect, his story has always been corroborated by Andrea, as he's told it."

"Well there's something there Manny, he's lying about something, I can feel it, something's wrong with our Mr Clay, there's definitely more than he's telling us."

"You reckon." Manny replied.

"No I know, that's 100% knowing it too, that fucker is lying. Let's talk to the wife. I'm keen to hear what she's got to say about that night."

-THIRTY FIVE-

Andrea Clay Remembers The Night Her Daughter Disappeared.

This was the first time Frankie had met Andrea Clay, he'd seen her on the telly, and read her interviews in the papers, she always appeared quite a formidable woman, but he had never met her in person. Of course there had been no need to meet previously, but with her sitting before him he could sense her passion, her drive, her unrelenting determination. She looked none too pleased to have been brought here, into that interview room, but that was how it was going to be.

She appeared in stark contrast to Paul, there was no fidgeting or shaking, no nerves, she did seem a little irritated, in fact very angry would have been a better description, but certainly not nervous in any way. Frankie was still thinking how there had definitely been something about her husband, and it wasn't just the nervous disposition and fucked up mental state that Manny had told him about, he had lied in there, he could tell it, if they had interviewed him so many times how they had not pulled him apart earlier? The bloke oozed deceit, but that still didn't make him their abductor, or indeed murderer, it only made him a liar, and what he was lying about Frankie intended to find out as quickly as he could.

"Why am I here Mr Manningwell?" Andrea asked Manny, ignoring Frankie completely, not even acknowledging his presence, "Please tell me why I have been dragged into this pokey little room, with no explanation or reasons?"

Manny initially said nothing.

"Well?" she said looking directly at Manny, an exasperated look on her face as she waved an open hand before her, as if she was expecting the policeman to place the answer upon it.

"Why-am-I-here?" She was speaking to the DI like he was some dumb Spanish waiter who had no grasp of the English language, Frankie looked up, that had just pissed him off.

"It's..." Manny began to talk, but Frankie finished the sentence for him.

"It's on my request Mrs Clay. Firstly can I thank you for coming in," he gave Andrea a reassuring smile, at least he thought it was, in reality it resembled more a pained grimace, "I'm DCI Adrian Howard, I'm taking the lead on your daughter's case, and before talking to anyone else I wanted to speak to you and your husband. I appreciate..."

Andrea interrupted Frankie mid-flow, "And you will appreciate that I'm not too happy being brought here like this, you'll appreciate you could have spoken to us both at home, there was no need for this, no need for this at all."

"Indeed I do, so whilst we're talking about appreciation I'm sure you will fully appreciate that nothing, and I mean nothing, is more important at this time than finding your daughter. There's a big bloody full stop after that comment, no caveats, no conditions, that's it. Now you coming here is at best an inconvenience for you, an irritation maybe, an afternoon lost, but to me it is a vital part of getting to know this case. I want to find Amelia, believe me whole heartedly when I say that, now having accepted that, and the fact that you now appreciate that nothing is more important to me than that, because we've already put that afore mentioned full stop in there just to be sure, you'll also understand that included in that 'nothing that's more important' is your inconvenience, your afternoon, and anything else that may be pissing you off at this very moment."

Frankie watched her to see how she would respond, he didn't intend to provoke her or upset anyone, but by the same token he had to be able to work this case how he deemed fit, he had seen how almost everyone had bowed and scraped to Andrea as she walked through the station, but her talking to them like they were some half-witted retards just wasn't happening.

She gave a wry smile, pausing for a brief moment, before saying, "Then you better ask your questions hadn't you Mr Howard."

***

COLIN PAYNE

The interview had followed a similar path to the one they had just conducted with Paul, yes homework, tea, bed at nine, Paul discovering his daughter missing at two thirty, the frantic call to the Police, but Frankie had heard all of that already, this wasn't his reason for talking to her.

"So Mrs Clay, this may sound an odd line, but your home could you describe the layout upstairs for me, left to right as you come up your stairs?"

Andrea looked puzzled, "Really?"

"Yes please, humour me, just so I can get a picture." Frankie answered.

"Well I'm sure Mr Manningwell could enlighten you on that, but anyway, to the right of the stairs is the bathroom, spare room and Paul's office, to the left, Amelia's room and our room." She answered matter of factly.

"It's a four bedroom house then." Frankie asked.

"Yes, if you include Paul's office."

"Just the one bathroom upstairs?"

Andrea shook her head, "No there's an en-suite in our room, although what relevance that has I can only guess."

Frankie nodded, "I agree, a bit of a stupid question, just building a picture that's all, anyway thanks for your time, we're nearly done here, if I could ask you to just hold on one moment, I just want to have a last word with your husband, then we'll get you home."

-THIRTY SIX-

Four Years, Four Years! Then Paul Clay Finally Tells The Truth.

"Right Mr Clay, just one question, just one thing I want to clear up before you go back to your home. Why did you walk past your daughter's room that night?" Frankie was standing up, leaning over the table, there was no doubt that this was a question that he needed an answer to. Manny wasn't sure why his DCI was so certain that Paul was lying, as far as he could ascertain in all this time there was no way he was connected to the abduction, no way at all.

Manny could see Paul, looking puzzled.

"Sorry, I thought I had answered that question, I was going to the toilet."

"And indeed you had, but you see that's what's bothering me, you have an en-fucking-suite bathroom Mr Clay, that's a modern invention with but one purpose, one reason for existing, and that purpose is to save middle class people traipsing around their landings at night going for a piss. That's why it's there, no other reason as far as I know. So tell me again why did you go to your daughter's room that night, and I want the truth, because I'm not some psychological expert in these things, but I know when someone's lying, and you sir, are fucking lying to me!"

"I can't recall..." Paul was stammering, his eyes now gazing down at the wooden table top before him, the table littered with the remnants of tiny pieces of the polystyrene cup he had drunk his water from, he appeared desperate to avoid Frankie's gaze, his eyes unable to make contact with the man's towering over him.

"Yes you can, you can recall every minute of that day, because as far as you are concerned that has been the last day you have truly lived, that is day fucking zero in your calendar, I know that, so don't tell me you can't recall, you could tell me every colour in Amelia's picture of the rivers if you wanted to, what exactly you had for tea, what was on the telly, what you all were wearing, so you need to tell me, where were you off to when you walked past that bedroom, because if you weren't going anywhere, then I want to know what you were doing, because people lie for a reason, and I really want to know what that reason is, are we clear on this Mr Clay, do we understand what I'm asking here?"

Paul said nothing just stared down, tearing another bit of polystyrene to bits, oh shit Manny thought, he's right, Frankie is so right, he was lying.

Frankie continued, "That's not an answer, I'm having dark thoughts here, horrible dark thoughts, about why you went to Amelia's bedroom, I need you to be truthful, I don't want

THE HUNT FOR AMELIA CLAY

those thoughts in my head, they're not fucking nice, but you lying to me ain't helping. So?"

Paul Clay was crying, at first they could see the tears appear, running down his cheeks, an almost inaudible sobbing, then he could hold it back no more.

As their interviewee sobbed Frankie and Manny looked at each other, Manny felt sick, physically sick, he had been on the case for four years, and here was their victim's father revealing he had lied about the night she vanished, thrown the entire investigation back to day one, what the hell hadn't Paul told them?

How involved was he?

Frankie sat down, saying nothing, just watching the man before him, Manny got up and reached over to a shelf pulling down a box of tissues, and laid the box before Paul, who noisily blew his nose. He sobbed for about another two minutes with no words exchanged before lifting his head.

"It's not what it seems, or what you may think Mr Howard," he said in no more than the faintest of whispers. "It's not like that at all."

Neither Frankie nor Manny said anything, leaving Paul to fill the silent void.

"I wasn't going anywhere," there was another long pause, neither of the two police officers breaking the silence they had maintained. "I was coming back, returning."

Frankie spoke at last. "Where from?"

"I'd been out."

"Where were you returning from Mr Clay" Frankie once more asked, a demanding tone in his voice.

"Oh my God." Paul Clay again broke down in tears, "Oh my God, I should have been there, I should have been there, it wouldn't have happened if I was there."

"Where the fuck were you then?" Frankie was again on his feet, his fist banging onto the table, bearing down upon the increasingly wilting form before him. "I said where in fucking hell were you!"

"Out! I'd gone out!" Paul wailed back.

"Where, where, where!" Frankie was shouting.

"I can't say, I can't"

"Bollocks you can't, where were you?"

"Milton Keynes, I was in Milton Keynes." Paul was now on his feet, as he screamed across the table.

"Where in Milton Keynes, what were you doing at half past two in the morning in Milton-fucking-Keynes?"

Frankie's face was just inches from Paul's, but only momentarily as like a puppet with its strings cut Paul slid back into his chair.

Manny who had remained silent could hold his peace no more, he spoke, but his voice was quiet in direct contrast to Frankie's bellowing, "Four years Paul, four years you've not said anything about this, not a thing, you need to tell us now, tell us the truth, and I mean right now."

How could this be? How could Frankie have got to the truth from the first person they had spoken to?

"I was in Milton Keynes." Paul whispered back.

"Yes, we know that, but why?" Manny asked, his voice calm, reasonable, hiding the feeling of sickening betrayal that he really felt.

"Please bear with me, this is very, errr, difficult." Paul said, still avoiding any eye contact, "I never intended to lie about anything, and nothing I have said makes any difference to the facts. It was just best not to tell the truth."

Frankie butted in, before Manny could say anything, although Manny was thinking exactly what his new boss was blurting out.

"Not best to tell the truth! Your daughter was snatched from her bedroom, by God only knows who, and you think it's best not to tell the truth. Are you for real? Like this man said, four years my friend here has been chasing a lie, four fucking years! So go on then, what is the truth, because I sure as hell want to hear it. What were you doing in Milton Keynes, what was so bloody need to know that you potentially fucked up a missing persons investigation, and let's remember that missing person was your only daughter, well come on, I'm on real tenterhooks here."

Paul was ashen, it was like he had been hung up and drained, of not just his blood, but his very life force.

Frankie again slammed his fist on the table, causing the quaking wreck before them to literally jump from his chair, "Now!"

Paul's mouth moved, but nothing appeared to come out, Manny didn't know what he felt about the man before him, hatred, sympathy, revulsion, but then that depended on what he was about to say, when what he was mouthing would eventually become audible words that is.

"I was with another woman. It was an arrangement we had, Andrea and me. The marriage was all but dead, we didn't, errr, we were no longer intimate, the physical side was over, it was agreed that I could see other women, although only on a casual basis."

"Go on." Frankie coaxed.

"We met in Milton Keynes, at a hotel just outside of town."

"And who was this woman?" Frankie asked.

"She called herself Cristal, but it wasn't her real name, we arranged it through the internet."

"And they say romance is dead." Frankie said, probably to himself, but clearly not as they all heard the words, before asking in a louder voice, "And you were with this mysterious lady all night?"

"Between ten and two in the morning, then I came home. That was when I discovered that Amelia wasn't in her bed, had gone, as I got to the top of the stairs, everything else is as I said, I was there when she went to bed, and I discovered she was missing when I said, it was just those few hours in between."

"Yeah, just those few hours in between, what do they matter heh? Paul's having a good time getting his sweaty jollies off with Cristal Tips, why did we need to know that, what possible interest would that have been to us on the night that someone broke into your house and took your daughter!"

Frankie stood up from his chair and paced around the interview room shaking his head, Manny remained seated, deflated, how had he missed all of this? But Frankie was still stalking around the room, cursing to himself.

THE HUNT FOR AMELIA CLAY

"Why didn't you tell us?" Manny asked, again calm and collected.

"Shame. Guilt. Self-loathing. Pick any of them." Paul mumbled.

Frankie again exploded, "What about rank fucking stupidity hey? What about selfish stupid bastardness of the highest order. You, well you just amaze me, oh Christ man, in the land of stupid twats, you Sir have to be the stupid twatting Emperor!"

-THIRTY SEVEN-

Missing Kit-Kats, Mysterious Cristal's And Tiny Tears Crying In An Interview Room.

"What do we do with him?" Frankie asked Manny as they both strode down the corridor away from where Paul Clay was still sobbing his eyes out, slouched over the small wooden table in the interview room.

"That depends, do you think there's more he hasn't told us about that night, is he in the frame?" Manny replied.

Frankie stopped by a vending machine and pumped a pound into it, "Anything you want, crisps, chocolate?" he asked.

"No I'm fine."

"Well," Frankie continued as he pushed the buttons to select his choice, "we need to find this woman he was banging, that ain't going to be easy, false name and four years later. I'll get Sylvia set up in front of a PC with Clay, she can trawl the net with him, she was interested in CEOPs, this should be right up her street, on-line nastiness, she can go into the sites he did, although like I said, four years, is this Cristal still likely to be into that shit? Plus we'll chat to the good Mrs Clay, she hardly seems the sort to go giving hubby a free pass to find himself some random fuck buddies off the internet, although I must say, that is some relationship, that is some truly innovative approach to marriage they have there."

As he was speaking Frankie was getting clearly agitated with the vending machine that had happily taken his pound yet was proving reluctant to dispense his *Kit-Kat*, leading him to begin to vigorously rock it from side to side in the hope that his confectionary would give up its fight to remain un-eaten and surrender to him.

"Fucking pile of crap machine," he was cursing as it became clear that brute force would not work in this case, just before a high pitched alarm began to wail from somewhere within the glass fronted cabinet. "Oh shit," being his only words as he pulled Manny by his sleeve, hurriedly walking away from the scene as quickly as he could.

"So let me get this straight, you're telling me you tried to buy me a bar of chocolate, but the machine ate your money, and that the reason you were buying me it was that you've got a really shitty job for me and Floyd?"

"Err that's about it in a nutshell" Frankie replied to Sylvia who was perched on a chair at the side of Floyd Carflour's desk. She looked puzzled like he wasn't making perfect sense. "Is there a problem?"

Sylvia furrowed her brow, "Well apart from the fact that I didn't even fancy a *Kit-Kat* until you mentioned it, but now I really want one and you've just buggered up the machine that sells them, oh and that you've got a really shitty job for me and Floyd to do, and we have no idea what it is, no everything's just fine."

"Good, now about this job." Frankie positioned himself between where Floyd and Sylvia were sitting and rested a hand on each of their shoulders, crouching down between them. He'd actually intended the chocolate bar for himself, but knew that Sylvia always worked better with the incentive of confectionary thrown into the mix.

"Now I'm not sure how well versed either of you are in this field, but out there in the big bad internet world it apparently is common practice for total strangers to hook up with each other, exchange details, then fuck each other's brains out. Now Mr Clay is currently in the interview room crying his eyes out, because he's just told us that on the night Amelia went missing he wasn't in his bed tucked in tightly next to his wife, but in fact was bollock deep up some desperate housewife by the name of Cristal…"

"Hold on Guv'," Floyd interrupted, Frankie could feel Floyd's shoulders physically tensing, "Paul Clay wasn't at home? But…"

"Yes DC Carflour, but for four years he has repeatedly told you he was. That is why we went back to day one, and that is why we need to track down this mysterious nympho, who we have good reason to believe comes from Milton Keynes, or at least did four long years ago. What I need you two to do is take Mr Clay to somewhere quiet, preferably without a massive audience, then trawl through these sites with him to try and track down this woman, because until we've spoken to her, Tiny Tears in there ain't going anywhere."

-THIRTY EIGHT-

It Was Complicated, Things At Home Were Far From Simple.

"Oh for heaven's sake, what is it now?" Andrea Clay asked the two Policemen sitting opposite her, "We've been here for well over two hours, please I have things to do, when can we leave?"

Frankie gave a shrug of his shoulders, "We've just a couple more questions Mrs Clay, it would appear there have been some discrepancies between your husband's initial statements, and what he has just told us. We'd very much like to discuss these with you."

"Really?" Andrea replied, Frankie noticed the slightest glimpse of panic in her eyes, 'Really?' indeed, he thought, she knows exactly what those discrepancies are, they are fucking great lies.

"We'd just like to clarify a few things. Now this may be a little delicate, so I feel it's best if we just say what's on our minds, and worry about any offence later."

She looked puzzled, but Frankie knew she was aware of exactly where this was going.

"So Mrs Clay. On the night that Amelia went missing, and please bear in mind that your husband has already told us what he believes is the real truth, was Paul at home between ten at night and two in the morning?"

She bowed her head, Frankie could almost see the cogs turning in her mind, weighing up her alternatives, thinking of what best to say.

"No."

He slowly nodded his head, lowering his voice, if she was going to tell the truth then he'd leave the theatrics out and just ask his questions as delicately as he could. "Was he out with another woman?"

"Yes."

"Were you aware of this?"

"Yes."

"And he says you agreed to him doing this?"

There was a pause, he noticed her lift her head, seemingly in an attempt to retrieve some dignity from this, "It wasn't something that filled my heart with joy, something I even liked, but it was complicated Mr Howard, things at home were far from simple."

"Please explain further?"

"Paul and I were going through a bad patch." She paused, looking at the two officers, her eyes glazed with tears but her voice unwavering. "But we stayed together for Amelia, hah, as we still do. Paul's little liaisons were his way of coping, his way of making things alright. He's a good man, a kind man, but he doesn't cope with stress in a good way, emotionally Paul struggles, you can't have escaped that fact, whether or not his sleeping with strangers helped I do not know, but at the time who was I to judge?"

-THIRTY NINE-

Looking For Cristal In The World's Most Unsavoury Identity Parade.

"Eurgh, per-lease, I don't know how much more of this I can take."

Leaning back in her swivel chair, her hands interlocked behind her head, Sylvia gave an exaggerated grimace, they had been trawling through dozens of websites, most of which featured a host of middle aged women in varying degrees of undress and very compromising poses, or totally naked men with their cock in their hands, as on their DCI's instructions they searched for the mysterious Cristal. Paul Clay had taken what must have been a much needed break and gone to the loo, and Sylvia and Floyd Carflour had gratefully also taken a rest from the screen that had presented them with a conveyor belt of all too willing housewives and maritally bankrupt spouses.

She'd about had enough. "For heaven's sake it's an endless stream of it, there's thousands of them!"

"I had no idea." Floyd replied, looking just a little shell-shocked, both he and Sylvia were sitting at Manny's desk, the venetian blinds closed to prevent onlookers witnessing Paul's humiliation. Prior to his 'comfort break' the clearly embarrassed Mr Clay had been sitting between them, playing his role in the world's most unsavoury identity parade.

Floyd was drinking from a can of *Coke*, "I mean are they all really looking to get hooked up with some stranger? That could be anyone replying to those women, surely it's a rapist's dream, it's all of their Christmas', Birthdays' and Easters' thrown in together. They don't even need to be hiding in bushes anymore, look at the lovely Dolores there, she'll happily make all your dreams come true, and as she says she means *all* your dreams, providing you're a clean male aged between thirty and fifty, don't smoke, and have a vivid imagination. Come one, come all, roll up roll up. Were you aware that all of this is going on out there? Because I had no idea it was, at least not on this scale."

Sylvia blushed, she was indeed aware, she presumed everyone knew that this went on, this modern day wife swapping without the need to actually go exchanging either your car keys or your actual wife. Of course she had never felt the need to open her front door, neither metaphorically nor literally to any Tom, Dick or Harry via the internet, but she had heard of such goings on. In fact she had recognised a couple of faces from the thousands of images they had perused, one was a rather rotund lass from *Tesco's*, who she would definitely now be avoiding like the plague if seated at any check out she was queuing at, the other, rather disturbingly, she recognised as a Sexual Health Nurse from her local GP surgery, although she had wisely held counsel over that little coincidence, especially as to how she had come to know that the woman held that position, that was definitely not an avenue she wished to venture down in any kind of detail with Floyd.

"Well I knew it went on, but not to this extent," she wisely replied, whilst still pondering how a sexual health expert could possibly be opening themselves up, again both metaphorically and literally, to such obvious risks.

Paul Clay returned, he was still withdrawn, he had said very little to either officer as they went through the seemingly endless procession of would be Cristals', with them agreeing early on that if he should spot her he would let them know, otherwise they would just keep on looking.

Sylvia wasn't sure how she felt about him, he looked so pathetic, his dirty little secret had no doubt eaten away at him all those years, and just as likely was continuing to eat away at any relationship he still had with Andrea. She had seen the strong and determined Mrs Clay on the TV on numerous occasions, she was an individual who carried so much respect, was seen as being so resilient and driven, whilst hidden away in the background at home was Paul, the weak and defeated man, guilt ridden and seemingly broken. She now knew why if prior to today she had been asked to pick him out in a line up she probably wouldn't have been able to, he wasn't the face that was plastered over any form of media, he was just Paul Clay, the adulterer, regardless of any sanctioning from his wife, if he hadn't been shagging strangers he may have been at home, and if he had been at home, then Amelia may not have been taken.

Yeah, she did feel sorry for him, of course she did, but that didn't change the fact that she was getting pretty bloody bored with looking at scores of women he may or may not have spent that night with.

Another two hours had passed, and still they searched on. Sylvia glanced at Floyd, he had gone from an initial eager enthusiastic voyeur, clearly fascinated by this macabre world of lust and infidelity flashing before them, to a man whose eyes had glazed over, both elbows resting on the desk as his head was supported by his hands cupped under his own chin. She was just clicking the mouse every couple of seconds, no one saying anything, as the next image would appear, to then be replaced by another, then another, then another… She occasionally checked that Paul was still awake, as he stared at the monitor. They had exhausted the 'fuck buddy' sites and were now searching through the pages belonging to escorts and prostitutes, Sylvia was surprised to see how many images cropped up in both sections, clearly there was a price to pay for some of this free loving, although Paul was adamant that no money had changed hands.

Then suddenly Paul broke his silence, his head jolting up to attention, his arm outstretched his finger tapping the screen.

THE HUNT FOR AMELIA CLAY

"Oh my God, that's her. That's Cristal."

-FORTY-

The Modern Day Odd Couple Go For A Drive To Leeds.

"So the new Guv', you've worked with him, what's he like then?" they were the first words Micky Page had said to her in close to an hour of driving, he was fiddling with the car stereo as he and Alice Parrachio were making their way up the M1 heading to Leeds, it was beginning to annoy her, he couldn't leave it on any station more than two minutes before he was tuning into something else, there was no consideration for her, what she may want to listen to, why couldn't he just leave the bloody thing alone?

"He's good, in fact he's very good." Alice answered, not really wanting to get into any long discussions about their DCI's abilities and personality traits, especially with someone who was clearly only asking in order to try and reinforce his preconceived prejudices.

Micky gave a nasal snort, it was clear that Alice wasn't being welcomed into the Major Crime Unit, at least by her DS, with anything much other than total resentment.

THE HUNT FOR AMELIA CLAY

"He's good? Of course he's good, he's a DCI, they all think they're good, I mean what's he like, as a bloke, you know to work for?"

Alice thought for a moment before speaking, describing Frankie in just one or two sentences wasn't easy, but at this point she would cling to any chance of a conversation, any opportunity to show this man that she wasn't some evil usurper, was actually a really nice person, because hell, she really was a nice person.

"This is between you and me Sarge'," she said, trying to remain guarded as to what she was saying, all too aware that anything she did say wouldn't be between just him and her, but keen to give him something, something to try and thaw his frosty attitude towards her.

"Well sometimes he can be a nightmare," she went on, "he's very driven see, when he gets hold of something it's nigh impossible for him to let it go, and he expects everyone else to have that same drive. He doesn't take kindly to backstabbers, weasels, or to quote him word for word here, treacherous bastards, it's never wise to cross him. He speaks his mind, and often what's in his mind isn't what people necessarily want to hear. But that's just part of him, he'll look after his team, really look out for you, as long as you're straight with him, but like I said go behind his back or cross him and well that's you out in the cold as far as he is concerned."

Micky laughed, but it wasn't out of amusement, "I'll best remember that then. So what about the Home Secretary, how did he get so friendly with her then, you know hooking him up with this posting?"

Alice shook her head and laughed, "Oh Sarge' you are so far off the mark there. Is that what people are saying? No he's no friend of hers! In fact he really pissed her off, the Ecclestone case last year, that was our investigation, Frankie brought the whole lot down around her ears, she didn't take kindly to it, it really was a political disaster, and how many ministers like political disasters. This move wasn't a reward, it was his punishment. He saw his Unit disbanded, the role lost to Special Branch, we all got shipped out here there and everywhere, but like I said he's loyal, so here we are."

Alice could see that Micky still wasn't convinced, he hadn't wanted to hear positive stuff, stuff that made the DCI seem alright, he clearly only wanted the dirt. He went back to pressing the buttons on the radio, asking no more about his new boss, but Alice was in no doubt as to whether Adrian Howard was a good man or not, he had now twice brought her into his team, following her just tipping up one day in his office, pleading with him to catch the killer of her colleague.

She could understand why Micky felt as he did, after all with Frankie demonstrating how loyal he was to his own people, three other officers had found themselves out in the cold, they had probably loved their jobs, were part of a team, and now no doubt felt both betrayed and very pissed off indeed with this new DCI, as would those remaining, Micky Page included.

THE HUNT FOR AMELIA CLAY

***

It was another five minutes before either of them spoke, Micky still was far from enthused about Frankie, and more importantly not exactly that enamoured with Alice. She knew it shouldn't bother her, but it did, she liked to be popular, although she often felt it was just shallow and conceited, it meant a lot to her that she was almost universally liked by all who she met. She wasn't one of those people who didn't give a toss how others perceived her, and she sure as hell wasn't going to spend the rest of her career being blanked by this man.

"So Sarge' Mrs Kilburton, have you met her?"

Again that nasal snort, Alice felt like telling him to just go and fuck himself, after all she was only trying to make a bit of conversation, relieve some of the awkwardness that he had filled the car with, but she knew she was now tied into working with him, had been allocated him as her 'new partner', yeah like some odd couple from a seventies American TV show. It was strange, he had quite a friendly face in direct contrast to his shitty demeanour, he was in his mid-thirties, mousey tousled hair, perhaps with a bit too much product keeping it in place, but Micky Page was quite a good looking bloke, a total arsehole sure, but he wasn't bad looking. He even had dimples in his cheeks when he smiled, something she hadn't witnessed that much towards her, but watching him talking to Denny and Floyd earlier it was clear that he wasn't such a bell-end to everyone.

She went back to staring out of the window watching the endless stream of lorries coaches and cars heading in the other direction. It was still raining out there, it seemed like it had been raining for months, beyond the opposite carriageway she could make out the occasional pit village perched on the hills, a dull grey vista on such a dull grey day. She imagined what it must be like to live there…

"She's a slapper."

"Sorry?" Alice replied, shaken from her thoughts.

"Shirley Kilburton," Micky continued, "she's a slapper. Was on the game, turning tricks when her daughter went missing, she's also a smack head, was married to a dirty kiddy fiddling nonce, and to be honest ain't got a lot going for her really."

"Why we seeing her today?"

"Your mate, Howard, he wants this to be day one, she was interviewed when she was down to identify Stacey, but she was so pissed by the time we managed to get to her hotel it was a total waste of time. We've loads of stuff from the South Yorkshire force, but have yet to have a proper talk with her ourselves. It was years ago, this woman can barely remember what she did this morning, let alone years back. It's a long way to go just to waste our time, but it needs doing I suppose."

No matter how grim their idea of where Shirley Kilburton lived may have been, it was still better than the actual reality of 26 Highmore Road on the East Riding Estate. Micky parked their *Ford Focus* on the grass verge opposite.

THE HUNT FOR AMELIA CLAY

"Urgh, for God's sake look at this place, what a shit hole." he said as he stepped out onto the sodden and muddy verge, and Alice had to agree with him, this was indeed a shithole of the highest order. She'd seen the pictures of the house in the file, from the time of Stacey's disappearance, but as rough as it looked in them, the place had somehow managed to go another step further downhill. Even the most eloquently verbose and generous estate agent would be hard pressed to come up with a more positive description than that offered by Micky, shithole was about as positive description as could be levelled towards it. Where once the crumbling render on the outside walls was cream they were now covered with little more than mildew, mould, and graffiti, the windows had filthy blankets hanging inside obscuring any view in or out, and it was impossible to see whether the front garden was paved, gravelled or grass, as it was literally covered in rubbish. Three shopping trolleys were parked amongst the debris, all of which were also filled with junk, and the broken pallets nailed together standing on their sides that ran parallel with the path resembled a barricade more than a fence.

Alice could see from Micky's face that this was not an interview he was particularly relishing, but then neither was she.

"Come on then, let's go see what she's got to say," he said as they picked their way through the less appealing items of trash that littered what they presumed was the path.

"You can lead on this one Parrachio, let's see how you get on, dealing with the Great British public instead of al-Qaeda or whoever, go on impress me."

There was little humour in his voice, no sign of good natured ribbing, or cheery banter, just that cynical tone he'd adopted with her since they had paired up. Yeah she thought, let's see how I get on. It would be good to impress him, perhaps he'd warm to her a bit if he realised that she was actually someone who could do the job, prove herself to him. Of course she shouldn't have needed to, but if this was what it took to make Detective Sergeant Page someone who liked her, then she'd damn well impress the cocky prick.

She banged on the dirty UPVC door, there was no answer.

She banged again.

Still no reply.

Alice crouched down in front of the letter box and called through, "Hello, Mrs Kilburton are you home?"

She could hear music playing from within, but no reply.

"Hello, Mrs Kilburton, this is the police, please can you come to your door?" She drew her face level with the letter box and peered through, looking beyond the cluttered hall way into what she guessed was the living room, she could see a form slumped in an armchair, an arm dangling at the side.

"Mis-sis Kil-burt-on, this is the Po-lice, please o-pen your door, we need to talk to you!" she shouted before seeing the arm move, then the person she was calling rise painfully slowly up from the chair.

THE HUNT FOR AMELIA CLAY

"Piss off!" eventually came the reply, as Alice could see Shirley Kilburton rubbing her eyes, "I in't got nowt to say to you, so just fuck off."

"Oh great." Micky said shaking his head, "this is all we need, three hours to get up here and she in't got nowt to say to us. Well that ain't happening is it."

He stepped besides Alice, saying no more to her than "Out the way." before hammering on the door. "Open up. Police, open this door now, before I kick it in, I'm not pissing about out here, this is your last chance!"

Alice was taken aback, "Sarge', she's the victim's mother, her daughter only died a few days back, please, go a little easy."

Micky cast her a withering glance, which was met with a similar look from Alice, a kind of silent Mexican stand-off over who could convey their disapproval most without the use of words. Maybe it wasn't that important to win him over after all, maybe it was good to have a little distance between her and people like him, Jeezus, did the man have no feelings. But as they glared at each other the front door opened.

"What do you want?"

Before them stood Shirley Kilburton, wearing a very faded and grubby peach coloured towelling robe, what was probably auburn hair, when clean, clung to her head as if she had just come out of her bath, only it was abundantly clear that she hadn't.

Alice answered her, "Hello Mrs Kilburton, we're here from Bedfordshire, we've come to speak to you about Stacey."

"Aye, funny that, six years she had been missing, plenty of people wanted to talk about Harry, but no bugger ever came to talk about my Stace, now they're both gone, no one gives much of a toss about either of 'em, but suddenly now it looks like the same bastard had her and that Clay girl, well you want to know again, want to suddenly find the animal that took them." Shirley was slurring her words, swaying as she spoke, Alice could smell the booze on her breath, mixed with the noxious combination of cigarettes and not having cleaned her teeth for far too long. Beyond the woman before her Alice now had a better view of the inside of the house, and there was one thing that was for sure, she really didn't want to be asking her next question.

"Can we come in please?"

"If ya come from down near London then I 'spose you'd best hadn't you, just don't go expecting too much." she answered, although Alice was already clear on the fact that she wasn't expecting too much at all. As they entered Alice was hit by the stench, it was hard to pin down exactly what it was they were smelling, but it wasn't pleasant.

Shirley was clearly already pissed, they didn't need the clue of the empties scattered all around the room, bottles of cheap supermarket vodka just dumped on the floor wherever the last drops had been poured from them. Shirley took a cigarette from a pack and lit it up sitting back in her armchair, she appeared to be deliberately avoiding any eye contact with the two officers.

"Sit wherever you can find a space," Shirley said between drags, "ask your questions, then piss off, I'm busy you know."

Alice perched on the edge of a battered sofa, a large crocheted blanket draped over it, vainly attempting to hide the tattered and threadbare upholstery beneath, Micky just remained standing, Alice thought if his nose turned up any higher it would be rubbing against his forehead, he could at least try and restrain his disdain, try and show a little bit of compassion.

"So what do you want?" Shirley asked, still not looking directly at them, "What's suddenly so bloody important that you roll up here without any warning, eh?"

Alice attempted a warm smile, but she wondered just how genuine it appeared, "Firstly can we just offer our condolences over Stacey, we appreciate it must be a very hard time for you. We're here as our department has taken over the case, and as such we're interviewing anyone who may be able to help us, starting afresh, no preconceived ideas, no…"

"Oh for God's sake." Shirley suddenly fixed her eyes on Alice, the clouded drunken haze she was caught in apparently evaporating, "Listen to you, starting afresh, no preconceived ideas, you lot didn't want to listen to me for the past six years, couldn't give a toss. Harry did it as far as you were concerned, end of. Although you couldn't prove it that didn't matter, he was your man. My girl, my little girl, what did she matter? For all that time, for all those months, years, all you cared about was Harry, not finding her. Now you've found her, found her..." she paused, taking a long draw on the cigarette in her trembling hand, before continuing, "Now you've found her dead, in Amelia Clay's back yard or wherever, now you want to know, oh yeah, now we're starting afresh."

Alice felt so much sympathy for the woman before her, because she knew she was right, had it pretty much nailed down, but that wasn't her fault, she had played no part in any prior investigation, but she was here now.

"I appreciate how you must be feeling Mrs Kilburton."

"Do you? Do you really? Do you have kids darling? How the hell can you appreciate anything? Look at me, go on take a good hard look, just a filthy skaghead, some old whore who couldn't even look after her own kid, that's what they say, that's what folk think. How do you think I feel, that was my daughter, that was my little angel, sure everyone appreciates how I must be feeling, but all that means is you don't give a bloody toss how I feel, because to the lot of you I'm nothing, no, I'm less than nothing, yeah that's me, less than nothing, and yeah that's probably true, but Stacey wasn't, she was something, but she paid the price for having the likes of us, me and Harry for parents."

Alice wasn't sure what to say, because that was pretty spot on as to what people thought, including Micky who was watching on saying nothing, he'd pretty much said that on the way up, Shirley Kilburton, the slapper. The poor cow.

THE HUNT FOR AMELIA CLAY

Shirley got up, and was pacing around, tottering on her feet as she did so, Alice wondered how much of it was the booze, the need for heroin, or was it all just real raw grief? She caught Mickey's eye, who merely raised an eyebrow, he'd made it clear outside this was her show, but at least that smug look was off his face, she wasn't exactly sure how much Micky was empathising with the wretched woman before them, but at least he was making an effort to appear as if he was.

"We'll try not to keep you any longer than is necessary Mrs Kilburton, but we do have some questions." Alice somehow wanted to convey that she wasn't like the others, she would listen, she would take her seriously, she did care, but by the same token she had no desire to be breathing in the revolting smell any longer than she needed to, yes she genuinely wanted to do something, anything to let Shirley know that her misery was shared, but that didn't mean that she needed to be spending any longer in that place than was absolutely necessary. Yes it made her feel guilty but she was beginning to suspect that that horrible sickly stench was actually emanating from Shirley herself, and that wasn't good.

"What we really want to do at this stage is go back to the day in question, the day Stacey went missing, we do appreciate that six years is a long time ago, but please try and think back. Can you tell us about your recollection of the day." Alice was trying to present her sincerest most caring personality, keen to try and reassure but also show that this was not just some exercise in lip service, this was genuinely serious.

Shirley initially said nothing, just stared into space, blowing smoke into the air, then as if shaken from some trance she responded, "Like you say, six years is a long time, I've already told the tale hundreds of times, can't you just check the files? They'd probably be a damn sight more accurate than anything my fucked up head can remember."

"Please just try, the transcripts will be most helpful, but we'd much rather hear from you."

"Well I'd spent most of the day at home, I was planning on working through the night, Stacey came back from school around four, I sent her down the chippy, she came home with her grub, Harry was supposed to be there to look after her, but you know what a useless bag of shite he is, anyway I went out about six." Shirley spoke very matter of factly, it was almost as if she was reading it off some invisible autocue, the fact that the child she had so tragically lost had been left at home, without even the security of some known paedophile to look out for her, attracting no more importance than the fact that she had eaten a bag of chips for her tea.

Alice nodded, "You say work?"

"Yes work, I was on the game, you know that." Shirley replied, taking yet another cigarette out and lighting it.

"Where were you working that night?"

"Chapel Town, Spencer Place."

"Any particular reason why you went there?" Alice enquired.

Shirley laughed, coughing as she rested the cigarette on an old torn up packet, "Because that my darling is where men pay to fuck prostitutes, it in't no secret."

"So that's the red light district."

"Yeah."

"And what do you remember of the night, the night at work?"

"What do I remember? I remember it was like any other night down there, only it was a bit quieter. I got picked up about eight, two hours of pissing around doing nothing, then during the night I went with about five punters. None of them were what you'd call different, odd, just the usual kind of saddos looking for a quick one."

"Was business always quiet that time of night, when you first got there?" Alice asked.

"Yeah, it don't pick up 'til night time proper down there, punters don't wanna be seen, only natural in't it."

Shirley again drew deep on the cigarette, Alice could see the pain on her face, the dark bags under her puffy eyes, she looked the kind of woman most people would actively avoid, she wondered who would possibly want to pay to have sex with her, it was a harsh analysis but true, she was not an attractive woman.

"So why go there at six?" Alice asked.

"I were 'sposed to meet someone, a guy I'd been with earlier in the week, he paid up front, double what I'd normally get, and said there'd be a bit more if I was there, even said what he wanted me to wear, he'd appeared alright, so I'd 'ave been mad not to have turned up."

"But he didn't show?"

"No, still he'd paid, it were his loss."

"Do you remember what he looked like?"

Shirley laughed, before shaking her head, "He was a man, had a cock, and paid me eighty quid, he looked like he wanted a fuck. That's what they all look like, that's what I remember, you don't look at faces, you don't look them in the eyes, it in't 'Pretty Woman' or 'Breakfast at Tiffany's', there's no fucking Richard Gere's down in Chapel Town darling."

"Can I ask if you still do that work Shirley, are you still a prostitute?"

"What do you think? Look at me." She pulled the grubby robe up over her knees, Alice thought she was going to vomit, her legs were rotten, ulcerated and raw, she now knew where the stench was coming from, she saw Micky look away. "No funny that, somehow even the weirdos and the really wrong 'uns don't wanna know."

They talked for another half an hour, established that Shirley hadn't noticed that Stacey had gone until the morning, and even then only called the Police that following evening, presuming she had just got herself up and gone off to school early. There had been no sign of a break in, and nothing to alert her to the fact that Stacey had been abducted. Harry Kilburton had been out that evening, hadn't returned home until after his wife, he may have been drunk and obnoxious when he returned, but she was adamant that he had nothing to do with her girl's disappearance.

THE HUNT FOR AMELIA CLAY

Alice didn't want to be judgemental, even though she supposed that was her job, but it was hard to reconcile the childhood she had known and enjoyed with that of the tragic Stacey Hamilton. As much as she appreciated that Shirley was suffering as any mother would, she also knew that the unavoidable fact was that Shirley had been a shit mother.

"Well?" Micky asked as they pulled away from Highmore Road.

"Well what?" Alice answered.

"What do you think?"

"I think I'm glad to be out of that house Sarge'. I also think you were right, well partially right about her."

"I'm always right," he smiled as he replied, "you'll learn that, even when I'm wrong, if we're going to work together you best remember that, but was there anything that interested you back there?"

Alice nodded, "The no show, the mysterious man who paid up front and never bothered getting his leg over. Why not turn up?"

"Maybe he'd sobered up from their last meeting, realised what he was paying for. It could be anything, car broke down, wife came home early, he smelt those legs, oh fuck what were they about?"

"Or maybe he wanted her out of her house." Alice said, looking over at Micky, who smiled back.

"Yep, maybe, great minds think alike."

-FORTY ONE-

Henry Manningwell Goes Fishing.

"Guv, you're going to want to see this."

Denny had got up from his desk, beckoning Manny over, he seemed excited, eager, Manny could see he had found something, and was keen to share whatever that was.

He needed some good news, oh shit did he need some good news. Although the whole Paul Clay thing had opened something up, and he had no idea exactly what it had opened up, it had made him look stupid, no more than that, it had made him look incompetent, and no one wanted to look incompetent, especially when in front of a new superior. Four years Clay had kept his secret, and yet with just a few minutes in front of Howard he had told the truth, no he certainly needed some good news.

"Got some results back, on Reginald Hargreaves, as far as the law goes he's clean, no history, no dirty secrets on the PNC, although we pretty much knew that, he's a Prison Governor after all. But, and this is going to interest you, look at his bank account, there, there and there," Denny tapped the PC monitor in three places, "Twenty grand paid in, on these three dates, cash transferred into his account."

"Hmm," Manny wasn't sure why he had gone delving into Hargreaves, he figured the man was just being pig headed over the business with Kilburton, the man ran a prison after all, he needed to be pig headed, couldn't just cede to any request, but it was all too wrong, literally within hours of them requesting that Harry be moved, he's dead, and he wouldn't have been had Hargreaves acted. He had looked into Woodley Grange, they had never had a riot since it had opened 20 years previously, now that, it had to be said, was some example of timing being everything.

He looked closely at the screen, where Denny had indicated, Hargreaves had close to eighty grand in his account, but then the bloke was well heeled, there was over five thousand pounds being paid in each month for his salary, the three big payments needed looking into, but if they were dodgy would he really have just paid them into his bank?

Was he just making it personal?

No, he thought, it wasn't just that, and sixty grand popping up in anyone's bank account is not a usual occurrence, it's not something that just happens.

"Denny, let's go fishing, get the authority sorted, I want a remote search of everything, his PC, emails, all computer access. Let's treat this with urgency. If he's dirty I want to know, if he's not, then let's get him out of the picture."

-FORTY TWO-

Floyd Carflour And Sylvia Hardacre Meet The Lovely Monica Maitland

She stepped out of the shower and wrapped the large fluffy white towel around herself, a second towel twisted around her head like some oversized turban. Monica Maitland was so glad to be clean again, what sort of perverted animal had that man been? She wasn't in the mood for any of that nonsense, he had sickened her, she should really have taken the rest of the day off, she could have gone out and done some shopping, grabbed a coffee, maybe have got something nice to eat, or popped down the gym, it'd had been a week since she last went down there. But then she'd got the call, from 'Floyd' - they never use their real name - wanting to call round, she'd considered just saying she was busy, but he sounded nice, young and cheerful, so polite too. He was a new client, and he wanted the full hour, that was £250, and although she did need to get out, another sixty minutes wasn't going to kill her, and there was no way he could be as gross as that horrible specimen who had left her apartment fifteen minutes earlier.

She walked through to her bedroom, her actual bedroom not the 'office', and sat at the dressing table, and once more began to methodically apply her makeup. Yes, he really had been that gross, that repulsive that she needed to totally get him off her, go back to bare skin and get ready from scratch. She unwrapped her hair from its fluffy turban and pondered on how long she had before it would just give up, fall out in clumps, how many times had she blown dry it, dyed it, curled it, each time destroying it just a little bit more, she looked at the black panties on the floor, and kicked them away, delving into her drawer for a fresh pair, she made a mental note to check that number on her mobile, bar it, filthy deviant, although £250 wasn't a bad hourly rate it would never be enough to repeat that.

At least the shower had improved her mood a little, 'The Carpenters' were playing on *Heart*, she loved that song, as she sang along to 'Goodbye to Love' she smiled, it was only a job, a well-paid one perhaps, but just a job. She pulled her stockings on, then stepped into the fresh knickers, clipping the tops of the hosiery to the regulation suspender belt, as the song drew to a close she switched the hair drier on, this Floyd would definitely be her last client for today, no matter who may call, she planned to settle down later with a bottle of white and the 'Great British Bake Off', was there ever a better remedy for a bad day?

COLIN PAYNE

***

As if on cue, no sooner had Monica finished her hair than the shrill warbling of the intercom kicked in, she walked over to the screen, to take a look, see what this Floyd looked like, and then she groaned, he looked alright, a black man in his late twenties, early thirties, he appeared quite fit, toned, well turned out, yes he was fine, but he wasn't alone, with him was a woman!

Oh that was all she needed, he never said anything about this on the phone, that's not on. Of course it wasn't something she had never encountered before, and to be honest it was money for nothing, they'd both be paying, and no matter what happened an extra body would equal slightly less work for her, but it would have been only fair to give her a heads up. She'd need to set out some ground rules, this wasn't some free for all, but she'd get it sorted.

Pressing the button she called into the invisible microphone, "Come on up please."

The door at the bottom of the stairs clicked open.

She quickly put her bra on and waited by the top of the stairs.

"Hello Floyd, I see you've brought a friend along, please come in."

The two clients walked in, Monica ran her eyes over the woman, she always did that when new people turned up, she called it her three second risk assessment, if they looked too dodgy she'd make up some excuse, get rid of them as quickly as she could, but in this case they both looked normal enough. The woman he was with had to be ten years older than him, where as he was smartly dressed in a suit and what looked like a very nice fitted silk shirt, she was in a pair of tatty Levis and polo shirt, with an ancient old parka finishing off her 'look' Monica presumed she was a lesbian, or more likely bi-sexual, and not just judging by the clothes, after all she was paying to have sex with her, unless Floyd had just brought her along to watch, it takes all sorts.

"Hi, I'm Honey, what can I do for you this afternoon then?" she asked, standing before them in just her underwear, "I must say I wasn't expecting you both, but well," she gave a little giggle, "I'm game if you are."

"We'd really like to have a talk Honey," Floyd replied.

"Well it's your time Floyd, I was kind of hoping we could perhaps be a bit more adventurous, you know have a little, or in your case a lot, of fun, especially as you've brought your friend with you. Hi sweetheart," she said nodding to Sylvia, "what's your name?"

"I'm Detective Constable Sylvia Hardacre, and this Honey is DC Floyd Carflour, Herts and Beds Major Crime Unit, just talking is fine by us, although you can help us by getting dressed, and perhaps sticking the kettle on." The woman was holding out a leather wallet with a shiny Police badge on it, oh bollocks! Monica thought.

"I'm not breaking any laws, I'm an escort, people pay for my time, anything else is…" Monica began to protest.

But the would-be lesbian, Hardacre, interrupted her. "Please we're not here to debate the finer points of your business, what you do to pay the bills isn't our worry today, although we do need to talk to you, please can you pop some clothes on, is it OK if we sit down?"

"Yes, where ever you like." Monica called as she rushed to her bedroom.

What did they want?

She pulled a pair of jogging bottoms on and hastily threw on an old sweatshirt, yep, this day had just got a whole lot worse.

As she handed the two police officers their drinks her mind was racing, what was this about?

Major Crimes Unit?

What had she done?

She certainly wasn't a major criminal.

The man called Floyd spoke first, he must have seen how awkward she was feeling, "Please relax, you're not in any trouble. So I presume Honey isn't your real name?"

"No it's Monica, Monica Maitland, Honey's my, erm, business name if you like, my Non de Plume as they say in France."

"Of course," Floyd replied. "Well Monica, we'll not keep you any longer than we need to, but we do need to ask some questions, now this may seem strange but we're going to need you to think back, think back four years."

Monica furrowed her brow, four years?

What on earth had she done four years ago?

The policeman continued, "We believe you registered with an on-line website, designed for people to meet up for sex, not an escort site though. You used the name Cristal, is this correct?"

Oh hell, she did recall that, but that was nothing really, certainly nothing illegal, nothing to warrant getting her arse bitten four years later.

"Yes, that's correct," she answered, not sure, not sure at all where this was going.

"Can I ask why? I mean if you are an escort, without wishing to appear blunt, but someone who is paid for their services, that is your livelihood, why would you go a on a site and give the goods, so to speak, away for free?"

She thought hard, she didn't want to lie to them, but it was all a while back, she was sure what she had done wasn't illegal, was within the law.

"A man approached me. I can't recall his name, in fact I don't know if I ever knew it. He paid me three and half thousand pounds to sleep with one of his friends, but it was on the proviso that he didn't know I was an escort, that he thought I was someone from this website. I was told who he was, and I contacted him through the link pretending to be someone who regularly used the site, and we met up in a hotel. I played the part, played it quite well if I remember rightly. He was happy, the man who paid the money was happy, and to be honest Floyd, I was happy, that's a lot of money, the man I met up with even paid for the room."

"Can you remember his name? The man who you met in Milton Keynes, not the one who paid you." Floyd asked.

"No, I meet a lot men, most aren't even using their own names, I'm sorry."

"And the man who paid you, what do you remember about him?" the female officer asked.

"It's strange I can picture his face, although to be truthful there was nothing outstanding about him, but it was familiar, I don't know why, I'd never met him before. He was very polite, brought the money around here in advance, told me it was his friend's birthday, that his mate messed around on that site a lot, but only ever usually met up with the women who were ugly, he wanted to give him a treat," she gave Floyd a wink, "and believe me I'm a treat."

"I'm sure you are Monica." Sylvia answered, before continuing, "Was he specific about times and places for the meeting?"

"Oh yes, it had to be at a certain time, and on a particular day, he couldn't stress that enough, kept going on about how if it was another time or date the deal was off, although he wasn't rude or anything, he was a bit of a gentleman."

"So," Sylvia asked, "you had, or indeed have no idea who the man was who you visited at the hotel?"

She genuinely didn't have a clue who he was, she had already said that, it was just another job, the best paid one she had ever had, it had paid for two weeks in Bali, just that one night, but unfortunately it was a one off.

"No never seen him before, and never seen him since, either of them, wish I had really, should have kept in touch with that pair," she laughed, "that could have been my pension sorted."

Floyd, who Monica had to admit was a damn fine looking man, rose to his feet, the other one following suit, "Well Ms

THE HUNT FOR AMELIA CLAY

Maitland, you've been a great help, is it OK to contact you on your business number should we need to?"

"Oh sweetie, you can contact me anytime you like, really don't you be shy, the way I see it you owe me an hour, and believe me that would be the best hour of your life."

Floyd appeared embarrassed.

"Oh look at him, he's gone all shy." Monica teased.

"We'll see ourselves out, thank you for the drinks," the female officer said, she appeared amused at her colleague's embarrassed exit, "I should forewarn you that there is a very good chance we may request that you come to Dunstable Police station, work with our composite artist, you know compile one of those identikit pictures, we'll be in touch. Thank you."

Monica saw the two Police Officers off then slouched into her settee, what a strange thing, all those years ago and they just roll up like that, although even worse, that was £250 down the drain, still there was always that wine and the 'Great British Bake Off'.

-FORTY THREE-

The Intransigent and Belligerent Starched Shirt And Regimental Tie Has Some Questions To Answer.

"This is bloody outrageous, I mean it, an absolute disgrace, on what grounds do you think you can just drag me out like some common criminal." Prison Governor Reginald Hargreaves was not happy, not happy at all at being escorted from his home to Dunstable Police Station.

He was sitting in the back of the unmarked dark grey *Vauxhall Astra*, DC Denny Black was driving, and DS Felix Fernando was sitting beside the irate Governor in the back.

"To be fair, we're not dragging you anywhere sir," Felix reasoned with their passenger, "you're just helping us with our enquiries, as we said you're free to decline our invitation, it's well within your rights, we just thought you being a respected part of the Criminal Justice world you may prefer that we didn't arrest you."

"Arrest me, oh for pities sake, you really are a pair of buffoons, I've never heard such codswallop in all my life. This is down to that jumped up Inspector isn't it, this is his way of putting me in my place, or something just as petty. You, you in the front, you were there too, so am I right, anyone who dares to say no to Inspector whatever-his-name-is gets humiliated, ridiculed, hah, what a waste of time, and my time at that. This is nothing but harassment in the plainest sense."

"Like we said sir, we just need to ask you a few questions, hopefully it won't take long and we can get you back home, it's certainly nothing personal I'm sure."

Felix could see how Hargreaves had wound Henry Manningwell up though, the man was arrogant beyond belief, he had responded with nothing but contempt when they had requested his presence. He wasn't sure what his new DI had on him, what they were going to present him with other than a few unexplained deposits in his bank account, but he hoped and prayed it was something substantial, the thought of him actually having justification for his claims of harassment made him shiver.

Watching on from behind the huge one way mirror, which separated them and Interview Room Four, Felix was sitting beside Denny, his mind was beginning to wander, as it often did. He still had trouble concentrating, always flashing back to the previous year's horrors, it was getting better, or at least he tried to convince himself it was, but then it would have been impossible for it to have become any worse. He wasn't sure if it was the pills or the on-going counselling that was helping, he just wished it would all speed up, he so needed it to get better.

The other side of the 'glass' sat Frankie and DI Manningwell, with a clearly disgruntled Hargreaves and his solicitor across the desk, it hadn't started that well with them having to wait over an hour for his brief to arrive, and even longer to debate the validity of the procedures that had followed, but clearly both Felix's superiors had crossed the T's and dotted the I's where needed as the interview had commenced.

He had seen Frankie in interview rooms before, many times, although officially the same, it was clear though the 'rules of engagement' differed vastly between interviewing would be terrorists and talking to highly paid Prison Governors, he was curious to see how Frankie would be playing it, throwing chairs across rooms and screaming in faces were not going to be particularly useful tools in this situation.

"Well thank you for agreeing to talk to us Mr Hargreaves, we do apologise for any inconvenience, obviously we appreciate that your time is very valuable, and hopefully once you've answered our questions we can get you on your way. For the benefit of the recording I'm Detective Chief Inspector Adrian Howard, and to my left is Detective Inspector Henry Manningwell, please give your full name and date of birth sir."

"Reginald Clyde Hargreaves, 10th August, 1966." Hargreaves replied very matter of factly.

"Also present is Mr Hargreaves legal representative." Frankie nodded towards the brief.

"Thomas Handle, of Fletcher, Fletcher and Hookshank," the young man in a sharp pin stripe suit said.

"Thank you gentlemen. I should make it clear that Mr Hargreaves is not under arrest, and we are just keen for him to answer some questions." Frankie gave the briefest of smiles before leaning down and pulling a salmon coloured card file up from by his feet and placing it on the desk before them.

"Right here goes. Mr Hargreaves on the 19th November of this year my colleague DI Manningwell and DC Black met with you in person at Woodley Grange Prison, do you remember this meeting?"

"Yes, it was more a brief conversation than any actual formal meeting, but yes I do recall it." Hargreaves answered, the arrogant aloof stance had been dropped, he was speaking in a clear confident voice, and Felix noted that there was good eye contact.

"And can you remember the main topic of any conversation that took place."

"Yes I do."

"Would you like to tell us of any requests DI Manningwell made."

"He asked me to move a prisoner, relocate him to another unit."

"And what did you reply to this request?"

"I declined it."

"Did DI Manningwell explain why he wanted this particular prisoner moved?"

"Yes."

"And yet you still declined that request."

"That's correct."

Frankie picked up the file that was positioned before him, opening it, and reading what was within for about thirty seconds, saying nothing, before once more closing it. Felix knew what he was doing, his DCI always did it in interviews, he left silences, awkward gaps, time for the person to think, to ponder what was being implied, what Frankie may be thinking, what he may be asking next, but Hargreaves appeared unfazed.

Frankie again opened the file, but didn't actually look inside.

"Who was the prisoner that my colleague requested be relocated?"

"It was Harry Kilburton."

"And where did he want you to move him to?"

"Our CSU, the Care and Separation Unit."

"Did he say why?"

"Yes, I believe Mr Kilburton had agreed to co-operate in a case but only if he was moved."

Frankie again paused, another fifteen seconds passed, he was just looking straight at Hargreaves, saying nothing, before once more speaking. "Was that an unreasonable request?"

Hargreaves appeared emotionless, once more the matter of fact tone, "That DCI is open to opinion. My opinion was that Mr Kilburton would remain where he was."

"But it was explained to you the importance of what Mr Kilburton may have been able to tell us, it was made clear the urgency of this, and also that your prisoner considered himself at grave risk?"

"It was. I also made it clear that Mr Kilburton was a known liar, a manipulator, someone who was adept at conditioning people in order to obtain what he wanted."

"Yes you did."

Again Frankie threw in a long gap, Manny was saying nothing, just watching on, his eyes locked on Hargreaves. After around another thirty seconds Frankie continued. "So would you be kind enough to tell us what followed. What happened to Mr Kilburton later that same day, the 19th November?"

Hargreaves took a sip of water from the polystyrene cup before him prior to speaking. "It is believed he took his own life."

For the first time since the interview had started his voice wavered, only slightly, but that all confident matter of fact air was absent.

"Yes he did didn't he. That very same day, the very same day that you decreed he would not be moving to an area of your prison that he would consider safe. Please Mr Hargreaves, enlighten us more on the circumstances of this suicide."

"I'm afraid that I am not able to at this time, you must know that it is still the subject of an investigation, the full facts are not yet known."

"Really?" Frankie asked with slightly mocked surprise. "We don't know the facts? Well can I ask a couple of general questions then? Question one, was there a riot on the wing where Kilburton was being held, the same wing he had reported he was in grave danger if he remained on it? Well is that a fact?" Frankie was now talking faster, slightly louder, Felix smiled, 'here we go,' he thought.

"It is still subject to an investigation." Hargreaves replied.

"Question Two, was Kilburton singled out during this riot, were combustible materials ignited in his cell, was he injured by items thrown in from outside his door."

"The events are subject to an investigation, I am unable to comment on that"

"Alright, what about this, a large group of other prisoners are seen at Kilburton's door, hounding him, driving him on, pushing him to take his own life, now that's on CCTV, I trust you have seen it, well, never mind facts, at least give us your opinion on that."

"As I've already said, these events are subject to an…"

"Yes I know, an investigation, what about this one, this one is easy, this one is so fucking easy to answer, is he dead now?" Frankie was now in full flow, his face was red, his voice raised to just short of an all-out shout, " Eh? Is Harry Kilburton dead, dead because he was on that wing, dead because when this man next to me asked you to move him you refused, dead because he wanted to give us information, is that a fact Mr Hargreaves, because I think it's a fucking fact, surely I don't need an investigation to tell me he's dead."

The brief answered before Hargreaves could speak, "DCI Howard, I consider your tone to be intimidating, my client is happy to answer questions, but please can we keep them just that, questions. You are voicing an opinion, suppositions, please can we remain within the parameters set out for this interview."

"Opinions?" Frankie answered, quieter, but clearly still not calmer. "Opinions? Sure it's my opinion, my opinion is that Kilburton is dead, it's my opinion because it is correct, unless someone's invented some magic pill they've not told me about, found some new elixir of life that works all year round and not just at Easter, then he is still very much deceased."

"Mr Howard," Hargreaves answered, he still appeared calm, still composed, "it is very likely Harry Kilburton killed himself, he committed suicide. I grant you that is a fact. It is being investigated by the Thames Valley Police, Prison Ombudsman and the Coroner. To my knowledge your department is playing no role in any of those investigations, I cannot give an opinion on these matters because that is all it is, now you can curse and swear as much as you like, I had served a long time in the Army and then the Prison Service, I have encountered bullies and blow-hards in both roles, you sir are nothing new."

"Very good, we'll move on then. For the benefit of the recording I am showing Mr Hargreaves an item which we have labelled as exhibit 1, it is a bank statement from November of this financial year, Mr Hargreaves can you please confirm that this relates to your current account, number 77785641, held at Barclay's Bank."

Hargreaves, pulled a pair of reading glasses from his jacket pocket, placing them on, and then peered at the papers before him, he looked puzzled, scanning the pages, before nodding.

"For the recording please Mr Hargreaves." Frankie instructed.

"Yes, that is a copy of my bank statement, although I…"

"Thank you sir, just the confirmation is required at this moment." Frankie pulled the papers back across the desk, and with a bright green highlighter pen began to make lines across the pages before him. He said nothing whilst doing so, Felix could see Manny looking over at the pages then back at the clearly confused Hargreaves.

Frankie stopped, slowly putting the lid back on the pen before rhythmically tapping his teeth with it, saying nothing, but watching Hargreaves intently.

Finally he spoke, again quietly, clearly he was now calm again, as he began to speak he pushed the papers back in front of the man before him, "As you can see sir I have highlighted three particular entries, dated the 15th September, 12th October and the 13th November, each one is for a sizeable cash transfer, that figure being twenty thousand pounds in each instance. Would you care to explain the origins of each payment, and why those figures were paid into your bank?"

THE HUNT FOR AMELIA CLAY

Hargreaves examined the papers before him, glancing over to his brief, who nodded.

"No I would not care to say where they came from, nor why they were paid into my account. This whole thing is becoming a charade. There is a perfectly good reason why that money was paid into my account, but it is neither illegal, nor may I add any concern of yours."

Frankie slowly shook his head, "I'm sorry I may have mislead you with the question, you know the wording, when I said 'would you care to', that was really a rhetorical question, it wasn't open to debate or negotiation, it was more an instruction than a request. Call me curious Mr Hargreaves, it's an affliction that us policemen have, it can be a curse, but sometimes it's a blessing. Curiosity is what solves crimes, curiosity is what leads to court cases, and good old fashioned curiosity is what fills your prison for you. Now I'm curious to find out why the hell you had sixty grand, sixty thousand pounds, paid into your bank in the space of under two months, now please sate my curiosity and answer the question."

Hargreaves whispered something in his solicitor's ear, who in turn whispered back, before he finally spoke.

"I sold a boat, as far as I know that isn't a crime, it was a sailing yacht, the buyer paid in three instalments, as you can see each of twenty thousand pounds. I understand cash is still a legal currency in this country, and the buying and selling of water bound craft has yet to be made illegal." Hargreaves sounded smug, Felix cringed, was that all they had. No wonder he sounded so smug.

"And you have all the relevant papers for this transaction?" Frankie asked.

"Of course, and before you ask it has been recorded in my financial accounts. The buyer comes from Cambridge, I will be happy to provide his contact details, if you feel it is necessary. Now is there anything else I can do to satisfy your healthy curiosity Mr Howard, or is this little pantomime now over?"

"Just one more thing sir, just one more question before you go." It was Manny speaking, he had been silent throughout, but he was now leaning forward, his head slightly tilted to one side. "What is the Tuesday Club?"

Hargreaves hesitated for a moment, just the briefest of moments, but enough for it to be noticeable.

"I have no idea Inspector."

"Have you heard of it? Take a moment to think if you like, the Tuesday Club, do you recall ever hearing that name?" Manny again asked.

"I don't recall it."

"You see when Harry Kilburton killed himself he made a point of doing something as his very last act, well the very last act before tying a sheet around his neck and leaving himself suspended that is, he wrote two words in his own blood. Now he must have thought those two words were quite important, meant something to him. Those words weren't 'Good bye' or 'Forgive me' or anything poignant as a farewell, those two words were 'Tuesday Club'. Are you certain you've never heard of it?"

"Of course I am, I have said so twice already." Hargreaves replied, the irritation showing through.

"Strange that," Manny replied, as he pushed a sheet of paper over towards him, "because this email addressed to you, and read by you, indicates that only this week you were invited to, and I quote, a very special evening of wine, fine food and exquisite entertainment at the Tuesday Club, the Greatest Show On Earth."

-FORTY FOUR-

Gentlemen I Give Not Just A Link, But A Genuine Suspect.

Walking out of the interview room, leaving a very anxious Reginald Hargreaves to talk to his solicitor, Manny felt good, they had done well trawling that email up, they'd only just managed to find it, it had been almost immediately before the interview, and he still had no idea of the relevance, but what it did do was stretch the possibility of some over-elaborate coincidence beyond the point of being feasible. He didn't know what role that man in there had in any of this, but he was confident they would find out soon enough, because Hargreaves wasn't leaving that room until they had.

As he and Frankie walked into the open plan office Floyd and Sylvia were sitting at one of the desks, it was covered in files, but they weren't paying much attention to them, instead she was laughing, apparently teasing Floyd, who appeared to be taking it in good spirits, whilst Denny was sitting at the work station opposite, engrossed in something, ignoring his two colleagues as his finger intermittently flicked on the mouse, his brow furrowed as he stared intently at the screen in front of him.

They walked through to Manny's office, which he had now found himself sharing with Frankie, and both men sat down, with Manny claiming the desk by virtue of getting in there first.

"We'll give him five minutes, let him try and come up with some excuse, then we go back and break his balls," Frankie said as he leant back in the faux leather settee the other side of Manny's desk, letting out a long yawn, stretching his arms out in a wide arc as he did so. He shook his head, "Urgh I really need to get some early nights, catch up with some sleep, I feel like shit."

Manny smiled, and nodded, as someone who hadn't had a good night's sleep for literally years he knew exactly where Frankie was coming from, although he had no desire to go debating the finer points of who was more tired and weary out of them, because he knew that was a contest no one would be beating him in.

"So Manny, this Tuesday Club, what do you reckon it is then?" Frankie asked.

"Who knows, well actually I'll rephrase that, *he* knows, Hargreaves, he must know, because he had that bloody invite, and he can damn well tell us, before he goes anywhere, he will tell us."

Frankie sighed, "As long as he doesn't leave it too long, if he does mate, you'll be staying in there with him, because me and my bed have an appointment, and it's one I won't be missing!"

But before Manny could think of a reply there was a tap at their door, and Denny poked his head inside, "Gents' sorry to disturb you, but there's something I think you both should see."

Once more sitting back at his desk Denny had turned around and was facing Manny and Frankie who were now both standing by his chair.

"Stacey Hamilton and Amelia Clay, there was never a link was there, nothing seemingly connecting them, no line on any white board running from one photo to another, am I right?"

"Err yeah." Manny answered, as both he and Frankie were looking down at the young Detective Constable.

"Wrong." Denny proclaimed, clearly pleased with himself, an air of excitement in his voice.

"I've been watching telly, well stuff on the net, and get this. In 2008 a company called *White Water Productions* made a series of documentaries for *Channel Four*, 'Working Girls', three one hour long films following a group of prostitutes in Leeds. I remember watching an episode at the time, although it was a bit too grim for me, hardly entertaining. Well one of the women who was featured, although her face was pixelated out, was Shirley Kilburton, she was filmed at her home, presumably where Stacey Hamilton would have been at the time."

He clicked the mouse and video footage appeared on the PC monitor, Shirley, was talking of her work on the streets, in the background a young child could be seen, although like her mother's her face was obscured by pixilation.

"That's Shirley." Denny proclaimed, "And I presume that is Stacey behind her."

Manny was underwhelmed, "And?"

"Well in 2010 *Sky News* interviewed Andrea Clay, also in her home, it concerned the Magnolia Ngonge case, the girl who was starved to death in a flat in Bedford because her parents were convinced she was possessed by demons. Andrea was head of Child Protection for Bedfordshire, and was under pressure to resign, she did this interview at home."

He again clicked the mouse and the footage of Andrea in the familiar surrounds of her home in Harwick Common began to play, Manny recognised the interviewer, it was Bill Penton, sitting across the coffee table he himself had interviewed Andrea over, Bill was talking not with the sympathetic tones he now adopted when conversing with Andrea, but probing, pushing, almost accusing, talking of resignations and responsibility, hounding the woman he would later become so supportive of.

"So they've both been on the telly." Manny said, still not convinced that the earth around him was shattering with Denny's revelations.

"No listen." Denny answered, again bringing the Shirley Kilburton footage up, "Listen to the voice, the interviewer cannot be seen, isn't even credited, but listen. Anyone we know?"

They could hear Shirley describing her average night, the type of people she met, how she felt, what she feared and worried about doing such a job. Then off camera the interviewer spoke, asking about her experiences with violence, but it wasn't what was being said that had grabbed Manny's attention, it was the voice saying it, the voice that unmistakeably belonged to Bill Penton.

"He's in both homes, talking to both women." Manny said, quietly, the penny clearly having dropped.

"Yes, a link," Denny was near to bursting point, "2008 Bill Penton visits Shirley Kilburton at home, three months later Stacey Hamilton goes missing. 2010, he interviews Andrea Clay at her home, just seven weeks later Amelia Clay is taken from her room. Gentlemen I give you a link, but is he a genuine suspect?"

-FORTY FIVE-

The Tuesday Club, A Place Where The Missing Can Be Found…

"So Mr Hargreaves, the Tuesday Club? Talk to us."

Manny was back in the interview room, his mind now partly focusing on the information that Denny had just supplied them with, Frankie once more beside him, although they had agreed that the DCI would remain silent, and that Manny would do all the talking.

"Come on Mr Hargreaves, you've had your chat with your legal representative, he must have explained your options, am I right?"

Hargreaves said nothing, but Manny knew the game had now changed.

"Did he not tell you that we would no doubt be going to a magistrate and getting the authority to tear your house to bits, seizing your home computer, seeing what other emails you've had, and more importantly replied to, what websites you've visited, what weird shit rocks your world, we'll be picking over your life with a microscope? Oh and you be sure, there is no such thing as a 'delete' button when we've got hold of a hard drive, everything's there for us, nothing can't be found. Did Mr Handle not tell you that was what we would be doing?"

Hargreaves looked to the afore mentioned Mr Handle, who gave a gentle nod.

"I acknowledge that I did receive that email." Hargreaves whispered.

Manny shrugged his shoulders, "We already knew that. Look I appreciate this is hard, so let's break it down into easily digestible questions, which you can answer individually, I always find this helps in these circumstances, does that sound OK?"

Hargreaves nodded.

"I'm sorry, if you could answer with a verbal response."

"Yes, that sounds OK," he replied, although none of his earlier calm confidence was present, nor the arrogance they had encountered at his prison, for Manny knew that this was now a man who would be talking, how much he would be telling them he had no idea, but whatever it was, he now hoped to find out exactly what the Tuesday Club was.

"So you acknowledge that what appears to be an invitation to the Tuesday Club was addressed to you?"

"Yes."

"Have you received previous invitations to this club's events?"

"Yes.

"Have you ever attended these events?"

THE HUNT FOR AMELIA CLAY

Hargreaves hesitated, looking once more to his brief, who with a stony face once more nodded. "Yes."

"Mr Hargreaves, what is the Tuesday Club?"

Hargreaves closed his eyes, and took a deep breath, before slowly breathing out, his head dropping as he did so.

His brief, Thomas Handle, spoke, "I would like it noting that my client is offering this information voluntarily, and that this should be reflected in any subsequent legal proceedings. His part in anything he is about to discuss is limited, and I would at this stage request that…"

Frankie suddenly broke his silence, interrupting the smartly dressed solicitor mid flow, "You can request what you like Mr Handle, but if it's some kind of deal you're after, that is something me and my colleague will only discuss once this man has answered our questions. Now Mr Hargreaves, please continue."

Hargreaves opened his eyes, and drew himself up straight, "The Tuesday Club is what you would describe as a paedophile ring."

He was staring straight ahead, towards the two police officers, but making no eye contact with them at all, just looking straight through them.

Manny said nothing, but his heart was beating ten to the dozen, he was surprised the others in the room couldn't hear it, he had him, he bloody had him! He tried to remain emotionless, but he wanted to punch the air, whilst Hargreaves had again bowed his head.

"Tell us about this Club Mr Hargreaves." Manny finally asked after what was close to a minute of leaving this now broken man to stew.

Hargreaves answered, it was like he was talking in his sleep, the words monotone, emotionless, so coldly factual, "It's selective, very selective, the members are chosen on the dual grounds of their integrity and their wealth. People are invited, on recommendation; it meets five or six times a year."

"And what happens?" Manny asked, now speaking quieter, with a gentle reassuring tone.

"Oh God." Hargreaves whimpered.

"He ain't gonna fucking help you." Frankie snorted.

"I feel so ashamed." The Prison Governor had his face in his hands, then once more rose up, shaking his head.

Manny gestured with his open hand, "Please continue."

"It's held somewhere different every time, I have attended three meetings in the past, always just as a spectator…" he again paused, before once more speaking, "there's no easy way of saying this Inspector, so I will just come out and say it, it's a place where people, people who can pay the asking price, can have sex with high profile children."

"What do you mean high profile children?" Manny barked.

"I mean Amelia Clay and Stacey Hamilton. Do you realise how desirable these girls are? Just how much someone is willing to pay to share a bed with them, or even just watch that happen? Oh my, that's the Holy Grail!"

Manny was speechless, he just stared at the man before him.

But Hargreaves was still talking, "That Inspector is the Tuesday Club, that is what Harry Kilburton wrote in his own blood, it's a place where the missing can be found, the unobtainable obtained, dreams become a reality. Of course you won't understand that, are no doubt repulsed by the very notion of it, but you asked, and that is the answer to your question."

Manny leaned across the desk, "Who organises it, who has Amelia Clay?"

"I have no idea."

"What do you mean you have no bloody idea, how can you have no idea, you've been three times, that was three times you could have saved those girls, three times we could have been there, do not tell me you have no bloody idea, because I am not buying that, I am not buying that at all. Now I'll ask again, who has that girl?"

"I really don't know, no one knows who organises it, the invitations come by email, you accept, pay the fee, then you are told where the event will be held. There are no names of organisers, never are any names given."

"Where is the next event being held?"

"I don't know, I never replied to the invite, you only reply if you are planning to attend."

"So let me get this straight, you have seen both Stacey Hamilton and Amelia Clay?"

"Yes."

"Oh God I can hardly get my head around this," Manny exclaimed, "She's dead now Stacey, murdered, snuffed out just like that, and you had seen her alive, and all you did was watch her being abused, watched her being raped, and you, well you…"

He stopped, he realised a tear was actually flowing down his left cheek. "We'll take a break."

"I'm sorry Frankie, I can't believe him, I just can't work out how anyone could just watch that happen, actually pay to watch it." Manny was in the corridor, just outside of the interview room, Frankie leaning against the wall beside him, saying nothing, but chewing gum.

"I mean," Manny continued, "he could have told us, he could have saved Stacey, and Amelia could be at home as we speak, what's wrong with that man?"

Frankie raised an eye brow, "He's a cunt Henry, plain and simple. Look, the bloke's a paedophile, he was only watching them being raped and abused because he can't afford to be doing the fucking himself, he was never going to tell us anything whilst he thought he could carry on going to their little parties, he's only talking now because he has no choice, he's only talking because he hopes to get off lighter through doing it, and you know what, he will. He will because we're going to need him, we're going to need him to answer that invitation, we need him to get us in there, he is a low life piece of shit, we know that, but we're still going to have to deal with him. Now when we go back in you have to offer him a deal, he's staying with us, that ain't even an option, but you need to get him to firstly accept that invite to that party, then find out where and when it is, I'm sorry, but that's our only way in."

-FORTY SIX-

Henry Mannigwell Talks To His Team With Eagerness And Optimism Flowing Through His Veins.

"Right people gather round,"

Pacing around the middle of the large office area Manny was calling his team together, Alice and Micky had just returned from Leeds so everyone was there. He walked over to a large blank whiteboard which he had dragged to one side of the room, Denny noticed how animated he looked, he hadn't seen him like this for a while, a very long while, it was as if he had received a massive transfusion of enthusiasm, with newly discovered eagerness and optimism flowing through his veins. He had a red marker pen in his hand, and he was waving it around as he spoke.

"This folks is a red letter day, this is the day we are taking control of this case. In one of our holding cells is a man by the name of Reginald Hargreaves, the same Reginald Hargreaves who has just explained what the Tuesday Club is."

He wrote 'REGINALD HARGREAVES' across the top of the board in bold letters, then he printed 'TUESDAY CLUB' directly below.

"This man has attended paedophilic events where both Stacey and Amelia have been present, this man has an invitation to the next one. Now he will accept that invitation, he will answer with a designated code word, which I now know, and we will turn up and do whatever we have to do. That is big, big news. This though stays in this room, I mean it, no one discusses this outside of these four walls."

Manny walked to one side of the board, leaving everyone to stare at the solitary name upon it, before continuing.

"Denny has discovered a link between Stacey and Amelia, in both cases within weeks of their disappearance their mothers had done Television interviews in their homes, on both occasions Bill Penton conducted those interviews. I want to know everything we can find out on Penton, and I mean everything, his history, his likes, his dislikes, what colour his underpants are, the lot."

He scrawled 'BILL PENTON?' to the left of Hargreaves name.

"Sylvia and Floyd managed to trace 'Cristal' our mysterious internet lover who was with Paul Clay the night Amelia went missing. She is an escort, Monica Maitland, now someone paid Miss Maitland to be with Paul that night, now that is no bloody coincidence. Floyd, I want you and Sylvia to go back and see her, I want you to take mug shots with you, including a picture of Penton, who knows we might strike it lucky. If no joy on that front I want her brought back here, she reckons she would recognise this bloke again, let's get a composite image done as soon as possible."

He wrote 'WHO PAID CRISTAL?' on the board.

"The night Stacey Hamilton went missing her mother remembers a prearranged punter never showed up, had paid her in advance, leaving the house empty bar her daughter, we need to remember she's met Penton, he interviewed her, so she would have recognised him, but who was this mystery punter, this man who would pay a street walking prostitute up front, demanding a very specific meeting time? That to me would indicate preplanning.

"We've been investigating this case for four years, and never have we got anywhere near where we've managed to get today, now come on, let's make this happen, let's get Amelia home as soon as we can!"

-FORTY SEVEN-

Paul Clay, Naked Bar The Silk Tie He Wore At His Wedding, Seeks A Release.

Laying naked, face down on the bed he used to share with his wife, Paul Clay sobbed, any resistance to total submission now abandoned on the floor of some grubby Police interview room. Neither he nor Andrea had said a word to each other since they had left the Police Station the previous day, after all what was there to say, what could he possibly say?

He had always known that it would all come out at some point, it had to, why hadn't he just been honest at the time? Why hadn't he just told the truth four years earlier?

But then he knew the answer to that one, because Andrea had insisted that he didn't, it would only detract from the one important thing that really mattered, getting Amelia back, she had insisted, told him not to be so selfish, what he had done, he had done.

THE HUNT FOR AMELIA CLAY

So for every day of those four long years their little dirty secret had eaten away at him, like some slow gnawing cancer, infecting his very soul, blowing itself out of all proportion. He had lived with it continuously, he wasn't there, he wasn't there when it had happened, only Andrea was, slumbering under the influence of yet another two bottles of wine, the very same Andrea who in that state would sleep through anything.

He wondered when it would ever all be over, but he knew that the only thing that was truly over was the sham of a marriage he still endured on a daily basis, locked into this horrible loveless life sentence for the benefit of Amelia. She didn't love him, she never did before Amelia was taken, so he knew only too well that she certainly didn't now, how could she?

Again he remembered that harsh and unforgiving Policeman's questions, opening up his deceit like a knife into a stubborn oyster shell. It wasn't the embarrassment, nor the humiliation that hurt, it was his own realisation that he had failed his missing daughter so badly. Everything that man had bellowed across the table was true, he had been an idiot, a bloody fool, what the hell had he been thinking all this time?

He felt so empty, so terribly lonely and indisputably alone. What did he have left?

All he had was the hope that his daughter would return home one day? But return to what? Some tawdry court case where not only would her abductor be judged, but also her parents failings so publicly exposed, the true guilty parties in her disappearance revealed in full tabloid sensationalism. They, or more truthfully Andrea, were now celebrities, and as such liable to be destroyed by their horrible lies and deception.

He buried his face deep into the pillow, and wished for all his worth he could turn back time, but that was a wish that was never going to come true.

He had often considered it, spent hours contemplating whether he was capable of such an act, would have the moral fortitude to do what he was convinced was now the right thing, now he was sure he could.

He rolled over and slid off the bed, walking to the large wardrobe that dominated one of the walls in the modern spacious bedroom, the bedroom that they had long since ceased to share. He gently tapped the ash panelled door and it silently and smoothly opened, revealing his suits, shirts and jackets, inside the door itself the tie rack. He ran his fingers along the dozens of silk ties, stopping at the wide purple one, the one that was around his neck the day they got married.

Yes, he thought, there was a certain symmetry to that, as he slid it from the rail, walking back to the large bed, before kneeling before the tall cast iron bedhead standing solid behind the usually perfectly fluffed up pillows.

He had slipped into an almost trance like state as he looped one end of the tie around the top of the frame and knotted it, pulling on it ensuring it was tight, that it would not give, then slowly and deliberately creating the noose, before looping it around his own neck.

He knew he was now being selfish, but he had spent so long just fitting in to accommodate others, Andrea would have no option, she would have to allow him this one instance of putting Paul first, because she had no choice. Of course she would be upset, probably devastated, but she would recover, her quest for Amelia would soon replace any memories of him, and he was sure that Peterson would supplant himself into her life with ease.

He had considered leaving a note, some heartfelt plea for forgiveness and understanding, but he didn't require either of those things, at least not from his wife, he just wanted a release, a release from the guilt, a release from the pain and a release from his now miserable existence.

He sat on the very edge of the bed, the tie painfully pulling against his throat, the well-constructed noose allowing the smooth fabric to freely tighten, already beginning to affect his airways.

Then he simply slid from the side of the bed.

-FORTY EIGHT-

No Space For The Candyman At Tuesday's Party.

"Bollocks." Frankie exclaimed as he looked at the email before him on the glowing monitor...

My dearest Candyman,

Thank you for your reply to the invitation, but unfortunately I regret to inform you that this party is now fully booked. There will be of course be more in the future, and I would as always recommend a swift reply to any invitations, as I am sure you are well aware how popular these events are.

Thank you for your interest, and once again apologies for any disappointment.

P

"Well that was too fucking good to be true wasn't it." Frankie said, walking away from the screen leaving Felix, his Detective Sergeant from his anti-terrorism days, to read the short message. "Where are we with this Penton?"

THE HUNT FOR AMELIA CLAY

"Floyd and Sylvia have gone to pull him in, he's on his way with them now, apparently he was none too pleased about being dragged off the street whilst filming." Felix replied.

"Yeah , well shit happens."

They were both standing by Felix's desk, outside through the long window that ran the length of one side of the open area Felix could see a clear blue sky, something of a rarity of late.

"How you coping?" Frankie asked him.

"OK. I think, you know it's been a while hasn't it."

It was the first time anyone had asked him that question since he had returned to work, and he wasn't really sure of the answer, so 'OK' seemed appropriate enough. He hadn't run out of the building screaming, or broken down into a heap in the Gents crying his eyes out, but he had been wandering around like a spare part, drifting off into his own little world, and whenever Sylvia was out of the office he felt a bit lost and alone.

"Look, I wouldn't have brought you back in if I didn't feel you were up to it. You know I'm not a charity, my own little Police Benevolent Fund or something, you're good for this. I've seen you moping around, you need to snap out of it, get a grip, you've had a year of all of that, so when this Penton comes in I want you to go in with Manny, I'll watch, you get involved. We'll also need to speak to that Hargreaves again, now that invite's died a death we need another way in."

Felix wasn't sure he particularly wanted to get that involved, but knew Frankie was right. He had lost someone he loved dearly, but he at last realised that he still had a life, a life he needed to get on with, and his work was a massive part of that life.

Felix could see Manny walking across to them, the resigned look on his face indicating that he had already seen a copy of the email.

"I've got someone upstairs trying to trace the ISP for that email address, but we're not expecting too much," he said, "Penton should be in soon, myself and Micky will take the chairs on that one."

"I want Felix to go in with you." Frankie replied.

Manny looked a little taken a aback, but said nothing, just nodding his head, Felix felt awkward, in reality he knew very little other than the headline facts in this case, he appreciated Frankie wanted him to 'get back on the bike', but he was sure Micky Page would have been more use in there, but he wasn't going to argue with his DCI, particularly in front of Manny.

"Well then Felix, so be it, come on, we'll work out how to play this." Manny said whilst walking back to his office.

Bill Penton sat opposite Felix and Manny, he appeared impatient, "Really? Do you think this is actually justified Inspector Manningwell?"

The 'Inspector' was accentuated, Felix knew that Manny and Penton knew each other, had a reasonable working relationship, he guessed the way the TV reporter had addressed him was just to ensure that Manny knew he was pissed off.

THE HUNT FOR AMELIA CLAY

He looked over to Manny who just nodded, "Yes Bill it is necessary, but hopefully we won't be keeping you too long, just a few points to clear up."

Manny went through the pre-amble before any questions were asked, turning on the tape machine with the usual spiel and introductions, this only appeared to irritate Penton even more, he had fixed a stare in Manny's direction, very slowly shaking his head as Manny spoke.

Once the formalities were completed Bill Penton spoke, giving the two Policemen no opportunity to ask their question.

"You've actually brought me in, eh? Couldn't even ask me over the phone or get your two lackeys to do your bidding. So what's so damn important that you drag me off the street and drive thirty miles, what have I done to warrant this treatment Inspector? What's the crime?"

Felix once more glanced over towards Manny, who straightened in his chair.

"I need to ask you about Shirley Kilburton and Andrea Clay. When did you first meet them?"

Felix could see that Penton looked puzzled, but after a couple of seconds of thinking he finally answered, "Shirley Kilburton I've only met a couple of times, I wasn't covering the story, someone else was reporting on that one, although I have interviewed her this week. But strangely enough I met her about six years ago, although nothing to do with the Stacey case, I interviewed her for a documentary, it was called 'Working Girls'. But like I said that was before

Stacey went missing. As for Andrea, we've spoken at least a dozen times, probably more."

"And when did you first speak to her?"

"I don't know the exact date, it related to her work, a child neglect case that went bad. As I said, I can't say when, but certainly four or five years back."

"Don't you think that's strange?" Manny asked, Felix noted the questioning look on his face.

Penton again paused, weighing up the simple question, "No not really, we were making a documentary about prostitutes in Leeds, Shirley Kilburton was a prostitute in Leeds, a girl died in Bedfordshire of neglect, I interviewed the head of the department that was being held responsible, it's what I do."

Manny pressed on, "I mean that both these women had their daughters abducted within months of those interviews?"

Bill gave a little smile, where this was going obviously now apparent to him, Felix could see him shaking his head again.

"Oh Manny really? I don't believe this. Is this what this is all about, you put two and two together and come up with total bollocks. Look, let me save you embarrassing yourselves any further, check the date that Amelia went missing, in fact check a week either side, contact *Sky*, or even easier type 'Major Thomas Endimann' in *You Tube*, go get someone to do it now, because I was reporting the Major's death at the hands of the Taliban in Afghanistan when Amelia was taken, I remember it well, because when I came home it had become the big story, I was given the assignment of covering it. I'm sorry guys, but if you think that I'm the answer to any more of your questions you are seriously looking at the wrong person. Me interviewing those two women was just a coincidence, they do happen, happen every day, but for heaven's sake that doesn't make me your new number one suspect."

As Bill Penton prepared to leave, Monica Maitland, who was standing beside Floyd in the small room next door, nodded when asked if she recognised the man who was the other side of the two way mirror.

"And where do you recognise him from?" Floyd asked, desperately trying to suppress his rising excitement.

"Off the television," she replied, "that's the man that does the News."

"So that's not the person who paid you to sleep with Paul Clay?"

She laughed out loud, clearly amused by the question, "Of course not silly, that's Bill Penton, why would he do that?"

-FORTY NINE-

The Tuesday Club Needs A New Venue.

Staring at the email, he could barely contain his rage, how could that damn fool let him down now? It was all organised, and it was tomorrow, yet the words were there in black and white...

Phillip,

So sorry to do this at such short notice, but can longer accommodate the TC this week, something's come up and I need to go to the States at short notice.

White Rabbit.

People had paid a great deal of money upfront, all the arrangements had been made, and not just that, he had his, or more relevantly the Tuesday Club's, reputation to uphold. He couldn't just cancel, it wasn't an option. He thought of alternatives, where could he find another venue with just hours to go? Who could accommodate the party at such short notice? But he already knew the answer to that one, he knew there was only one location, one venue, one place... his own home.

THE HUNT FOR AMELIA CLAY

It went against all the self-imposed rules he had written himself when he first initiated the club, *never bring it home*.

Yet what else could he do?

He was only a few miles from where they had planned to hold it, all the 'entertainment' could be rerouted, the catering could still be set up, and the wine and champagne would easily be diverted to his house.

He would still be anonymous, no one would know he was 'Phillip', the reluctant host, it was what he had to do.

It would of course be hard work arranging such changes within such a tight time frame, but that was what would have to happen.

Whilst Phillip began to compose his revised invitations Amelia Clay was sitting up against the wall that ran parallel with her bed. In her hand were the shiny scissors she had stolen from Gerald Draper, she pushed the ends against her soft finger tips, a bobble of blood appeared, coating the sharp points. Again she considered cutting herself with them, disfiguring herself to such a degree that 'The Pig' would never want to use her again, or even cutting herself so deeply it would go away completely, but that was not what she had taken them for.

She told herself again and again, "I can do it, I can do it," her whispered mantra, as she envisaged in her mind's eye plunging the scissors into him, stabbing, tearing, twisting, gouging, ripping him apart, pay back for all the parties, all the long nights when he would come to her, all the hurt and pain he so cruelly inflicted upon her, for nothing but his own selfish deviant pleasure.

She knew the party was tomorrow, but she couldn't face another one of those, was actually incapable of going through it all again. She looked out of her window, the sun shining on a world she was excluded from, shimmying along that ledge was always still an option, but by the time he unlocked her again it would have been dark hours before, and no doubt raining once more.

No, she knew what she was going to do.

"I can do it, I can do it, I can do it…"

-FIFTY-

And Then There Is Space For The Candyman At Tuesday's Party.

"Guv, Guv!"

It was Denny Black, barging into Manny's office with a sheet of paper in his hand, The DCI and DS Fernando were also in there with Manny going over the train crash of an interview they had conducted with Bill Penton.

He couldn't help himself, he had to tell them as soon as possible, "It's on!"

He had been near to bursting point, waving his A4 declaration of joy in the air, he had to show them immediately, if for no other reason than to share his excitement.

"What's on?" Manny replied.

"The Tuesday Club, Hargreaves has been invited again, Guv' it's on." Denny's voice was practically a squeak, a high pitched statement that this was actually pretty bloody big. And indeed it was.

He lay the sheet of paper on Manny's desk and the other three gathered around viewing his two dozen or so typed lines of renewed hope.

They all looked at each other, the excitement was palpable, they now had an in, they now had that door to the mythical Tuesday Club wide open, and with it their route to Amelia Clay.

Candyman,

I have some most excellent news for you, due to circumstances beyond his control one of our guests will be unable to attend tomorrow, which for your good self is great news, as there is now a Golden Ticket available!

As per usual this will be priced at £50,000 payable to the account detailed below. I cannot stress what a fantastic opportunity this is for you to experience a joy so few get to ever participate in.

I am also so pleased to confirm that AC will once more be the star attraction, though as per usual there will be supporting performers for all to enjoy prior to the main event.

I look forward to hearing from you, and may I suggest that there is no better use for that money you received for your 'boat' than this!

Details of venue to follow once the fees have been transferred, and of course don't forget the theme is the Circus!

P

THE HUNT FOR AMELIA CLAY

"Let's get some money to him straight away," Frankie said, rubbing his hands together as he spoke, Denny could see that he was thinking what they all were, this was the end in sight.

"We need to know that address, we need to get ready for this. I want them all, every one of those perverted bastards, and more importantly any kids that are there. This isn't just about Amelia, from what Hargreaves tells us, and of course what's in that email, there will be other kids. For fuck's sake, *supporting performers*, what kind of animals are these?"

Manny turned to Denny, "Get the Chief Constable on the line, we need that money authorised, we need to pay it through Hargreaves bank, get all the details off of him and make sure he gets no chance to contact anyone, no one at all, we don't want him tipping them off. We need it transferring within the hour."

"This stays very fucking need to know," Frankie said. "We know there's high profile people involved, we only include those that really have to be included. We're going to need lots of bodies tomorrow, but we hold with any organising until the morning, get the others in here, I want everyone on the same page on this."

Denny went to call the rest of the team into the office, but before he could go through the door Micky Page had entered, blocking his way.

"Sorry to interrupt the party gents, but I think you should know, it looks like Paul Clay hung himself this morning. He's dead"

-FIFTY ONE-

Modern Policing, It's All About The Blame Game.

Closing his eyes, Manny bowed his head.

'Bollocks!' he thought. The office had gone deathly quiet, Oh jeezus he didn't need this. He kept thinking, 'had we been too harsh, had we gone over the top with him?'

But he knew they hadn't, because the late Mr Clay had lied, and they needed the truth.

They were not responsible for this, no blame would be landing at his or Frankie's doors. They were clear on this one, the tapes would show that, everything above board and proper, thank God.

Then he caught himself, a man was dead and all he was thinking of was whether anyone would be able to blame him, but that was modern policing, it's all about the blame game.

Yet in this case the Force weren't responsible for that man's death, and neither was Paul Clay really, even though it was self-inflicted, the blame on this one rested squarely on the shoulders of the bastard who had taken that poor wretched man's daughter, the same nasty bastard that saw her as the *Main Attraction*, sold tickets to violate her for

£50,000, that's where the blame lay, and that's who would be brought to account.

He knew someone would have to go and see Andrea, oh dear, poor Andrea, and he knew *that* someone would need to be him, of course he would be taking Denny, there was no way he was going within ten miles of that place without him, but everything else would have to wait.

Denny was watching him, no doubt dreading that visit to Harwick Common just as much as he was.

"I'll just get my coat Guv," being all he said.

-FIFTY TWO-

Cinderella Is Given The Opportunity For A Little Bit Of Redemption.

Whilst Denny and Manny went to Harwick Common to talk to what would certainly be a very emotional Andrea Clay, Frankie and Felix went to speak to Reginald Hargreaves in the holding cell which had become his temporary home.

"Right Cinderella," Frankie said as they walked into the small cell, no pleasantries or hellos, just straight to the point, "I've some good news for you, your invitation to the ball has arrived, Prince Charming does want you there after all. Unfortunately you can't make it, sorry but no Fairy fucking Godmother is going to be springing you from here any time soon. But all is not lost, you can help us to help you, we need you to do something for us, won't take a minute, but may shave years of any sentence coming your way. We're kind like that, even to people who we fucking despise, and believe me, have no doubt about this, at this very moment I think that's a fair reflection of how I'm feeling about you."

Hargreaves looked up from where he was sitting on the graffiti covered solid plinth that doubled as his bed, Frankie could see the defeated look in his eyes, he knew that this man had accepted he was fucked, it was just how fucked they were now debating.

"You see Mr Hargreaves," Frankie continued, "what's done is done, we can't turn back time, but what we can do is offer you the chance of some genuine redemption, a chance for someone who has done some pretty bad shit to try and at least show a bit of common decency. Now we know that sixty grand wasn't just for a boat, and when we're done with you I need you to be sure that I'm throwing you over to Thames Valley, because they are going to want to talk to you about Harry Kilburton. But what I want to know is one thing, one simple thing, I want the name of who paid you that money?"

Hargreaves looked up, "I can't say."

"Yes you can!" Frankie shouted back.

"No, you don't understand, I can't say because I don't know. All I know is it was paid to me by someone called Phillip, the boat was little more than a glorified sailing dinghy, I signed it over to a fictitious name, he paid me the money."

"And why did he pay you that money, this Phillip."

"No comment."

"What do you mean no fucking comment?"

"I mean I will have that conversation with Thames Valley, when I have a solicitor present."

Frankie stood up and paced around the room, he didn't want to lose him, let him clam up, the Kilburton business was Thames Valley's, he could let that go, but he still needed to know stuff.

"Then tell me about the parties. How do we get in?"

-FIFTY THREE-

The Electoral Roll Reveals Who Occupies Charles Glen House, And It Ain't A Pleasant Surprise.

Manny was chatting to Micky Page who was poring over the latest email from the would-be abductor, Phillip, giving 'The Candyman' the information relating to the forthcoming party. It was right on their door step, just six miles down the road, and now just a few hours away.

He had that gnawing feeling in his stomach, part nerves, part anticipation, and part poor choice of chilli for lunch, something he was reminded of by the small orangey brown stain he was trying to hide under his tie. He was tired, really tired, and that situation certainly wasn't helped by spending twenty minutes with the distraught and traumatised Andrea Clay. He was now running on some secret energy reserve, which he had somehow conjured from nowhere, powering him through what he knew would be another very long day, only by the end of it there was a genuine chance that Amelia Clay would be returning to her home.

But what kind of home would that be? The distraught mother wracked with her own guilt over the self-imposed death of the spouse that she had long since ceased to love. What kind of homecoming surprise would that be for Amelia, 'Surprise! Daddy topped himself yesterday. Welcome home darling!'

Around him the office had become a hive of activity with people scurrying about everywhere arranging the raid that was now so near to happening, everyone now aware of what their part was. He thought back to the beginning of the case, four long years back, how then in that golden period of the first 48 hours they had trampled over the local fields and woods, Harwick Common flooded with Police and the dozens of eager volunteers, he recalled the frogmen trawling through the same river by which Stacey Hamilton was recovered. Then as the hours turned to days, then to weeks, the realisation that with all that time, so had the chances of finding Amelia.

He was suddenly shaken from his thoughts.

"Guv', can I show you something," it was Alice Parrachio calling, waving him over to her desk, she had a slightly smug look on her face, like the child who always had their hand permanently up in school, the one with all the answers to all of teacher's questions. He had detailed her the job of scouring the electoral roll, seeking out who owned the venue for this unsavoury little soiree they would soon be gate crashing, and by the look of it she had only taken a couple of minutes to come up with something, he was quite impressed with the latest addition to his team, even though he had been given no say prior to her arrival.

He walked the few paces to her desk, and looked over her shoulder at the monitor she was now pointing at.

"I've got a name for you sir, Charles Glen House is occupied by a Christoff Peterson, a quick scan of the PNC records that Peterson has no criminal…"

"Hold on!" Manny exclaimed, "Christoff Peterson. Oh bloody hell."

He felt like he had been hit by a giant wrecking ball, knocking all sense from his head. Christoff-bloody-Peterson!

"Are you alright Guv?" Alice was asking, but the words were floating over him, not registering at all. Christoff Peterson.

Really?

Manny was staring at the screen, it was there in black and white, well black on pale green, *Resident Mr Christoff Oliver Peterson*. Andrea's rock, her support, the champion of her cause, that very same Christoff Peterson.

He was involved, he was part of it, was very bloody involved. He felt sickened, he remembered how that toad was always there at Harwick Common, always in the background, yet all along Peterson knew, he must have known, because they were taking Amelia to his house that very night, or had she always been there?

"Mr Manningwell, are you alright?" Alice repeated, the words finally filtering through.

"Err, yeah, well actually no. Peterson is the man who has led the publicity campaign to find that girl, Andrea Clay's so called friend, I've seen him around their house, supposedly doing his all to help find that poor girl, and all along he's involved, he's part of it."

Within another half an hour Alice had been able to present Manny with the fact that although a Phillip Mortimer had purchased what was increasingly looking like a mythical boat from Hargreaves, Christoff Peterson had withdrawn the three payments of twenty thousand pounds from his account in each case a mere matter of hours before Hargreaves had deposited that same amount in his bank.

But when it came to bank accounts, that wasn't their only discovery.

"He's a multi-millionaire Guv'." Alice announced as she sat opposite Manny in his office. "He's absolutely loaded, family money, he's heir to a Swedish paper production company, a forty percent stakeholder."

Manny was silent for a moment, it didn't make sense, Peterson had worked for the council, a highly paid position sure, but a multi-millionaire?

"What else do we know about him?" he asked.

"I know that before working for Bedfordshire County Council, he owned his own television production company, a small set up call *White Water*." She gave a little smile obviously having seen Manny's facial reaction. "Yes Guv, a small world eh?"

COLIN PAYNE

-FIFTY FOUR-

Send In The Clowns.

He usually didn't have much time for Japanese cars, but this one was certainly an exception to his rule, it really was a nice motor. Frankie was sitting behind the wheel of Reginald Hargreaves *Lexus GS*, but when it came to comfort and pleasure those two particular feelings were only applicable to the car, because at that moment this particular item of high end Japanese automotive engineering was being driven by what could only be described as a clown.

He knew from the moment they had decided that someone would need to dress up and take the place of Hargreaves at the party that it was going to have to be him. He was a similar age, height and build to the man they were holding in their cells, it made sense. And just as certainly their choice of Circus themed costume wasn't going to be the World's Strongest Man, a Trapeze Artist or Lion Tamer.

He looked in the rear view mirror and was once more confronted with the image of himself covered in greasepaint, a big sad mouth painted over his own big sad mouth. 'I fucking hate clowns', had been his only reply when Manny had inevitably suggested that he take the role, and that was an understatement, because along with mime artists, ventriloquists and all forms of impressionists they had no place in modern society. They were neither amusing nor funny, they were just annoying to a point where, in his mind at least, a damn good hiding should be administered to each and every one of them. They were a sub-species of creepy horrible beings who only eked out a living because well-meaning left wing councils funded them through schemes, which for some inexplicable reason allowed them to have close contact with children. Yet here he was, now joining their grotesque and freakish ranks, going to some grotesque and freakish party full of grotesque and freakish men, where any close contact with children would be way beyond anything any normal decent human being could ever comprehend.

He considered the plan, which was basically for him to get into Charles Glen House, the ridiculous face paint offering him the anonymity to take his place using Hargreave's 'Golden Ticket', then assess what was happening, to see if he could locate Amelia or any other children present. He was fitted with a tiny camera positioned in one of the giant pom-poms that ran down the front of his silk red and yellow polka dotted shirt, and through its audio capability when the time was right he would issue the instruction to the dozens of other Police officers to come rushing in. The majority of those were still holding at Dunstable police station, eager that their ten vehicle convoy didn't go passing any of the guests on the roads leading to Peterson's home, with just Manny and his immediate team parked up in two unmarked cars in a lane about half mile from their target.

COLIN PAYNE

He wasn't sure, initially he preferred the option of just charging into the address straight away, every single body they could muster rushing into the place en-mass, retrieving the girl and as forcefully as possible nicking anyone else they could, but Manny had persuaded him that if they wanted all those involved then this was the only way. The major problem with that plan was the fact that it was him playing the role of the paedophile, him dressed up as Coco-the-fucking-nonce, as he had dubbed himself, and him that would be going to this meeting of the depraved and perverted, this so-called party which was in fact nothing but a version of hell itself, existing for no other purpose than for very rich men to do very evil things.

Frankie popped a stick of gum in his mouth and slowly chewed. He could see the huge mansion just ahead. Shit he thought, why did both Manny and Felix have to be bearded fat men? How did Floyd get to be lucky enough to be black? And why couldn't that DS, Page, and young Denny both be six inches taller. But most relevantly, why did it have to be him?

He glanced down at his satin electric blue trousers, ballooning out around his legs, beside him on the passenger seat the large oversized foam boots, "Ah fuck's sake," he muttered to himself.

As the gravel coating the long drive crunched under the tyres of Hargreaves car, he picked up the handheld radio and spoke to Manny and the others parked down the lane.

THE HUNT FOR AMELIA CLAY

"Lima One to Romeo, I'm in position, arrange for all supporting units to be ready to move, on my signal I want this place swamped. I will enter shortly, so will activate the camera, please confirm that you have both visual and audio feed, test now commencing."

He tapped the tiny camera once, it appeared a tacky bit of kit, Chinese crap no doubt, and he didn't have too much faith in it.

"Testing, testing, one, two, fucking three."

"Romeo to Lima One, that's affirmative, we have both sound and vision," he heard Manny reply.

"Right here goes…"

… # -FIFTY FIVE-

Bring On The Dancing Horses…

Amelia bit her nails, as she silently sat on the side of her bed, the chain still running from her wrist to that huge bolt in the wall, she was clothed in a sequined leotard with a large stiff tutu, dressed up for *their* entertainment. 'The Pig' had informed her she was supposed to making some kind of grand entrance, wheeled into the ballroom upon a life sized model of a white dancing horse. He had actually expected her to be excited, like he had delivered some fantastic surprise to her, was he really that mad?

Even though she could now hear the music below, bellowing through his huge house, the other Pigs arriving, she wasn't going to be there, and neither would he.

What would follow would no doubt follow, but she wasn't thinking that far ahead. She wasn't overly scared or nervous, although she knew she should be, she wasn't sure exactly what she was feeling, but then had she really been aware of her true feelings at any point over the past four years?

She fingered the steel scissors hidden beneath her white cotton pillow, those cold, hard scissors that were now her only way out, her key to another place, although what that place consisted of she had no idea.

But she knew what she needed to do, and she also knew she was fully capable of doing it.

-FIFTY SIX-

Welcome To The Greatest Show On Earth!

"Gentlemen, gentlemen," Phillip Mortimer, AKA Christoff Peterson, bellowed through an old metal megaphone, "Welcome to the Greatest Show on Earth!"

The two dozen or so men gathered around him in the meticulously decorated ballroom broke into applause. Peterson was standing in the middle of a small circus ring, he couldn't believe how good it looked bearing in mind how little time he had to prepare following being let down at such short notice. Gathered around him the other side of the brightly coloured perimeter were his guests, seated around small circular tables, they had really gotten into the spirit of the event, dressed in a variety of costumes. Of course none looked as impressive as he did in his brilliant white breaches, highly polished leather riding boots, the bright red tailed coat, and of course his wonderful black top hat.

Yes! He was the ring master, the lord of all he surveyed, this would be the best party, his greatest event, because he had total control over organising it, the profit would not be as great, but then this wasn't about the money. He looked above his head as he spun around, his arms held out wide, the long whip in his right hand. He noted the trapezes hanging from the ornate ceiling, the two cages to one side, to hold the little 'beasts', and right in the middle of the ring, the three beds, brightly coloured orange, pink and red silk bedding draped on top of them.

"Tonight I present to you exotic treats from around the world, fantastical entertainment for your delight, it will be an evening to remember and never forget. This I guarantee will be the best Tuesday Club yet! Please, as we await our first act, enjoy the food and drink on offer, prepare to be dazzled and amazed, for the show is soon to begin."

Again the applause, he looked to one side where the large wooden white horse stood, ready to wheel his star attraction into the ring, he had wondered if he had gone a little over the top, but that was the whole idea, pure extravagance, put on a show, a genuine event, make the Tuesday Club something really special.

It had all really progressed so much over the six years, he thought back to the first meeting of the Tuesday Club, little more than some glorified meat market, prostituting little Stacey out to the highest bidders, he felt a tinge of shame, a pang of regret, but not for Stacey, just that he had sold himself so short. He really could have done so much better, and was now proving that point.

The themed parties were a recent thing, and he really wished he had cottoned on to the idea a lot earlier, they had brought an element of class to the proceedings, plus offered an air of anonymity to those members attending, the 'Alice in Wonderland' party last year had been the first, and after that there was no going back.

The circus theme was the 'White Rabbit's' idea, it had been his turn to host it, damn him, he thought, but then would he have presented the show that was now going ahead?

He very much doubted it.

It was nearly time, a few more minutes and he was going to bring the children down, he had paid handsomely for the other two, 'hired' them for the night, but they were just the entrees for the main course that was Amelia, they would each be placed in one of his 'cages' fashioned from doweling and silver paint, he would leave them 'locked up' for fifteen minutes, whet his guests appetites, before the fun really began.

Oh yes, tonight was going to be special.

-FIFTY SEVEN-

The Lion Tamer, The Clown, And The Repulsed Policeman Share A Glass Of Champagne.

Frankie's leg was actually physically trembling, he had no way of stopping it, an involuntary response to all that was going on around him. He was sitting at one of the tables, he recognised Peterson from the pictures they now had pinned upon the whiteboard back at the station, the 'genial host', dressed up to the nines, the dirty horrible bastard.

Sitting either side of him at the table were two other guests, a Lion Tamer, complete with pith helmet and a khaki safari suit, and a fellow clown, they had attempted to engage him in conversation, but he was in no mood for pleasantries, he just wanted this done with.

Before them stood two bottles of champagne and tall crystal flutes, the Lion Tamer insisting on charging their glasses whenever either of them took a sip. He knew he had to play along, couldn't just tell them to 'fuck off and leave me alone', but it wasn't easy, everything about this repulsed him, because he was so aware what ultimately this was all about, and it wasn't some over expensive fancy dress party.

It was clear to see how much cash this must have all cost to put on, but then he remembered how much of the Force's money they had needed to part with to get him through the door, and if you multiplied that amount by at least twenty then that added up to a cool million.

As he cradled his glass the other clown laughed raucously, nudging Frankie as he did so, nodding towards the Lion Tamer, at first he struggled to see what was so amusing, then he glanced over to see the cause of the amusement standing up, strapped onto his baggy shorts was what had to be at least a twelve inch dildo.

He could only look on in horror, as the other clown declared, "Well that's decided, and it's definitely my turn on her before you!"

Frankie's table companions again laughed, but he wasn't laughing, he had recognised the voice, the voice of the clown, Terry Bagshott, star of kid's TV, decades of Pantomimes and most recently languishing in the jungle with Ant and Dec. Yep, after Peterson he would be next in his interview room, closely followed by the horrible little shit with the giant rubber cock, who unbeknown to him was none other than top crimper to the stars, Gerald Draper, they would all be his soon enough.

Felix was with Manny watching the footage via a laptop in the back of one of the cars parked just off the road a few hundred yards from where the images were being transmitted. Sylvia and Floyd were sitting in front of them, and in the other car were Micky, Denny and Alice, who were seeing the same images as they were. Felix had a pretty good idea of what Frankie was thinking at that very moment, they had seen the guy with the huge prosthetic penis, and he had already declared to Manny that when they went in 'he's mine'.

This was new to him, he was used to dealing with terrorists, not people such as this, terrorists always had an ideology, a reason, a cause, but these people were just sick. He couldn't get into their minds because he really didn't want to, what could possibly possess someone to do what these animals planned?

As Felix wondered at just how low the human race was capable of scraping, the other vehicles were leaving Dunstable, they would be meeting up with them soon, then it was just a case of waiting for Frankie's say so, and as far as he was concerned the sooner that came the better.

Peterson had moved from the 'ring', unbeknown to him his movements were being monitored by Frankie, who had watched as he exited the ballroom through the two large doors at one end. His two new 'friends' had clearly decided to leave him alone, and he was conscious that he should really have played along, shared in their fucked up joviality and got into 'character'. But this wasn't his character, this could never be his character, this was so revolting it was making him want to vomit.

He stood up, nodding and forcing a smile as the other two looked at him, and then made his way towards where Peterson had left the room, he wanted to see where he had gone, whether he could locate Amelia or any other kids that may be there, because that was the reason he was there.

As he made his way to the doors the circus themed music faded out, replaced by 'Thank Heaven for little girls' by Maurice Chevalier as the lights dimmed to near blackness. Suddenly a huge projection appeared on one of the walls, it was a Police Poster, Frankie recognised it from the offices they worked in back at the station. The bold letters declaring:

MISSING

AMELIA CLAY

Aged 11

Last seen Harwick Common

Then a description above that iconic photo of the forever smiling eleven year old Amelia.

The guests cheered as one, as the image appeared, before singing along to the French crooner's Gallic tones.

THE HUNT FOR AMELIA CLAY

Frankie hurried from the room, he was sure that if he had still carried a gun he would have been sorely tempted to have put a bullet in each and every one of their heads.

But then as he looked at the poster still on display he hurried his pace, she was there somewhere, that poor girl was somewhere in that very house, among these monsters, and he needed to find her.

COLIN PAYNE

-FIFTY EIGHT-

The Girl In The Sequined Leotard and Tutu Messes Up.

Amelia could hear all the noise below, that French song once more playing, she knew he would be there soon, 'The Pig', coming to take her down, coming to make her wretched existence even worse.

As she sat there in that horrible costume he had earlier given her to wear she thought about how it could all have been different, how other fifteen year old girls lived, in loving families, with friends, at schools, why had it been so different for her? Out of all those fifteen year olds, living their lives like fifteen year olds should, why had she instead been living like this?

Then she heard the door handle turning, her stomach knotted, it was him.

'The Pig' entered the room, he was dressed like some kind of fancy huntsman, and he looked so pleased with himself, he was clearly excited, clapping his hands as he pronounced,

THE HUNT FOR AMELIA CLAY

"It's time my darling, all the guests are so keen to see you, I must say you look stunning."

She ignored him, just looking down, as he hurriedly came over taking her hand in his, raising it to untie the handcuff.

"Oh please Amelia, not the sulky routine tonight, I need you to be happy, it's a party for heaven's sake, no one wants a sour puss ruining it for everyone. Come on give me a big smile."

She had no desire to give this Pig a big smile, she wondered whether she would ever smile again as she clasped the steel scissors tightly in her hand, and just as the cuff slid from her slender wrist she swung around with them.

He was level with her, crouching down, the sharp tips plunged into the thick wool coat, she felt it push into him, into his flesh.

Christoff Peterson recoiled, he felt the searing pain in his shoulder, what had she done?

He leapt to his feet and threw himself backwards, bringing his hand to the top of his arm. Blood coated his palm, he looked horrified towards the girl rising to her feet, slowly, deliberately, the scissors raised in her hand, blood coating them, his blood.

"You bitch!" he screamed, drawing his whip up before swinging it round. Within the confines of the room he couldn't swing it its full arc, but it was enough to knock her back, the tightly plaited leather rope lashing across that little whore's face.

He rushed forward, she had ruined it, she had ruined everything!

"I'm going to kill you!" he spat, no longer cheery, no longer excited, because that little bitch had destroyed it, and she needed to pay.

The pain was all too apparent in his bloody shoulder, he didn't care about the party, the guests, money, or even having her just for one last time, he just wanted to snuff out her worthless life like he had done to Stacey, only this time it would be painful, the ungrateful slut would pay and pay big! There would be no quick departure, not now, she would know exactly what was happening to her, every single painful little detail.

He had rushed forward, Amelia knew she had messed up, her face was bleeding, where the whip had slashed across her cheek, it stung like mad. She had needed to kill him, and no one died from a cut shoulder. She raised the scissors high, and as he came into her reach, that contorted look of rage and hate all over his face, she plunged the shiny blood coated shears into his eye socket, deep, as deep as she could, there was little resistance, they just slid in, after making an initial horrible 'squelching' noise. The blood sprayed over her hands, over her own face, and over that hideous awful leotard. As he instantly fell to the floor, his legs crumpling beneath him, the scissors pulling free from his face as he went, she straddled his lifeless form, plunging them into his body again and again. She pulled the thick scarlet woollen coat open, allowing her blades an easier passage, his chest now open to her assault.

He had to die, he had to!

As she stabbed and stabbed, the door flew open, she looked up, it was another Pig, it was another one of them, watching on, apparently frozen to the spot.

-FIFTY NINE-

Adrian Howard, The Policeman With Nothing But A Bright Red Nose and Orange Wig For Protection.

Frankie was creeping up the stairs, slowly scanning around looking for a sign of Amelia Clay, or any of the other children he now knew were present, it was a huge house, and he was well aware she could be anywhere. He could hear the music, the guests singing and laughing, as they awaited their entertainment.

He was now on the second floor, just slowly walking down the landing, pictures and paintings adorned the walls, but none offered any clues as to what actually went on within this house, what its true purpose was. Each step was accompanied by a creak as the floor boards under the floral carpets reacted to his every movement. He felt vulnerable without a gun, all alone with nothing but a red nose and bright orange wig, this was not how he would choose to go on any operation let alone one where he was outnumbered almost thirty to one. He didn't even know whether his little camera was still transmitting, were the others seeing what he was seeing, were they ready to come rushing in on his say so?

Then as he passed a portrait of some woman that looked like Harry Secombe he heard the shouting.

You bitch!

It was coming from above, he ran for the stairs.

I'm going to kill you!

Oh shit!

"Go, go, go!" he shouted into the air, just desperately hoping that Manny would hear his order.

He came to a narrow staircase, he could hear what sounded like a fight, he sprinted up the steep steps two at time bursting into the room to see a blood soaked girl in a tutu manically stabbing the decimated form of what was once Christoff Peterson.

"Stop!" he screamed.

She was looking at him, a look of horror on her face, the face that was covered in what he hoped was just Peterson's blood.

"It's OK, you can stop," he said in a calm voice, that surprised even himself, because he wasn't feeling calm at all, he was feeling very un-calm.

She initially just stared at him, a crazed manic look upon her young face as he walked towards her, she was still spread over the ex-ringmaster, her deathly scissors in her hand, she was dressed like some ballerina, only her whole body was covered in the bright red blood of the butchered ring master.

He crouched down. "It's OK, I'm a …"

"No!" she suddenly screamed in a high pitched wail, and before he could react or defend himself Amelia Clay plunged those same scissors in Adrian Howard's chest.

-SIXTY-

A Blood Soaked Amelia Clay Is Recovered From Charles Glen House.

Once the long convoy of Police vans had met up with them, Manny and the rest of the MCU had followed them to Charles Glen House, parking up literally a few dozen yards down the lane, just awaiting Frankie's say so. They had via the 'live feed' observed the goings on within the large ballroom, and accompanied Frankie on his hunt around the house, so when he issued the command to go, they were able to react instantly. The ground floor was secured in seconds, with over fifty uniformed officers blitzing the place, it was text book, most of the guests were in cuffs before they had even realised what was happening.

But Felix had seen none of that, because he had immediately rushed upstairs, Manny and the rest of their unit following, he had heard the shouts, had seen Frankie head up the narrow staircase whilst he watched via the laptop as their car sped into the gravel drive, he had seen Amelia Clay plunge something into his DCI's chest, before the footage suddenly cut out.

"Frankie! Frankie!" he frantically called as they climbed the stairs.

He burst into the room, oh please God, he thought, please don't let him be dead.

Felix stood just inside the doorway, the room was a horrific sight, blood was splattered everywhere, what the hell had happened? Although he knew exactly what had happened.

Then he saw Frankie sitting on the floor, holding his blood soaked hand up for them to stop, his orange wig was off, his other arm was wrapped around Amelia Clay's shoulder.

"It's OK, it's OK," being all he said to reassure his sergeant.

The 18 layers of Aramid and four millimetres of foam within Frankie's anti-stab vest had no doubt saved his life, as it was designed to do, but Peterson had definitely not been so fortunate. Frankie looked across at his body, his face and chest decimated, by Amelia's stabbing. As the Paramedics came and tended to the clearly shocked Amelia, he followed Manny and Felix out of the room.

"What happened?" Felix asked.

Frankie shrugged, "We'll probably never know, she hasn't said a word, my money is he attacked her with that whip, she reacted, grabbed the scissors, self-defence."

"Really? Self Defence?" Felix replied, Frankie could hear the scepticism in his voice.

THE HUNT FOR AMELIA CLAY

"Yes, Felix, really, she's in shock, I don't want anyone talking to her until doctors clear it. That's the story, as far as I'm concerned that's what happened. We clear?"

He could tell that neither Manny nor Felix were clear, but it was a scenario he was happy to run with, he had heard Peterson threatening her, clearly stating he was going to kill her, it was on the camera, or least he hoped it was, anything else was just conjecture, guessing, Amelia was in no state of mind to contradict his view of what had happened, she was clearly in need of help, not questions.

-SIXTY ONE-

Not A Bad Night's Work.

Manny leant against one of the *LDV* Police vans, in his hand a *B&H* which he was drawing upon heavily, Denny walked over and was standing beside him.

"Twenty seven arrests," the young DC said, "three kids found including Amelia, and apparently a shit load of evidence linking at least a hundred people to all of this. Not a bad night's work Guv'."

Manny said nothing, just flicked his cigarette butt away, before pulling another 'smoke' from the pack.

Four years they had been searching for that girl, hunting the bastard that had her, and both were right there just a few miles down the road all along. He had been at Harwick Common when Peterson had been in the Clay's home, how much of that lost time was down to his failings?

He shook his head. "We let them down Den, we should have sorted this so much sooner."

He never looked at Denny as he spoke, just stared at the black Private Ambulance that he knew now contained Peterson's body, then over to the vehicle Amelia was being loaded into, Alice Parrachio and Sylvia Hardacre escorting her to hospital, where she would no doubt be reunited with her mother.

"She'll be going home to what? What's Amelia going to find there eh? Her Dad's funeral, Andrea's guilt, and four years of messed up memories. Oh God man I never thought I'd be feeling like this, when it was over, this ain't how I should feel is it?"

"Of course not, this is it done Guv', it's a result. You, no we, did everything we could, with what we had, don't you dare blame yourself for any of that, what matters is we got her back, Manny we did it."

Denny slapped his arms around his boss, giving him a hug, slapping his back, as he said, "We did it Manny!"

Manny could feel the salty tears flowing down his face, Denny was right, they had done it, they had got Amelia back. It was over.

COLIN PAYNE

-EPILOGUE-

Two Months Later…

"Cut."

Whilst the rest of the crew packed away the equipment and prepared to return to their West London base, Bill Penton just stood and stared at the huge Georgian country house. It was more than eight weeks since Amelia Clay had been found within those large imposing stone walls, and the fall out was still landing on those involved. Over one hundred people had been arrested, as the Police continued to cast their net over those connected to the Tuesday Club.

Obviously Christoff Peterson would never see a court, the man behind it all killed by his victim as she fought off his final onslaught. Nor would Harry Kilburton, the step-father who had sold his wife's daughter for the price of a battered second hand car, a lot less than the fee a corrupted Prison Governor received when it came to his turn to look the other way.

Bill turned around and walked to join the rest of his crew, this story still had 'legs', that wasn't the final cut by any means, but for Bill that was it. He had landed his place on the 'sofa' on Breakfast TV, he was now only one step away from becoming a contestant on 'Strictly Come Dancing' and

THE HUNT FOR AMELIA CLAY

doing a song and dance routine for 'Children in Need', yeah things had worked out alright.

Whilst Bill contemplated his new profile and the prospect of all those early starts, across the English Channel in Provence an English woman laid breakfast out on the small circular table upon a patio, the winter sun vainly attempting to offer some warmth. Her daughter sat on a wicker chair, ensconced in a thick fleece jacket, her legs curled up to her chest, with earphones relaying music via an *i-pod*.

As Andrea Clay placed the small tray of croissants and a couple of pots of yoghurt before her, Amelia gave the briefest of smiles by way of acknowledgement, before once more closing her eyes and gently nodding along to her tunes.

The psychologists and doctors had said it would take time, and considering all she had been through she was already making far better progress than would normally be expected, but Andrea wondered whether either of them would ever again enjoy a life that could possibly be classed as normal.

Made in the USA
Charleston, SC
08 September 2014